ALWAYS

What Reviewers Say About Kris Bryant's Work

Home

"Home is a very sweet second-chance romance that will make you smile. It is an angst-less joy, perfect for a bad day."—*Hsinju's Lit Log*

Scent

"Oh. Kris Bryant. Once again you've given us a beautiful comfort read to help us escape all that 2020 has thrown at us. This series featuring the senses has been a pleasure to read. …I think what makes Bryant's books so readable is the way she builds the reader's interest in her mains before allowing them to interact. This is a sweet and happy sigh kind of read. Perfect for these chilly winter nights when you want to escape the world and step into a caramel infused world where HEAs really do come true."—*Late Night Lesbian Reads*

Lucky

"The characters—both main and secondary, including the furry ones—are wonderful (I loved coming across Piper and Shaylie from Falling), there's just the right amount of angst and the sexy scenes are really hot. It's Kris Bryant, you guys, no surprise there."—*Jude in the Stars*

"This book has everything you need for a sweet romance. The main characters are beautiful and easy to fall in love with, even with their little quirks and flaws. The settings (Vail and Denver, Colorado) are perfect for the story, and the romance itself is satisfying, with just enough angst to make the book interesting. …This is the perfect novel to read on a warm, lazy summer day, and I recommend it to all romance lovers."—*Rainbow Reflections*

Tinsel

"This story was the perfect length for this cute romance. What made this especially endearing were the relationships Jess has with her best friend, Mo, and her mother. You cannot go wrong by purchasing this cute little nugget. A really sweet romance with a cat playing cupid."—*Bookvark*

Against All Odds—(co-authored with Maggie Cummings and M. Ullrich)

"*Against All Odds* by Kris Bryant, Maggie Cummings and M. Ullrich is an emotional and captivating story about being able to face a tragedy head on and move on with your life, learning to appreciate the simple things we take for granted and finding love where you least expect it."—*Lesbian Review*

Temptation

"This book has a great first line. I was hooked from the start. There was so much to like about this story, though. The interactions. The tension. The jealousy. I liked how Cassie falls for Brooke's son before she ever falls for Brooke. I love a good forbidden love story."—*Bookvark*

"People who have read Ms. Bryant's erotica novella *Shameless* under the pseudonym of Brit Ryder know that this author can write intimacy well. This is more a romance than erotica but the sex scenes are as varied and hot…"—*LezReviewBooks*

"This book is a bag of kettle corn—sweet, savory and you won't stop until you finish it in one binge-worthy sitting. *Temptation* is a fun, fluffy and ultimately satisfying lesbian romance that hits all the right notes."—*To Be Read Book Reviews*

Falling

"This is a story you don't want to pass on. A fabulous read that you will have a hard time putting down. Maybe don't read it as you board your plane though. This is an easy 5 stars!"—*Romantic Reader Blog*

"Bryant delivers a story that is equal parts touching, compassionate, and uplifting."—*Lesbian Review*

"This was a nice, romantic read. There is enough romantic tension to keep the plot moving, and I enjoyed the supporting characters' and their romance as much as the main plot."—*Kissing Backwards*

Listen

"[A] sweet romance with a touch of angst and lots of music."—*C-Spot Reviews*

"If you're looking for a little bit of fluffy(ish), light romance in your life, give this one a listen. The characters' passion for music (and each other) is heartwarming, and I was rooting for them the entire book."—*Kissing Backwards*

"Ms. Bryant describes this soundscape with some exquisite metaphors, it's true what they say that music is everywhere. The whole book is beautifully written and makes the reader's heart to go out with people suffering from anxiety or any sort of mental health issue."—*Lez Review Books*

"This is the first story I've read in a long time with a virginal character, and it made a refreshing change both in and out of the bedroom. If you suffer from anxiety, know someone who suffers from anxiety, or want an insight to how it may impact on someone's daily life, I urge you to pick this book up. In fact, I urge all readers who enjoy a good lesbian romance to grab a copy."—*Omnivore Bibliosaur*

Forget Me Not

"Told in the first person, from Grace's point of view, we are privy to Grace's inner musings and her vulnerabilities. ...Bryant crafts clever wording to infuse Grace with a sharp-witted personality, which clearly covers her insecurities. ...This story is filled with loving familial interactions, caring friends, romantic interludes and tantalizing sex scenes. The dialogue, both among the characters and within Grace's head, is refreshing, original, and sometimes comical. *Forget Me Not* is a fresh perspective on a romantic theme, and an entertaining read."—*Lambda Literary Review*

"[I]t just hits the right note all the way. ...[A] very good read if you are looking for a sweet romance."—*Lez Review Books*

Shameless—*Writing as Brit Ryder*

"[Kris Bryant] has a way of giving insight into the other main protagonist by using a few clever techniques and involving the secondary characters to add back-stories and extra pieces of important information. The pace of the book was excellent, it was never rushed but I was never bored or waiting for a chapter to finish...this epilogue made my heart swell to the point I almost lunged off the sofa to do a happy dance."—*Les Rêveur*

Whirlwind Romance

"Ms. Bryant's descriptions were written with such passion and colorful detail that you could feel the tension and the excitement along with the characters..."—*Inked Rainbow Reviews*

Taste

"*Taste* is a student/teacher romance set in a culinary school. If the premise makes you wonder whether this book will make you want to eat something tasty, the answer is: yes."—*Lesbian Review*

Jolt—*Lambda Literary Award Finalist*

"[*Jolt*] is a magnificent love story. Two women hurt by their previous lovers and each in their own way trying to make sense out of life and times. When they meet at a gay and lesbian friendly summer camp, they both feel as if lightening has struck. This is so beautifully involving, I have already reread it twice. Amazing!" —*Rainbow Book Reviews*

Touch

"The sexual chemistry in this book is off the hook. Kris Bryant writes my favorite sex scenes in lesbian romantic fiction."—*Les Rêveur*

Breakthrough

"Looking for a fun and funny light read with hella cute animal antics, and a smoking hot butch ranger? Look no further. …In this well written, first-person narrative, Kris Bryant's characters are well developed, and their push/pull romance hits all the right beats, making it a delightful read just in time for beach reading."—*Writing While Distracted*

"[A]n exceptional book that has a few twists and turns that catch you out and make you wish the book would never end. I was captivated from the beginning and can't wait to see how Bryant will top this."—*Les Rêveur*

Visit us at www.boldstrokesbooks.com

By the Author

Jolt

Whirlwind Romance

Just Say Yes (Wedding Series novella)

Taste

Forget-Me-Not

Shameless (novella writing as Brit Ryder)

Touch

Breakthrough

Against All Odds

Listen

Falling

Tinsel (novella)

Temptation

Lucky

Home

Scent

Not Guilty (writing as Brit Ryder)

Always

ALWAYS

by

Kris Bryant

2022

Credits
Editors: Ashley Tillman and Shelley Thrasher
Production Design: Susan Ramundo
Cover Design By Kris Bryant

Acknowledgments

We know 2020 and 2021 were difficult years for all of us. I slowed down because the weight of the pandemic drained me, but 2022 is going to turn things around starting with this book.

A massive thank you to everyone at Bold Strokes Books for staying on task and getting all the books in front of readers. I love that we've had virtual events to be able to still talk about our books and writing. I love the connection we have with readers, so the bookathons and virtual readings were wonderful.

I will probably never say this again, but I had a lot of fun with my editors on this book. Most of the time, I dread edits, but this book is so unique and emotional that I wanted to get feedback and try to improve on the story with their help. Ashley understands me like no other. We worked through so much content-wise and I now understand why she is called the Kris Whisperer. Shelley T. has my back on copy edits and it's always a pleasure working with her. Ashley and Shelley are complete opposites in the way they edit, but I need both of them to polish the story.

Massive thank you to my local friends who encourage me and check on my progress weekly. I love you, KB Draper, Stacy, Alisa, and Kasey. We've had great times together and I look forward to many more pop-up superhero parties, lake visits, even pickle ball games. Shout out to Fiona Riley who calls me, texts me, has writing dates with me, keeps me sane, and reminds me that friendship love is beautiful. I love you, Jenn, and the ginger snaps so much. Where would I be if I wasn't solving crimes with Paula, getting much needed personal and professional guidance from Carsen, love and chats from Melissa, animal pics and stories from Georgia, football rants from Friz, adorable phone calls from my bff Morgan, the only Millennial who will talk on the phone, and so many others who have ensured I stay in the game and stay on task? I love you all for so many reasons.

Molly is with me every step of the way. I know it won't be like this forever, but for now, I cherish each day. Thank you to Deb who gives me space to write knowing this is my dream. Your support is so appreciated even if I don't tell you enough. Thank you to my mother who pushes me like a mother should. Have you written today? Why not? These are daily questions and I playfully roll my eyes at her, but I'm so fortunate she is still in my life to hold me accountable. No, she is still not allowed to read my books (neither is my father).

Readers have changed my life. Buying my books, talking about them, and reviewing them have made my dreams come true. I am a writer because of you all. Your encouragement and kind words about the stories I tell make me want to keep writing. Thank you. I'm grateful for you, my life, my friends and the love I have in my heart.

Always.

Dedication

This is dedicated to everyone who believes
in the raw power of always and forever.

CHAPTER ONE

THE JOB—PERI

My first client was dead. My great-grandmother, Hildegarde Bennett, whom I affectionately called Amma, died two weeks ago when her heart simply gave out after one hundred years of living. I spent a lot of my childhood with Amma, and even though her death saddened me, it wasn't a surprise. She was the oldest person I knew. I felt horrible for my grandmother and my mother, who were very close to her, especially during the last decade of her life. At the reading of the will, I was given a packet with a note, a heart-shaped gold locket, and a stack of cash. The lawyer's writing on the envelope had more words than the message from Amma did. I held the piece of paper carefully and read the scratchy, wavy letters written on forty-year-old stationery that still smelled like Amma's cedar desk and the lavender sachets she kept tucked in the corner of the drawer.

Find her. Love, Amma

That's all the note said. The square, block lettering on the packet congratulated me on my new business and wished me the best of luck with my first case. The contents of the packet sat on my large, secondhand mahogany desk, along with a phone with three incoming lines, a rustic leather accessory desk set from my parents, and a cup of hot coffee. The pen holder held ten blue ink pens that showed the name of my new business, phone number, and website. The pens were mostly so my mother could give them to her friends and clients. More importantly, I paid Google Ads a monthly fee to be on the first page of the search engine for Putnam, Connecticut. Amma didn't really have a concept of money since she had people to do everything for her. While five grand was a lot of money, my going rate plus expenses would gobble up this retainer in no time.

My business phone rang for the first time, and my heart skipped a beat. I squelched the anxiety in my throat and answered it. "Logan Investigations. How may we help you?"

"Hi, honey. It's Mom. Just wanted to see how your first day is going. Why didn't Ginger answer the phone?" Ginger was my mom's best friend from the salon. My mom was a stylist, whose clientele ranged from sixty to eighty years old. They all asked for the same poofy style, so she hadn't learned any trendy cuts in twenty years. She practiced on my hair once, and I vowed never again. The cut was too short. My natural, soft curls were finally growing out. Whenever I catch her eyeing my hair or running her fingers through it now, I pull away and scowl. She thinks it's funny. I still have emotional scars.

I glanced at the clock on my wall. It was 8:24. I'd been officially open for twenty-four minutes. The coffee that I brought from home was still steaming. "It's early, Mom. Ginger works nine to three. You're my first call though, so that's something, right?"

"First call. I'll take it. Do you need anything?" she asked.

I sat up straight when an idea hit me. "Actually, I do. What do you know about Amma when she was in her twenties? Do you have any old letters or journals or anything about her life before she got married?" I opened the ornate locket and stared at two women, a black-and-white portrait on either side of the tiny golden hinge. Amma was one of the ladies. The other one had a classic beauty with long, dark hair and dark eyes. They both looked relaxed and happy.

"I can look up in the attic. I might have a few things. You should really visit Granny and ask her. She probably has a lot of stories," she said.

My grandmother lived in the next town. She was still distraught over her mother's death, and I wasn't sure I wanted to interview her yet. As if sensing my hesitation, my mom dialed up the guilt trip. "She would probably really like to talk about Amma. Maybe you could go over there on your lunch hour and keep her company."

Mom wasn't wrong. I could console Granny and ask questions at the same time. "I might do that when Ginger gets here."

"Oh, please have her call me when she gets in, will you?"

I didn't point out that when Ginger arrived, she was on the clock, but I promised to give her the message. It wasn't like the phone was ringing nonstop. I flipped the locket over and inspected the back for any clues. Who was she? Why did Amma want me to find her? Hoping something was on the back of the photo, I gently lifted it from the locket with the straight edge of a small screwdriver from my eyeglass repair kit.

Isabel, 1945 was written in pencil on the back of the tiny photo. "Isabel." I liked the way her name rolled off my tongue. I started a list of questions to ask Granny. Where was Amma stationed during World War II? She worked for the Red Cross at the end of the war and a year after. Did she ever talk about any friends she made? Did she love her job? Where did she meet The Captain, my great-grandfather?

"Who's late on their first day?" Ginger, whose name was really Betty, blew through the front door at 9:07 with a smile and a beach bag full of things I was sure to cringe at once she pulled them out.

She answered to Ginger because, when she was younger, she looked like Ginger from *Gilligan's Island*. Her hair, until recently, was red and cut exactly like Tina Louise's. When she was young, people mistook her for the actress all the time, according to my mother. In fact, that was the only reason I had a clue who Tina Louise was. Now, Ginger's silver hair was short, but coiffed and hair-sprayed to perfection. She accepted my receptionist position because it was from nine in the morning until three in the afternoon and she needed the late afternoons off to watch her two grandkids after school. I stood in my office doorway and smiled away my irritation. "It's no problem. I'm just glad you made it."

"I wouldn't miss it for the world."

She popped her gum and twirled in the chair, almost falling in the process. I reached out to catch her. I didn't offer insurance yet, and sure as hell didn't want a lawsuit on day one. "Please be careful." Visions of her hitting her head and slumping over the desk filled my brain, and at times like this I hated my overactive imagination.

Ginger laughed. "It would probably knock some sense into me."

She steadied herself and touched everything on her new desk, including the phone, the pens, the keyboard, the monitor. I found it interesting. What was she thinking? "You've worked on a computer, right?" Ginger was fifteen years older than my mother.

She waved me off. "Oh, sure. I have one of these at home. The kids use it all the time."

I showed her how to operate the two programs I'd purchased to run background checks. She looked a little overwhelmed until we reviewed my calendar and billing programs. Those she was a wiz with.

"Listen, Ginger. I'm going to get started on my first case." I corrected myself. "On *our* first case. Here's a set of keys to the office. I don't think things will get crazy, but call or text me if they do." I handed her a key ring with three keys. "I should be back after lunch." I grabbed my purse and turned with my hand still touching the knob. "Oh, and call my mother."

"Will do. Good luck."

I thought about phoning Granny before showing up, but she would brush me off, and talking about Amma was a good idea. Not only for the case, but for her well-being. A surprise pop-in was the best course of action. I started my nine-year-old Volkswagen Passat and slipped smoothly into mid-morning traffic, stopping only to pick up pastries from the bakery near Granny's house. I knocked out of politeness but used my key to let myself in. "Granny? Are you up? I brought those delicious buttery, gooey Danishes you love."

"I'm in the kitchen, Peri. I just put coffee on."

Granny drank only coffee and iced tea. Too much caffeine made me jittery but didn't seem to affect her at all. "I'll just pour an iced tea." I kissed her cheek and hugged her a little longer after seeing her red-rimmed eyes. "Are you doing okay? Can I get you anything?"

She tapped my arm and motioned for me to sit at the table. "No, dear. I'm hanging in there. It's just hard, you know?"

During Amma's funeral, Granny sat tucked between me and Mom and squeezed my hand with strength that surprised me. All three of us cried because a woman we admired for very different reasons was gone. "I know. I hope it gets easier for you. Are you going through the photo albums now?" I pointed to a stack of albums on the chair next to me.

"It's so overwhelming. These are the albums from her room. Several are still up in the attic," she said.

I opened the first one and smiled at the four-generations photo we took when I was five. Amma had been beautiful even at eighty. She always looked like a movie star from noir films of the forties or fifties. The Captain always said she married down when she accepted his proposal. "She was so beautiful. And she loved all of us so much."

Granny nodded. "She always said she had a magical life."

I thumbed through the thick, stiff pages and ran my fingers over the old photos behind their plastic sheaths. Some were black-and-whites, and some were Polaroids whose colors were fading. There weren't many, but my excitement grew when I found a sleeve of square black-and-white photos obviously taken when she was about my age. I pulled one out and tilted it under the light to get a better look. "Where was Amma stationed during the war? This looks like somewhere in Europe, with the cobblestone streets and the architecture of those houses." I handed Granny the photo and waited for her memories of any stories Amma might have told her to kick in.

"The Red Cross moved her around, but she spent most of her time in Italy. They opened a location after the war to help the

Americans who were there to fix ships docked for repairs. She used to joke that the Italian wine would help fix the burns and broken bones quicker than they could."

Italy. The woman in the other photo had dark hair and dark eyes. And I didn't think Isabel was a common American name back then. "Does Amma have any paperwork from when she was in the war, like employment papers or paycheck stubs?"

Granny took a sip of black coffee before answering. She didn't look good. The dark circles under her eyes had gotten worse. I knew sleep was fleeting and decided to spend the weekend with her. Maybe I could talk my mother into joining us for a movie night. "We might find some paperwork in her desk. I haven't had the energy to start digging through it. Her lawyers had the important papers, so at least her estate is settled."

It took all my energy to not jump up and race to Amma's room. Granny needed me to be there for her, not to rifle through her mother's things. I squeezed her hand. "I'm glad it's settled, too. You didn't need that added pressure. Are you up for a trip to the cemetery? It's a nice day."

"Do you have the time to take me? Don't you need to be at work?"

"I'm the boss, so I can do whatever I want. Besides, Ginger's there, and she can field the calls to me. I don't have to be in the office to work." Guilt made my heart pump faster, but I held her hand and waited.

"I would like that. Just let me finish my coffee and this wonderful Danish first."

She pulled one of the photo albums from the stack, smiling and touching the photos. I'd be wrecked when my mother died, so I understood the need to find comfort in whatever she could. I pointed to a picture and gave a low whistle. "Is that Amma? She was gorgeous."

Granny looked at me. "Honey, you look just like her."

I scoffed. "No, I don't. She was so beautiful. I look dull compared to her."

"Well, if you took the time to style your hair and wear makeup, you two could pass for sisters."

I studied the photo. We shared the same eyes, lips, and chin. Her hair was almost a platinum blond whereas mine was more golden. I needed to get highlights. Now that my hair had grown out from the Hair Incident, I could do more with it. "Is that your way of telling me I should try harder?" I knew I'd let myself go a bit. Almost a year ago, I ended it with a high-maintenance girlfriend who pushed me constantly to eat the right foods, use the most expensive skin-care products, order top-of-the-line makeup, and wear high heels with jeans. When we broke up, I ate snack foods for a solid week and refused to wear mascara or lipstick, or even brush my hair. My mother staged an intervention and forced me to shower, eat more than doughnuts and chocolate, and get my shit together. It wasn't a bad breakup; I just needed time to not care so much.

Once I got over the initial shock, I put my energies into something productive. I quit my job as a forensic scientist, much to my parents' chagrin, and opened my own private investigating firm after shadowing a PI and a detective on the local police force. My mom told me I was bonkers and even cried, saying it was too dangerous, and people wouldn't take me seriously because I was young, attractive, and a woman. My dad squeezed my shoulder and asked if I could afford to walk away from a good-paying job. He knew better than to say anything sexist. I told him it was better for me to do it now before life got overwhelming with marriage and children. He sighed heavily and poured himself a whiskey.

Now I was twenty-six years old with a private investigator's license and zero business. Nobody believed in me except Amma. I developed my thirst for crime-solving when I spent my summers with her. We watched reruns of *Murder, She Wrote*, *Criminal Minds*, *Law and Order*, and *NCIS* when it was too hot outside to play or swim. I enjoyed the challenge, and Amma said I had a head for solving crimes.

"I'm ready to go if you have the time," Granny said.

I closed the photo book and took both cups to the sink. "Do you want to stop and get fresh flowers?"

She waved me off and shot me a sad smile. "Honey, that's sweet, but her grave is still covered from the funeral. We can get fresh flowers the next time."

Amma was very active and popular in her retirement groups until the day she passed. She cared about the way she looked, always dressed to the nines, and had a student hairdresser fix her hair every Friday. She seemed to be waiting for something to happen. I didn't know why, but something told me that my first job would give Amma peace even though she was already gone from this world.

Chapter Two

Bad Decisions—Camila

W as it Thursday or Friday? The days melded together, especially in the summer when I wanted to be at the beach and not cooped up in the shop. I was always ready for the weekend because I didn't have to work and could hang out with my friends as late as I wanted. Our olive oil shop opened at nine, even though nobody raced to buy oil first thing in the morning. Most of the patrons came for the wine we sold next door. Our olive oils were an afterthought. I was in charge of them, but it was a boring job.

My two older brothers were lucky and got to schmooze with the townspeople and tourists at our winery up the hill. The wine shop next door was for the convenience of people who couldn't take the time to go up to the winery. My mom worked mornings, and one of my aunts picked up the afternoon shift. We kept the door between the two businesses open, hoping the overflow from the wine shop would trickle into my store. Sometimes it worked. Most of the time people walked through as though they were going to buy something but immediately left through my front door. It wasn't as if our oils weren't popular, because they were, but people could go through a bottle of wine a lot faster than a bottle of olive oil.

My father caught me sitting in a chair with my motorcycle boots up on the counter. "The oil isn't going to sell itself."

I threw my hands up. "Nobody's here. Who am I supposed to sell it to?"

"Be professional, Camila. People are always watching." He knocked my boots off the counter and wiped the spot where my heels had rested. "Maybe you can dust or straighten the bottles?"

I rolled my eyes and smirked at him. "Maybe you should ask Ethan or Luke to come in here and make it perfect." Even though our vineyard was small, our wines were popular. We shipped worldwide, but most of our business was local. My bisnonna, my great-grandmother, insisted on starting an olive grove years ago. Now we were able to turn a solid profit on our olives. My family pushed me to learn the olive business, even though I was more familiar with our wines.

He leaned over and touched the tip of my nose with his forefinger. "But you are my beautiful daughter, and this is the face that sells the oil. You know the wine sells itself. The boys are only there for something to do."

"It's not fair."

"This gives you time to work on your art. Your hours aren't bad. You have freedoms that most of your friends don't. Be thankful, Camila," he said.

He was right. I nodded after delivering the longest sigh. "It's just so boring here all by myself."

He pointed to a corner that housed a simple olive oil display but had a great view of the vineyard up on the hill. "You should set up an easel and paint. We could sell your drawings and paintings here."

I had a better chance of selling my art on the streets, but it couldn't hurt to try. We drew a fair number of tourists from neighboring Naples. Even though I wasn't a famous artist, I sold enough at local street fairs to buy indulgences like my nice leather motorcycle boots and jacket. My parents thought my art was a nice hobby. Only Bisnonna understood my passion. Whenever she asked me for a painting, I dropped everything and gave her what she wanted. She was ninety-six and my whole world. I loved my mother and Nonna, my grandmother, but because Bisnonna was so frail and her time limited, I was fierce about her. "I'll bring my paints tomorrow."

He hugged me before he left and pointed at the counter to serve as a reminder not to put my feet up there. My father was hard on all of us, but I was his weakness, and the whole family knew it.

He and my mother's story was a true-life fairy tale. They met at a youth hostel in Rome. My mother was there to see an American boy-band concert, and my American father was backpacking through Europe. He bought her gelato from a cart in a cobblestone piazza and, according to my father, fell instantly in love. He extended his stay to get to know her. They communicated by pointing to words in translation books until they learned each other's language. He not only found himself, but a beautiful Italian wife and, within a few years, two sons. I was born six years into their marriage.

My brothers and I were bilingual and switched between English and Italian at the villa. My father's Italian wasn't the greatest even after thirty-two years, but he was constantly trying to improve it. Nerissa, my mother, had learned some English in her youth from Bisnonna and Nonna.

Bisnonna's English was better than my father's Italian. She learned it during World War II when she and her friends went to the beach every weekend and hung out with the Americans working on their warships. Nonna said Bisnonna also took language classes after the war. And not just one class, but several. She spoke English with her grandchildren but switched to Italian whenever my father was nearby. She joked that she did it to make him try harder. She wanted to practice English more than anything, so when my mother met my American father, she greeted him with open arms.

My cell phone rang, bringing me out of the fairy tale that was my parents' story.

"Are you ready for tomorrow?"

So, it was Friday. When we were young, everyone thought Mateo, my best friend since kindergarten, and I would get married. It wasn't until my parents caught me making out with his cousin, Aria, when I was fifteen that they realized I was a lesbian. They didn't care. They had their hands full with my brothers, who were young men trying to figure life out. They were struggling until my father sent them to Texas for a summer to work at a cattle ranch with our uncle. They came home stronger, disciplined, and ready to get back to easy vineyard life.

"Yes. I have everything matted and ready to go. What about you?" I asked.

"I just got my order of dolphins in so I can rest easy." Mateo had written and illustrated a successful children's book about a dolphin, Luigi, who gets lost, and people from the Italian seaside towns help him get back to his pod. He made a respectable living selling signed books with small stuffed dolphins, but his steady income came from working part-time at the winery. I was proud of him, and slightly jealous.

"Even without the stuffed toys, your book would sell. It's adorable. The next time I visit my aunt and uncle in Dallas, I'll take a suitcase of them and sell them to the bookstores there." That wasn't how it worked, but I could tell he was excited about the idea.

"I hope I sell out again. Tourists are the biggest buyers."

"That's because everyone here and in the neighboring towns already has your book," I said.

"What are you displaying this week?"

"Mostly sketches and a few oil paintings." Too many artists here painted watercolors of the ocean, and I wanted to stand apart from them. They catered to the tourists, while I indulged the locals with town and vineyard paintings. Besides, the tourists were more trouble than they were worth. Most of them haggled like my art was cheap and I was trying to gouge them. It was nearly criminal. And then there were the actual criminals. People came through and scammed the locals or other tourists, knowing they would be out of the country before their petty crimes caught up with them. It was better to stick with people I knew and trusted.

"You'll do well. You always do. What time do you want me to pick you up?" Mateo asked.

It was hard to carry anything on my motorcycle, so he transported my art in his tiny pick-up truck on the weekends we participated in the street fair. Most of my summer weekends were for drinking wine and heading to the beach with my friends, but at least once a month, Mateo convinced me to set up a booth and sell what he thought was magnificent art. Bisnonna told me I got my talent from her, but I never saw any of her artwork. I hated to lose a day on the beach, but I tolerated the heat and the boredom that came from running a booth at the fair to indulge Mateo.

"You're going to make me get up early tomorrow, aren't you?" Mateo and three of our friends were going to a party on the beach. I'd rather party with them and sleep in, but I feared Mateo had other plans.

"How about I stay the night? If everyone is going to the beach tonight, then I can at least make sure you get home at a decent time." His suggestion had merit even though he had an ulterior motive. If he was with me, then he controlled what time we got up and headed to the market. It wasn't in full swing until nine, but Mateo always got us there at seven thirty to set up.

"Okay, but you have to wake me with coffee and a pastry."

"Deal. I'll pick you up at nine tonight."

"Come over at seven for dinner." I disconnected the call and closed out for the day. We had a total of twenty-four sales. Tomorrow we would do five times that when the tourist buses arrived. Two of my cousins and one of my aunts worked on the weekends. We paid a hefty price to have our vineyard and olive grove on several tour-bus stops, but it was worth it.

I locked the door and started my motorcycle. Technically, I could walk to work, but my confidence kicked up several notches when I rode my bike. She was a hand-me-down from my brother, but she still had some miles left. I was saving for a new Ducati, and whenever I told Mateo I didn't want to spend my weekend at the market, he texted me a picture of the bike I wanted.

The door to the wine shop opened, and my mother came out. "How was business?" She wiped her hands on her apron and kissed my cheek. At fifty-four, she was amazingly beautiful. Nobody believed she was our mother. People mistook her for my older sister all the time. Every day she fixed her hair, put on makeup, and wore either a dress or slacks with a silk blouse. Image was everything to her.

"We had a decent day. About right for this time of year."

"Are you going out tonight?" she asked.

"Yes. Oh, and Mateo is coming over for dinner and staying the night. He wants to make sure I get up on time for the fair."

"Do you blame him?" She knew how difficult it was to wake me in the mornings. I played hard and slept even harder.

"Not at all." I kissed her good-bye and excused myself to find the artwork I wanted to sell tomorrow. I settled on a dozen oil paintings ranging in size, depicting scenes of our quaint town, the olive groves, and the goats that were shepherded on neighboring land. The sketches were of animals, still lifes, and a few of my family. I'd found a beautiful photo of Bisnonna when she was younger and sketched it. There was also one of my bisnonno, Lorenzo Rossini, when he was a pilot in the war. Those weren't for sale, but I used them to draw people to my booth. By the time Mateo showed up, I had chosen a total of thirty-six items. He gave a low whistle when he saw my stack.

"You are ambitious about tomorrow." He picked up the sketch of my bisnonna. "If she were sixty years younger, I would go for it."

I smacked his shoulder and cursed him in Italian. "You're not her type. She likes tall, burly, strong men." I was lying and he knew it. Mateo really was her type—kind and gentle and romantic. She had a soft spot for him. He loved her, too, and made a point to sit and chat with her every time he visited. Often, she asked him to read the book he wrote and held the stuffed dolphin on her lap when he opened the pages and began Luigi's journey. I was almost certain she had helped him financially when he was writing his book. It didn't bother me.

"All the Rossini women love me." He puffed out his small chest and tilted his chin up.

He wasn't wrong. Mateo was a nice-looking young man who spent a lot of time playing Romeo. I was five foot seven and could look him in the eye. He had dark, wavy hair and dark eyes, but his body was soft. He enjoyed pasta, wine, and bread too much. While our muscular friends blew through a lot of the attractive women in town, as well as the hot vacationers who summered in Italy, Mateo noticed the women who weren't expecting it. At least he spent more time wooing them than sleeping with them. "We love you like a little brother."

He reached out for me and twirled me as if we were dancing. I went along with it. Mateo was graceful and loved to dance. "You love me for me." Just before he dipped me, he gave me a smoldering look that only made me laugh. I grabbed his shoulders and pulled myself up.

"Your charms are worthless on me. Save them for the unsuspecting tourists who will inevitably be invited to our bonfire tonight." I straightened my shirt and tucked the front into my jeans. "Let's go. We don't want to be late for dinner."

"They were working, right?" Mateo asked.

"What was working?"

"My charms."

"Dream on."

❖

"Get up."

I groaned and snuggled deeper under my thin blanket. No way was it six thirty. Didn't I just get into bed? "Go away."

"It's time to flirt with customers."

Mateo's voice pushed its way through the hangover haze that clouded my brain. How many glasses of wine did I drink last night? "I changed my mind. It's too hot and I need sleep. Why did you let me drink so much?" His fingers brushed my unruly dark hair out of my face. I cracked open an eye. He was already dressed, and the mint on his breath made me close my mouth and groan. I could taste my bad decisions from last night and knew every part of me stunk.

"Start the shower and find me something normal to wear."

I bounced slightly as Mateo's weight left the mattress. I heard him turn on the shower and rifle through my closet. I dragged myself to the bathroom and stepped under the stream of barely warm water, cursing Mateo's name. He did that on purpose.

"Quit complaining. We have to leave in thirty minutes. I'll be downstairs with coffee and a roll. Hurry up."

I ran a quick razor over my legs and rinsed out the conditioner, hoping it would calm the waviness of my long hair. I was down to fifteen minutes by the time I dried off and slipped into a thin, sleeveless top and a skirt. The sandals I wanted to wear were somewhere downstairs, from what I vaguely remembered about last night.

"Camila, hurry up! You are making Mateo late."

"I'm almost done." My mother's voice instantly irritated me for no reason other than she was right and I was a jerk for drinking too much last night and for committing to the fair this weekend. "Here I am." I kissed my mother's cheek and grabbed a warm roll off the plate as I followed Mateo out. "Good luck today. Looks like it'll be busy."

"We've got it. Have fun and be nice. You get more flies with honey," she said.

"She's right. You need to sober up and put a smile on that beautiful face." Mateo handed me a cup of coffee to go with my breakfast.

"I know. I'll snap out of it by the time we set up." It wasn't Mateo's fault I didn't feel like peddling my art to people I either knew too well or didn't know at all. "I'm just tired of the same thing. This town is so small. Nothing exciting ever happens around here."

"Stop being so negative. You never know. Today might just be your lucky day."

CHAPTER THREE

PASSPORT STAMPED—PERI

My heart fluttered, and I stopped and stared at the sketch of a woman displayed in a booth at the street fair. I was outside Naples, Italy in Sequina, a small town Amma had spent some time in. I'd parked my Fiat rental and started walking only because the street was blocked. After three days of squeezing the steering wheel and barely surviving traffic in a foreign country, I was starting to get used to the speed of cars here and their drivers' lack of turn-signal usage. I even looked to see if maybe the cars in Italy weren't equipped with them, but they were.

I leaned closer to the sketch, amazed at my luck after several days of hearing and learning all the different ways to say "no" in Italian. I'd started with the towns Amma had been stationed in for the longest periods of time. My list of residences and archives to check out had dwindled to this little town that I wasn't even sure she'd lived in. After all that, here was a sketch of a woman who looked exactly like the photo in the locket.

I turned in the empty booth and looked out into the crowd, willing somebody to see me and help me. Somebody who should be in this booth. I needed answers. After days of showing an enlarged photo of the mysterious woman to people in half a dozen towns in Italy, I'd finally caught a break.

"Do you know where the artist is?" I asked the man selling puppets in the next booth. He shrugged and muttered something in

Italian. It sounded like he wasn't fond of his neighbor. The man in the booth on the other side, selling books and stuffed toys, was too busy to bother. I looked around one last time for help before I gently pulled the sketch down to look at the detail. The artist had done an amazing job. She'd captured the same happiness in the woman's eyes and the small dimple in her left cheek. Her hairstyle must've been a popular one because Amma had it, too, though the length was shorter.

From behind me came an angry question in Italian. I turned to see a tall, beautiful woman with her arms crossed. My peripheral vision picked up long, tanned legs, red toenails that peeked out from strappy sandals, toned arms, and beautiful wavy hair that she had pulled over one shoulder, but my eyes never left hers. As if in a trance, I couldn't stop staring at her light-brown eyes. They quickly flashed with annoyance, and I figured at this point that I was staring. There was a clip to her words that I knew was more than the language. I couldn't find my own words. To hear about somebody being tongue-tied around a woman was different from experiencing it. I opened my mouth and closed it again quickly. Where were my words? Something must have clicked because she took a small step back and forced a smile.

"Can I help you?"

Was she the artist? I tore my gaze from her penetrating stare just to catch my breath. She was very attractive and extremely intense. Her light, fashionable, yet casual clothes made me feel like a frumpy American. At least I'd tried harder today after learning that people were more likely to help me when I took the time to fix my hair and apply makeup. My wardrobe was very limited, and I didn't want to spend any of Amma's money on new clothes. The woman's perfectly arched eyebrow indicated she wasn't happy. Why was everyone here so angry at me?

"Just so you know, that's not for sale." Her English was perfect, but she had a slight accent. She gently pried the sketch from my hands and hung it again.

"I need to find this woman. Please. Do you know her?" I heard the desperation in my voice that had been building since the moment I opened the locket.

"Why?"

I took a step back and a deep breath to calm down. I probably sounded bonkers to the artist, but I needed her to know that this woman was the sole reason I was in Italy in a way that wouldn't overwhelm her. Another deep breath. "I have a client in the United States who asked me to locate her," I said.

The woman folded her arms again and leaned her weight on one hip. Her movement drew attention to her legs, and I took a quick moment to appreciate the skirt that hugged her curves and was short enough to show off the smoothness of her skin.

"So? How do you know she's the woman you're looking for?"

I handed her an enlarged photo replica from the locket. She harrumphed and thrust the photo back.

"That could be any Italian woman. And it doesn't answer the question. What does your client want with this lady?"

I stepped closer, anxious to prove my point. "First of all, it's definitely the same woman. Look at the shape of the eyes and the depth of her dimple. It's the exact same as your sketch. I only want to meet the woman and give her a memento from my client. Personally give it to her. If you know who she is, can you please tell me where I can find her?"

"Where are you from?"

"I'm from Connecticut. On the East Coast." I wanted to see recognition but was only afforded a bored look. "Can you tell me who she is?"

The woman looked me up and down, pursed her lips contemplatively, and nodded. "I can do better than that. I can take you to her."

Without thinking, I grabbed her hands and squeezed. "Thank you so much." I dropped her hands at the second eyebrow arch.

"I'm here until six. If you come back then, I will take you to her."

My jaw dropped open, and I laughed at my good fortune. "Definitely. Six o'clock. I'll be back then. I'm Peri Logan. What's your name?"

She stalled for a few moments. "Camila. Camila Rossini."

"Thank you," I said.

One nod. "I'll see you later."

Her arms were still crossed, and she ignored my attempt at a handshake. That really wasn't a thing in Italy. I was going to have to learn that not all cultures were the same.

❖

"Where's the woman who was in this booth?" It was five minutes until six. The ten-foot by ten-foot space was empty. No walls or anything indicated that somebody was ever there, but I knew it was the same spot. "What time did Camila break down?" I asked her puppet-wielding neighbor. He shrugged and shook his head as though he didn't understand me and continued carefully storing his puppets in containers. I tried again. "Camila?" I pointed to the now-empty booth. "Is she here?"

He hissed a reply as if asking him a few questions was such an inconvenience. "No. Gone." He held up both hands and spread out his fingers, indicating the number ten.

Even though his English was choppy, I understood she left ten minutes ago. Shit. Damn it. She tricked me. Or maybe she just forgot. I cleared my voice to loosen the bubble of panic stuck in my throat. I quickly used my translation app and asked the question in Italian, even though I knew the answer. "Do you know where she lives?"

"No."

I had a feeling puppet man knew but wasn't going to tell me. He was shaking his head too hard, as though telling me would be the death of him. As confident as Camila seemed, I didn't get a murderous vibe from her. Maybe he was only protecting her. "Okay. Will this street fair be here tomorrow?" I pointed to the cobblestone sidewalk and twirled my finger around to indicate here if he didn't understand me. I hit my app again for the Italian word for "tomorrow" and said it the best I could.

"No," he said.

My heart sank along with my hopes.

"Saturday," he said in Italian. I had learned the days of the week during the flight over. That meant the fair was only on Saturdays. Well, fuck. I couldn't take another week off. Italy was killing my bank account and time. I didn't have either to spare. If only I had skipped the gelato and returned twenty minutes earlier, I wouldn't be standing here alone in an empty booth. Where was she? Did she live in this town, or was she from another?

I made another lap around the fair, hoping to glimpse the young, beautiful woman who had either tricked me or simply forgot about meeting me. I watched as people swiftly broke down their booths and packed up. Some made eye contact with me and smiled, while others ignored me completely. It was infuriating. I shouldn't have come to Italy. This whole idea was dumb. I should've plugged Amma's money into the business and given the locket to Granny as a keepsake. I smacked my fist into my hand in frustration and headed back to my car. I googled Camila Rossini on my phone, but the information was overwhelming. I was going to need my computer to do a more intensive search, even though my database was limited to the United States. I called Ginger to have her run a search.

"How's it going, Ginger? Anything happening?" I could tell from the background that she wasn't in the office, which irked me, but then I remembered something. "Crap. I forgot it's Saturday."

"It's no biggie. Just grabbing lunch. You haven't missed much, but we did get payment from Richard Bridges. I guess he liked the incriminating photos of his wife with that guy from the bar. Should make for an interesting divorce." She slurped on what sounded like a milkshake. "I deposited the check into the account yesterday. How's Italy? Did you locate the mysterious woman?"

"Sort of. I met somebody who says she knows her, but I can't find her now."

She snorted and coughed. "What happened?"

"I met somebody who said she knows the woman, and we agreed to meet tonight, but she stood me up."

Ginger made a noise of frustration. "That doesn't make sense."

"I know, but I'm going to spend the weekend trying to find her." My mind was racing. What did young adults do on Saturday nights around here? The possibilities were limitless.

"Call your mother. She's been worried about you," Ginger said.

"Shit, yeah. I need to. Thanks for the reminder. I'll do that now. See you soon." I hung up and quickly called my mother before I got too busy. "Hi, Mom. How are you?"

"How's Italy? Are you having a good time?"

I closed my eyes to keep them from rolling out of my head. "I'm working. Yes, Italy is beautiful, but I haven't had a lot of time to sightsee." It's what she wanted to hear.

"Oh, can you bring me back a bottle of wine? Nothing beats Italian wine."

"I'll see what I can do."

After five more minutes of convincing my mother I was fine and with the promise that I would text her photos even though I wasn't on vacation, I hung up and started my trek around town. Most shops were closing, but the bistros and restaurants with their outdoor seating that gobbled up sidewalk space were open. I walked around for an hour looking for Camila but couldn't find her. I pulled out the picture of Isabel and continued flashing it around town to anyone who would make eye contact with me. After two hours and zero luck, I made my way back to my car and drove slowly back to my hotel. People didn't seem to care about things like bumpers or safely staying ten feet behind the car in front of you. I grabbed a few snacks from the shop in the small lobby to serve as my dinner and headed to my room. I was emotionally exhausted, but at least I had a lead.

For the record, a lot of Rossinis lived in the area. If Camila Rossini was her real name, I wasn't having any luck. Great. She probably lied about her name, too, but it was worth checking out. I found Rossini Winery in Sequina, a town northeast of here, but saw nothing about the family online. Instead, I read an extensive description of the grape and olive cultivars grown at the vineyard.

I woke up sitting in a chair after six hours of uncomfortable sleep. I packed my bag and did a final sweep of my hotel room, making sure I wasn't forgetting anything important like my passport or wallet. I headed downstairs with my bag.

"Are you leaving us, miss?"

The hotel clerk who checked me in a few days ago was very polite and spoke English.

"Yes. I'm headed north for a few days, and then I fly home." I signed my receipt, grabbed a bagel and an apple, and left the hotel. The streets were empty this early in the morning. A lot of the small towns weren't open for business on Sundays, so finding either woman would be difficult. Maybe I'd head to the beach for a few hours of relaxation, since my options were very limited. Using my phone, I reserved a room at a B&B in Sequina, but check-in wasn't until this afternoon.

I pulled on a hoodie, rolled up my jeans, and found a spot in the sand for my quiet, contemplative breakfast. It was too bad I'd spent most of my time here knocking on doors looking for somebody who might not even be alive. Italy was beautiful and exactly how I pictured it. And to think I almost gave up until I saw that drawing. In my heart, I knew it was the same woman. I understood that Camila Rossini was protecting her. If some rando showed up looking for someone in my family or anyone in my social circle, I would've clammed up, too, but I would've wanted to find out why somebody wanted to see her. Camila didn't press. Apparently, she didn't share my curious nature.

I put my bag under my head, slipped my sunglasses on, and did what I should've done sooner. I relaxed. I dug my toes in the sand and thought about the woman I'd met. Camila. She was around my age, very chic, and way out of my league. I felt completely out of place here, and if I wasn't so damned determined to find the mysterious woman, I would've left after the first day. No, that's not true. I would've never flown over here in the first place.

One more thing to file under my repertoire of bad decisions: falling asleep on a beach. I woke up surrounded by bold, squawking seagulls with gritty sand in my mouth. They were eyeing the half-eaten bagel I still clutched, each one bravely moving closer to nab it. Shrieking, I tossed it as far away as I could from an almost horizontal position and tweaked my back in the process. Fuck. Stupid birds. I heard a few people around me laugh and wondered if videos of this were already on social media. I could only imagine the hashtags: #sleepinggirlattackedbybirds #hitchcockwasright #birds1woman0. I stood, gingerly trying to stretch my back and not look like a complete idiot. I grabbed my shoes and my purse and limped, slightly hunched over, back to the car to nurse my ego. It was close to check-in time, and I needed a hot shower to loosen my muscles.

The woman working the tiny front desk in my B&B greeted me in rapid Italian.

"I'm sorry. I don't speak Italian." I showed her the reservation confirmation on my phone.

She handed me a key and pointed to the stairs. "Two."

"I'm in room two." I pointed up the stairs for affirmation.

"Si" She nodded.

"Grazie."

To say the room was small was an understatement. I could almost wash my hands in the bathroom sink from the bed. But it was clean, beautifully decorated, and within my budget. It also included meals and was close to the Rossini vineyard. It couldn't hurt to check it out. According to Google, they were open only to bus tours today, but open to the public tomorrow at nine. That would be my first stop. Maybe they knew either Camila or Isabel. I needed to regroup, dig around some more, and find something to eat that wasn't either pure sugar or salty chips.

Chapter Four

Why Is She Here?—Camila

I liked nothing better than being on the beach, drinking wine, and hanging out with my friends.

"What wine did you bring us today?" Mateo dropped next to me on my blanket and looked through my bag without asking.

I smacked his hand. "Never go through somebody's things without permission."

"But we're family." He shook his hand to minimize the sting. "And it's time for wine. The sun is setting." He had two paper cups, and I shook my head at him.

"Really, Mateo? You just met her. And she seems very young."

He followed my line of sight. A young woman sat on his blanket, drawing designs in the sand with her finger. His shirt was draped across her shoulders for added warmth.

"She's twenty-two and here until next weekend. She is visiting her cousins, who are over there with their group of friends. I invited her over because she looked lonely." He pointed to eight people sitting in a circle laughing and seemingly having a great time about twenty feet from us. She looked uncomfortable but determined. Was she trying to make somebody jealous from her group, or was she legit bored? I handed him a bottle of our Sangiovese blend.

"You be nice to her, or I will disown you," I said.

"Come have a drink with us."

I shook my head. "I just want to chill here and enjoy my last night of freedom."

"Try to be friendly. You're too pretty to frown all the time."

"Go away." Even I felt the scowl on my face. Mateo went back to his woman of the moment and said something to her. She waved to me, thanking me for the wine. I made it a point to smile at them.

"Camila, how did the art fair go?" My friend Gemma came up behind me. We'd been close since we were five. We weren't besties, but we hung out in the same circles. She and her husband Brando were expecting their first child in two short months. They were the first in our group to start a family. Rossini Winery provided the alcohol, and Isabel's Oils were used at the wedding dinner. I held my hand out in case she needed it as she settled into a comfortable position on the blanket next to me. We both let out a sigh of relief when she was finally seated.

"It was good. I sold several paintings and a few sketches." I didn't tell a single person about the woman who approached me about my bisnonna. It was unsettling. I didn't know who she was, and she didn't explain herself well.

"That's wonderful. I love your paintings. And I'm glad they aren't the typical touristy type art."

"It's probably a mistake not going with what everyone else is doing, but I like different."

She gently touched my arm. "With your art, people get to see the real Italy. Not what's on the internet or what they think our country looks like. Those are overdone. You paint real life. I adore the sheep painting so much."

"That was my biggest seller," I said. When I sold the painting of lost sheep strolling through town for four hundred Euros, I turned around and bought motorcycle boots. I should have saved the money, but I wanted the power of spending that much money on something I didn't have to. My parents had money but made damn sure we earned ours. One day, everything would fall to us, but for now, we all had to work for a living. My brothers had their own places in town, whereas I still lived in the family villa. The upstairs was mine, but sometimes Ethan would crash in the spare room next to mine when it was harvest time and he worked late.

"You should go to school for your art. I know your parents have this idea that you and your brothers will take over the businesses, but I think art is more important to you."

I scoffed, but Gemma was right. I loved art, but no one else except Bisnonna did. My parents thought it was a hobby that couldn't possibly make me rich or happy. "One day I'll start a family like you, and I'll need the steadiness of a good job. I don't know that my art will support me."

"If you lived forever at the villa, you could do it all," she said.

I picked up a handful of soft sand and watched it sift slowly through my fingers. "I want my independence. I want my wife and me to have our own place. I mean, yes, the villa would be easy, but I like privacy, and you know how I don't have that really."

Gemma laughed. "Especially since Mateo has no problem busting through any closed door. It's a good thing your parents love him so much."

"It's a good thing I do, too." We watched him talking to the young tourist. "I bet he's telling her all about the wine."

"I wish his book would take off worldwide. He would charm the pants off the international market."

"I know, but he refuses to promote it beyond Sequina. He could be talking to schools and libraries and even read it to classrooms and preschools."

"He's so charming. He should be writing romance novels. Then he would be surrounded by eager women looking for love."

I turned to Gemma. "That's the best idea I've heard so far. Mateo is a good writer. Maybe if we work with him on the plots and give him the woman's perspective, he could write a best seller."

"Mateo, come here." Gemma motioned him over.

He frowned at us but excused himself and walked over. "Hello, baby and mama. What's going on? I'm behaving. Tory's a very nice woman."

I smiled because he thought we were going to criticize his philandering ways. "You're fine. Gemma just had a fabulous idea, and we couldn't wait to share it with you."

"What?"

I tugged on his chin to get him to look at us and not his date. "Focus. This is good stuff."

"I'm sorry. What?"

"We think you should write a romance novel."

He threw his head back and laughed, gaining us the attention of everyone in our group. "You're not serious."

"We are. It's a great idea. You are a gifted writer, and a man writing a romance under our tutelage? It'll be amazing. Think of all the women who will line up to be charmed by best-selling writer Mateo De Luca," Gemma said.

"Oh, no. He would have to write under a different name. Too many people know Mateo De Luca. It needs to be sexier. How about Mateo Moretti or Mancini?" I asked.

"Good-bye, ladies. I'll see you later." He wiped the sand off his shorts and walked back to his date.

"Or you can be Lucinda De Luca. The name is up to you," I called.

He flipped me off behind his back and was rewarded with a laugh from both of us.

"It's too bad. I think it's a great idea," Gemma said.

"Oh, he's totally in. He just doesn't realize it yet."

The idea had merit. A children's book was fine, but if Mateo was serious about writing, romance was the genre that sold the most and made the most sense. He could write it in both Italian and English. And he was very smooth with the ladies so his experience would come in handy when writing the intimate scenes.

"Do you think so? I mean, it seems like our idea had zero effect on him. Look at him. Schmoozing that poor girl."

"I know we joke about him, but he's got a good heart. One day he'll settle down. I bet he'll beat me at that."

"Oh, please. Sister Gabriella has a better shot of settling down," Gemma said.

Sister Gabriella was in charge of Sunday school when we were little. She was old, sour, and hated everyone and everything. At least that's what it seemed like to seven-year-old students. "Is she still alive?" I asked.

"She was only forty-five or so. I bet she's still teaching."

My gasp was genuine. "Really? Why did she feel so old to me?"

"Because we were seven and hated authority," she said.

"I'm twenty-five and I still hate it," I said.

"Learn to drive that crappy motorcycle slower, and then you wouldn't hate all the speeding tickets and parking violations."

"But the motorcycle is so much fun," I said. It was easier to drive, and I didn't travel much unless I was going to Rome for a long weekend with my friends.

"That money you are saving? That should be for a car. What happens if I go into labor and you're the only one around? I can't be on the back of your motorcycle as you race me to the hospital." Gemma nudged me with her shoulder.

"I'll just take the keys to your car and drive you there." Gemma upgraded when they found out they were pregnant, but the car wasn't that much bigger. The car seat alone would take up most of the backseat.

"Camila."

I didn't recognize the voice behind me. I leaned back to see who it was and almost fell over. I grabbed Gemma to steady myself. It was the American from the fair yesterday. How did she find me?

"You're Camila, right? Camila Rossini? The one who asked me to meet her and then ghosted me?" She was angry and sunburned. And embarrassing me in front of my friends. Gemma looked at me wide-eyed with legitimate concern. I didn't remember the American being so attractive or so assertive. Her wavy blond hair fell around her shoulder in a messy braid, and her ocean-blue eyes were even more pronounced against her sun-kissed cheeks.

"Yes. But I didn't ghost you. I shut down early, but you were nowhere to be found." That wasn't true. I purposely shut down to avoid her. Somebody wanted to find Bisnonna, and I wanted to protect her.

She folded her arms in front of her. "Well, I'm here now."

Mateo came out of nowhere and reached out for my hand. "Hello. I'm Mateo. I'm Camila's best friend."

"I'm Peri. Peri Logan. Nice to meet you," she said.

She wore a hoodie tied around her waist, aviator sunglasses, and jeans rolled to just below her knees. She had toned calves and red polish on her toenails. I gritted my teeth while Mateo lavished attention.

"Mateo, your girlfriend looks upset." I nodded at the woman he had quickly abandoned for the American.

He shot me a warning look that I returned with heat.

"Nice to meet you, too. I better see to my friend." Mateo smiled at Peri. When he walked by me, he scowled and, under his breath, told me he'd remember this.

I played innocent and shrugged. What I said was true. Plus, I wanted Peri all to myself. I needed more information on her interest in Bisnonna. "Come join us for a bit." I pointed to a spot on the other side of Gemma.

Peri seemed surprised at the invitation and hesitated. "Uh, sure, I guess."

I motioned for her to sit and even gave her a smile. She untied her sweatshirt and carefully placed it on the sand. The fact that she had found me in my hometown on the beach was incredible. I doubted this was a coincidence. The woman was in Italy on behalf of some mysterious client who wanted to give something to my bisnonna, but all she had was an old photo? It didn't make sense. No way was I going to help her. I'd be seriously creeped out if she didn't look like such a lost puppy. In my heart, I didn't think she was a threat, but I was cautious because she was a stranger. An attractive stranger if you liked the American girl-next-door look. Villanelle from *Killing Eve* was also smoking hot, but look how that turned out. "Are you staying close by?"

"Not too far away." She thumbed behind her to either the rows of B&Bs or the hotel up the street.

"What's she saying?" Gemma asked.

Since Mateo had been my best friend for twenty years, he grew up learning English with me. They taught it in school, too, but a lot of my friends forgot it because they never used it. "She's telling us where she's staying."

"Why? How do you know her?"

"She showed up at the fair yesterday looking for Bisnonna," I said.

"Why? That doesn't make sense." Gemma's smile was more of a grimace. I elbowed her arm gently.

I switched back to English. "So, Peri, you never said why you wanted to contact the woman."

She held her hand up to shield her eyes from the sun. I felt a flutter low in my stomach when our eyes met. I blamed the betrayal of my body on the color of her eyes. Hers were light blue, like the ocean closer to the beach. "I can't share that information. It's a client-confidentiality thing. But I promise you it's nothing bad. I just have something to give her."

"Camila, what's going on? Why is she looking for your bisnonna?" Gemma asked.

I prayed Peri didn't understand Italian as I explained our meeting yesterday and how I tried to get away from her.

"Do you think she's following you?"

I grimaced. "I'm starting to think so, but she seems like such a mess. I doubt if she's capable of following me."

"Should we alert the authorities?" Gemma looked frightened.

"No. And stop frowning. I don't want her to realize I'm not going to help her," I said. Gemma quickly shifted her expression. "I don't intend to introduce her to Bisnonna, but I'll be more than happy to show her every nook and cranny of this town until she has to go back home." I could tell by Peri's furrowed brow that she was getting frustrated. I switched to English. "We think the woman you are looking for is on vacation."

"So, she's still alive. That's good to know," Peri said.

Anger bubbled up, but I suppressed it. I had to stop giving her information. "I can meet you tomorrow, and we can visit her house."

"If you just give me Isabel's address, I can do it myself. I wouldn't want to bother you."

I bit the inside of my cheek to keep the surprise off my face. She knew her name? Then she must know where the villa and the vineyard were. What game was she playing? "Oh, I don't mind at all. You're a stranger, and I have lived in this town my entire life. It's my duty to be hospitable." That was true. I knew how to be charming. I added a sweet, innocent smile. "I'll give you my phone number, and you can call me tomorrow."

She smirked at me. "I have a feeling you'll give me a wrong number."

Touché. The idea had crossed my mind. I pulled out my phone. "Do you have WhatsApp? What's your number?" I asked when she nodded and waited for her to recite her number. She was surprised when her phone rang.

"Hello?" she asked.

I never understood why that word was a question. "Hi, Peri. This is Camila. How are you enjoying Italy so far?" I could hear the echo of my own voice coming from her phone.

The smile that blossomed on her face was nearly perfect. When not frazzled, Peri was lovely. I found myself smiling back at her but stopped when I remembered she wanted to get to my family for reasons she wasn't willing to share.

"It's a very pretty place, but I'm anxious to find Isabel and finish my job," she said.

She hung up but quickly added me to her contacts. What was I thinking? Now I was obligated to help. Gemma nervously picked at the hem of her shirt, obviously uncomfortable between us, but I needed her exactly where she was to act as a buffer.

After a long, awkward silence of my friends all staring at her, Mateo broke the quiet. "Peri, would you like something to drink? We have wine, water, and Coke." His timing was perfect. He pointed to the cooler.

"Water sounds great. Thank you."

She met Mateo halfway. That gave me the opportunity to study her. A vulnerability about her made me question my decision, but only for a moment. Even though everything about her screamed tourist, her entire look gave her an innocent, sexy vibe that infuriated me. I unfairly resented her for being attractive and realized I was wrong inviting her to sit with my friends. Mateo's new friend, Tory, said good-bye to the group, which gave him the opportunity to work his charms on Peri. I frowned at him when he stood. He winked at me in return. Don't do it, Mateo. Don't you do it, I willed.

"Peri, what are you doing in Italy? Are you here with your family? Husband? Girlfriend?"

He sat down next to her in the sand and clinked his cup of wine against her water. She smiled at him and took a sip, but her eyes found me. I stared at her until she turned her attention back to Mateo.

"I'm here on business. So far, it's been a very nice country. I'm so surprised that so many people speak English," she said.

"They teach it in school, but I've been friends with Camila since we were babies, and her father is American. I begged them to teach me. Now I'm glad because I get to speak to beautiful women who come to our town to enjoy the beach, our wine, and our company."

"All the girls fall for this, right?" Peri laughed.

"Only the ones I want to fall for this," he said.

She laughed with him so easily. It wasn't jealousy I felt, but betrayal. Mateo ignored my quiet, warning looks, and I crossed my arms and stewed in self-pity.

"She seems nice. I don't think she's out to hurt you or your family. Oh, maybe she's like a long-lost sister," Gemma said.

I nudged her with my shoulder. "Don't even joke about that. My brothers are enough siblings for me." Plus, I would have had impure thoughts about my sister, and that creeped me out.

"Or maybe she's one of your cousins from America."

"Can we please not assume she's a family member?" I sighed deeply and stared at Peri again. She was looking for my great-grandmother on my mother's side, not my father's. "I hate to admit it, but I'm curious why she wants to meet Bisnonna."

"Long-lost family fortune? Look, I'm trying not to overthink this, but what could she possibly want with Isabel? Maybe it has something to do with the olive oils? She was the one who started the business, right?"

"Let's not talk about the oils either. I have only one more night before I have to go back to work."

Gemma touched my hand. "You really should tell your parents you want to focus on your art. I know it's hard because you have been working for the family so long, but don't you think your parents have your best interest at heart? They love you. They want what's best for you. Your brothers can run things."

I snorted. "Can you imagine that conversation with Gregory and Nerissa? I'm going to art school. See ya!" I mock-saluted Gemma, who shrugged.

"Couldn't hurt to try."

But it could. My father would be devastated if I packed up and moved away to attend art school. Failure wasn't my forte either. What if I said good-bye only to return a few months later because the quality of my work wasn't good enough? Then I would be devastated. "Let's talk about the baby."

She nodded. "The shower's next weekend. I'm registered online. Wait. You're coming, right?"

"I wouldn't miss it." I had totally forgotten about it and was pleased I hadn't missed it entirely. "Is Mateo invited?"

"Definitely."

"I'm going to guess the baby is going to get a signed copy of *Luigi*," I said.

"You're probably right. But that's okay. He doesn't know it yet, but he's going to be our number-one babysitter. He's so good with kids."

The more we stared at Mateo, the more I loved the idea of him writing a romance. I was also growing irritated at his ease talking to Peri. I interrupted them. "Peri, what do you do back in the United States? You said you have a client. Are you a lawyer?"

Her smile from the conversation between her and Mateo slid off her face when she heard her name and turned her attention toward me. She was still upset and wasn't likely to improve her disposition after the plan I had for us tomorrow.

"I'm a private investigator."

She had pride in her voice. I ignored the spike in my pulse. Fear had entered the equation. She knew more than she was letting on, and for a moment I doubted my plan to get her out of our lives was going to work.

Chapter Five

Helpful People—Peri

I had to believe Camila was telling the truth, that she simply forgot our timing was off and I must have missed her by a few minutes. I texted her last night to confirm where we were meeting this morning. Café Sequina wasn't hard to find, but I was nervous she'd be a no-show again.

"Good morning."

Camila's smile made my stomach flutter, and I hated myself for letting her affect me. I kept my smile small because I wasn't sure if I could trust her, and a big, toothy smile meant my guard was down.

"How are you?" I was being polite. I needed to build trust, and I had only a few days left. I was at her mercy, and she knew it.

"It's a beautiful day, the sun is shining, and I'm about ready to have the best coffee in town."

The morning had a small chill, but in the sunshine, it was perfect. Camila looked fresh in her cream-colored summer dress and taupe heels. Her long hair was loose and cascaded in waves down her back. Long eyelashes fanned out from her light-brown eyes that twinkled in the sunlight. She wasn't just beautiful, but a whole different level of classy. As much as I wanted my guard to be up around her, I felt it slip away as easily as a whisper in the summer breeze.

"I'm going to have to take your word for it," I said. Italians liked their coffee strong. At least that had been my experience. Espresso was the popular drink and too bitter for me. I was dying for a Frappuccino that tasted more like a blend of whipped cream, almond milk, and sugar than coffee.

Camila reached in front of me and opened the door. I stopped only because the movement was unexpected. I pulled my hand back when our fingers brushed. I wasn't expecting her brief touch to feel so foreign and so warm at the same time.

"Thank you."

She nodded and marched in front of me. There wasn't a line even though it was still early. I watched as she placed her order and, after I nodded my consent, placed mine. I looked around and tried not to be obvious as I translated what I could about their conversation. I picked up words like good morning, coffee, and American, but I really paid attention when I heard her say Isabel. The barista smiled, nodded at me, stifled a giggle, and turned to fix our coffees. Camila tapped her fingers in perfect rhythm as she waited. Her painted nails were short, but manicured and long enough to make the tap, tap, tap noticeable on the countertop. I hid my hands because my chipped polish was embarrassing. They were fine when I left, but five days of driving in congested traffic in a different country and hauling my bags around from hotel to hotel took its toll on my manicure.

"Thank you." I reached for the cup she handed me.

"Let's have a seat over there. It's too bright to sit outside." Camila picked a table near the window and sat. I joined her to keep the peace, even though I wanted her to grab her to-go cup and find Isabel. She wasn't in a rush. I swallowed my impatience and sat with her. "How do you like Italy so far?"

"It's definitely a beautiful place and very different from where I live." That was friendly. "But I'm here to work, so my play time has been limited." I couldn't help myself. I had to say something to let her know I wasn't here for leisure.

"Oh, yes. Finding Isabel. Let's drink our coffees, and then we'll go see if she's home. She visits with her family on the weekends so I'm giving her time to sleep in. She's in her nineties, and I don't want to scare her by pounding on her door this early."

Camila had a point, although Amma was an early riser. She always told me she was happy to wake up for the day, even if it was extremely early, like four or five. A bit morbid now that I recall the one day she didn't. "Is she far from here?"

"Oh, no. Just a few blocks. We can take Mateo's truck."

"I can follow you in my car. It's no problem." I was vulnerable enough. I didn't need my only mode of transportation left behind.

"We should walk then. I can tell you about Sequina and show you all its charms. Besides, her place is close."

Camila took a slow sip of her coffee. It was her way of letting me know we were going to go at her pace. I leaned back in the chair to show her that I could play her game. My ticket home was in three days, and, according to her, we were only a few blocks away. If Amma was watching me, I knew she would be proud at my patience and the fact that I had found Isabel. Almost.

"You're smiling," Camila said.

I shrugged. "I'm just thinking of someone." She didn't need to know who.

"Must be somebody special. Do you have somebody at home who's worried about you here in Italy all by yourself?"

"No. I'm too busy," I said. I could have told her anything, but I went with the truth.

She laughed. "Come on. A cute, All-American girl like you doesn't have anybody worried about her?"

I glossed over the part where she said I was cute and ignored her inquisitive probe into my love life. It wasn't her business. "Being alone here in this beautiful city doesn't scare me. I love to travel." I neglected to reveal that Italy was the first stamp in my passport. I'd traveled across the United States with family and a few people I dated, but I was super proud of myself for getting on a plane and flying over the Atlantic with minimal help. Thank God for Ginger and her jet-setting past. She'd booked my ticket and given me the dos and don'ts of international travel.

"So, no boyfriend? No girlfriend?" she asked.

She quirked her head at me as if she was waiting on confirmation of something important. Why did she care? And why was I being such a jerk to somebody who was trying to help me?

"No. We ended the relationship about a year ago, and with all the free time on my hands, I decided to change my career, too."

"What were you doing before being a sleuth?" She seemed genuinely interested.

"I was a forensic scientist."

"Wow. That's quite a change."

I liked the way her lips curled around the rim of the cup as she took another sip. I don't know how her lipstick stayed on her lips and didn't transfer to the cup. When she put the cup down, nothing was smeared on the edge.

"They are similar, if you think about it. Searching for answers, finding the truth. In this case, finding a person."

"How long have you been doing this?" she asked.

"What do you do for a living? Are you an artist full-time?" Completely ignoring her question, I threw a few at her to change the subject. Her inquisition was starting to rattle me. This was not an interview. She laughed harshly. Obviously, I'd hit a nerve. I didn't back down.

"I work for the family business. I sell olive oils."

"And you're an artist. A really good one," I said. A small flush brushed her cheeks. She looked down at her coffee and shrugged. Sadness pinched my heart. Apparently, she wasn't getting the support she deserved. "I liked that your art was so different than what I saw in most of the booths. And maybe puppets are cool here, but your neighbor's creepy puppets kept me up the last few nights."

Her laughter was so pure and beautiful that I blushed with her because it was the first genuine moment we'd had, and it felt nice. Too nice.

"I know. It's more of a cultural thing, and he takes advantage of tourists. We all do."

"There's nothing wrong with that unless you're price-gouging, and your prices didn't seem to be any different than other vendors at the fair."

She slowly twirled her almost-empty cup. "That's nice of you to say. Most people think they can haggle with us, that our art isn't worth the price tag."

"I liked how there were so many different things at the fair. I saw watercolors, drawings, pottery, puppets, and stuffed dolphins. And don't even get me started on all the food. It was a nice distraction."

She smiled brightly. "You didn't recognize Mateo in the booth next to me?"

"He was the one selling dolphins?" That surprised me. I thought he looked familiar.

She pulled out her phone to show me something, which gave me the opportunity to look at her without overtly staring. Camila was very pretty. Her smooth skin was void of any freckles or moles and seemed flawless. Her full lips pressed together in a flat line as she scrolled on her phone. My stomach tensed when her lips popped into a smile.

"This is his children's book. He sells a stuffed dolphin as a visual aid for it. It's a super-cute read." She turned the phone to show me a photo of Mateo holding a children's book at a launch party. His happiness seemed so authentic.

"Is he successful?"

"He's sold a book to everyone in town, and he sells out during the fair. He's self-published, but he doesn't take the time to promote it as much as he should. Gemma, my pregnant friend from yesterday, and I are trying to convince him to write a romance novel," she said. Pride dripped from her voice.

"I should have bought his book Saturday." I had no idea who I would have given it to since I was an only child and had no nieces or nephews, but I liked Mateo. He seemed like the kind of person who helped a neighbor out and made it a point to talk to everyone in a crowd. He'd made my afternoon a lot smoother. Camila had barely said anything to me, but I did crash her beach bash. She seemed to have a different attitude toward me today. Maybe she found me awkwardly charming. She was taking time out of her life to help me find Isabel.

"Well, maybe on our walk this morning we can hit the bookstore. They carry his book. He's even signed them," she said. Her chair scraped the tiled floor when she stood. "Are you ready to find Isabel?"

I jumped up and threw out my cup. "Definitely."

She watched as I fumbled and checked all my pockets for the important items like car keys and my phone. My hair got tangled in the strap of my messenger bag, and Camila reached to tug it free.

"It's tangled in the buckle. Don't move," she said.

My arms fell limply at my sides while she tended to my mini crisis. She was in my personal space and acted as if it wasn't a big deal, while I was a heartbeat from sprinting away. She smiled at me and carefully pulled at the tiny, tangled strands. She unnerved me. My throat dried up even though I'd just swallowed four ounces of liquid adrenaline. A light dusting of mascara brushed across her lashes, lengthened them and made the sparkle in her eye even more noticeable. My palms started sweating. "It's okay. I can do it." I was ready to just rip the strap away from my head and say good-bye to the tangled mess, but her soft touch on my arm stilled me.

"Relax, Peri. I'm almost done."

I liked hearing her say my name. I smiled because, with her slight accent, it sounded sexy. Or maybe it always was, but she was the first to make me realize it. Ten seconds and one more tug and my hair was free. I took a step back and thanked her. "Sorry. I was just getting frustrated."

She walked toward the door, seemingly accepting my need to distance myself. "No worries. Let's go see if Isabel is awake."

I glanced up at the clock. An hour had passed, even though it felt like ten minutes. "I hope so." I quickened my step until I was next to her. "What's your favorite part about Sequina?" A soft smile widened her mouth a bit, and I wondered if I was pronouncing the name right. Seldom did you hear people say the name of the town they were in. I never said Putnam, Connecticut to anybody. "Am I saying that right?" I asked.

"Yes. I smiled because I love this town. I love the people, my life, my family."

"That's nice. Do you ever travel?"

She pointed to a bump in the sidewalk so I would avoid it before she answered. "I traveled more when I was in school. I spent my breaks across Europe. And I've spent some time in Dallas."

"Texas?" That shocked me. "Why Texas?"

"I have relatives there. I went when I was about eight and again when I was thirteen."

"Texas in the summertime is the worst."

She laughed. "When I was eight, we went there for Christmas. Even then it was warm. But a Texas summer? Hot doesn't even begin to describe it."

"I'm in Connecticut so we get all four seasons. And they are very distinct. Hot to very cold with snow and ice."

"I only like the snow when we go on family trips to ski," she said.

"Do you have a large family?"

I saw the moment she shut down. Talking about the family wasn't an option.

She shrugged. "Average size," she said and pointed to an upcoming street. "Isabel lives up here." She went into the history of why some streets were still made of cobblestone and others were paved. I didn't care. My heart was racing knowing that I was going to meet somebody who was extremely important to Amma. I took a deep breath and followed her up a short set of steps. She rang the doorbell next to a name I couldn't read from where I was standing. She took a step back so we were shoulder to shoulder. No answer. She buzzed again. Still nothing. "She's probably still with her family," Camila said.

To say I was disappointed was an understatement. "Do you know where her family lives?"

"No. This is a small town, but not that small. From what I remember, they take her to a place they have in the mountains in the summers. I don't know where that is though."

"Maybe her neighbor knows? Should we try ringing them?" I looked at the three other doorbell buttons next to faded names. I barely made out I.R. next to S. Moroni. My finger hovered over the black concave circle.

Camila wrapped her fingers around mine and pulled my hand away. "No. He's not a nice man."

She looked genuinely alarmed. I shook my hand free. I was too close to give up now. "What about L. Amato?" I squinted at the handwritten name faded by the hot Italian sun.

"Camila!"

An elderly man looked over the fence and waved her over. Camila muttered something under her breath and quickly walked over to him. I followed but kept my distance. They were talking low, he nodded, looked at me, nodded again, barked a loud laugh that startled me, and then shook his head. The somber expression on his face made my heart fall to my feet. Something had happened, and it wasn't good.

"Is everything okay?" I was two seconds from freaking out. I was going to be super pissed off if I came all this way and Isabel had died in some freak accident or drowned in the ocean because her family wasn't paying attention to her.

Camila smiled at me. "Everything is fine. Leo just told me she hasn't returned with her family yet." She shrugged and walked back toward me. "And he said he doesn't know where they go either, but he thinks she'll be back tomorrow. So, we can come back then."

"Wait. No. I'm leaving Thursday. I don't have the time to spare." Desperation in the form of sweat trickled down the small of my back, and I balled my fingers into fists of anger. This was so unfair. I was so close. So close to solving the riddle my Amma left me and one step closer to getting out of here.

"When is your flight?"

"Midnight."

"See? There's plenty of time. Why don't you let me take you to lunch and give you a tour? We have several wineries, beaches, and excellent food. There's a lot of history, too. Also, I can show you the best places to buy gifts for your family."

"That sounds nice." I was trapped. There was nothing else I could do right now, and her offer was kind. "What does the R stand for?"

"What?" Camila tilted her head as if she didn't hear me when I knew I spoke loud enough. Was Camila stalling?

"The name on the door. It says I. R. What's her last name?"

She held her finger up as a phone call saved her from answering. I heard a man's voice, and she turned and took a few steps away from me. I snapped a picture of the street sign and memorized the number on the apartment building that looked like it was really a house divided into four units. If Isabel knew my great-grandmother, that put her well into her nineties, and I hoped she had the ground-floor apartment for her safety. Once I shook free from this impromptu tour, I could Google this address and maybe do a deep dive on the tenants. My databases only reached so far, but if I was able to get her last name, I could reach out on Intellenet, an international intelligence network, and see who could take the case and gather info for me quickly.

"That was Mateo. I have his truck. I told him I was using it to give you a tour. He says hello," she said.

"Where's your car?"

"I don't have one."

Who didn't have a car? I couldn't imagine not having transportation. "Oh. I see." I wanted to know why, but I also didn't want her to think I was interested in her. Once I left Italy, Camila Rossini would be a distant memory. Just a woman who hopefully helped me solve Amma's case. A very beautiful woman who exuded sexy. I still couldn't tell if she was playing me. Her reactions always seemed calculated, so my guard was up.

"What's Isabel's last name?"

"Rastelli." Camila didn't stutter.

"Isabel Rastelli," I repeated.

She nodded. "Would you like to see the wineries up in the hills? I'd take you to the mountains, but I don't think you want to spend the entire day with me."

I wanted to go back to my small room and work, but I was also at her mercy. I compromised. "A drive to some of the wineries sounds like fun, and maybe lunch, but then I need to check in with my office and get some other work done.

She clasped her hands together and smiled. "You won't regret it. I promise."

CHAPTER SIX

THE RUNAROUND—CAMILA

L a Locanda Gesu Vecchio."
I pronounced each word slowly and waited for Peri to repeat. She struggled with the sharpness of the words and overpronounced Vecchio. I didn't blame her. Most of what she knew about Italians was probably from television and movies, and most of it was true. "That's good. I think you've got it." She really didn't, but I was tired of hearing her slaughter the words. "How have you been getting around Italy without speaking the language?" I kept the sarcasm out of my voice so my question sounded genuine. She showed me her phone.

"I have an app. I wasn't expecting to travel here for business. If I was here on vacation, I probably would have taken a few classes. Instead, I jumped on a plane with a small suitcase, my messenger bag, and my phone. This app is very handy." She was smug about it.

"What happens if you lose your phone?" I asked.

"How many times have you lost your phone? It's practically glued to our hands. Even if I did lose it, I could always have the office overnight me one." Peri sipped on her wine and leaned back as though she delivered a punch.

"Do you work for somebody?"

She sat up straighter on the bistro chair and lifted her chin. "I have my own business and staff."

I wondered if they included her family. "Impressive. Have you always wanted to be an investigator?"

Peri nodded, and a visible sadness washed over her. "I've always loved crime shows, but I never wanted to be a cop. Too corrupt. Striking out on my own seemed like a great idea." Her voice trailed off as though she either didn't want to talk about it, or she regretted sharing more of herself than she wanted.

"It sounds like a thrilling job."

"That's what television makes it out to be. I spend most of my time watching, waiting, and using databases. Most of my business has been background checks."

"Except for this one."

She smiled at me. "Except for this one."

"Must be pretty important to fly all the way here just to deliver a message," I said.

She folded her arms in front of her. "It's an item, not a message. And I'm a professional."

"Not even a little clue?" I turned on the charm.

"Nope. Let's talk about something else. Thank you for giving me a tour of your town and taking me to this wonderful restaurant. Do you cook?"

My mother was always trying to teach me to cook, but I just didn't have the patience or desire to learn. The kitchen was her pride and joy. The only time I cooked was when I was the only one in the house and there weren't any leftovers. Even then to call it cooking was a stretch. I threw pasta on the stove, mixed one of our oils and one of our popular white wines with mussels, and called it a meal. "Only when nothing's left in the refrigerator. I don't do the shopping."

"Do you live with someone?" Peri automatically looked at my left hand.

"I live with my family in a villa." For some reason, I couldn't stop from telling her the truth. I wanted her to know that I was proud of my heritage. The Rossini family had roots here, and people knew us.

"No boyfriend? Girlfriend?" she asked.

"No. What about you?"

"I own a house and I live alone. Actually, my ex-girlfriend is the reason I decided to become a private investigator."

"She cheated on you, and you caught her?" I couldn't help myself. Reality television was my weakness. I had seen too many people in the arms of somebody else and caught on video.

Peri laughed. "No. Not at all. She was just too much. She wanted me to be somebody I wasn't. So, I scrubbed my life of her, other peoples' expectations, my boring job, and took a leap."

I didn't even address that she said girlfriend. I'd had her completely pegged wrong since the beginning, but nothing surprised me anymore. "Are you happy with your decisions? All of them?"

"One hundred percent. I'm finally where I need to be. Well, not here, but doing the job I've always wanted."

"What do you do for fun?" I asked. Being a private investigator didn't strike me as a nine-to-five job. I was sure she worked long hours for little money.

Peri played with the napkin in her lap. Her hair seemed lighter than it was yesterday, and her sunburn had subsided. A smattering of freckles crossed the bridge of her nose. "We had a recent death in the family, and I've been spending a lot of time helping sort through things and paperwork. Normally I would hang out at my friends' house on Plum Island most weekends, but this year has been a struggle."

A flash of pain crossed her delicate features, and a ping of guilt stabbed my chest. Peri seemed like a decent person, and if I weren't trying so hard to push her away, she would be somebody I would ask out. But I had to stay strong and remember that I didn't know her motivations. Whatever Peri had for my bisnonna—if she had anything at all—could be detrimental to her. Bisnonna's body was frail, even though her heart and attitude were strong. Until I knew what exactly Peri wanted with her, I wasn't letting my guard down.

"I'm sorry to hear that. I'm lucky to have most of my family still with me," I said. I couldn't imagine losing my nonna or bisnonna. It would crush me. I tried to live life to the fullest, but a loss that great would set me back. I applauded her resolve.

"I know that's how life works, but it's never easy," she said.

"I agree. When Mateo's mother died, he was crushed, and I never thought he would recover, but my mother and my grandmother really made him feel like a part of the family. He's like my brother."

"Mateo? For some reason I thought maybe you were dating."

"Mateo?" I laughed. We'd been raising hell since we were small children. "Oh, no. Mateo and I both like women. We've never dated or tried. I'm gay and he's not."

Peri looked surprised at that confession. She opened her mouth, then shut it, but opened it again. "Wow. I wasn't expecting that."

"Which part? The fact that Mateo and I aren't dating or that he's straight?"

Her sweet laughter made me smile even though I didn't want to. This woman was doing something to me. I'd spent only half a day with her, and as much as I didn't want to like her, it was hard not to.

"You know what I mean."

I winked. "Oh, the part about me. Yeah, about that."

"You're telling me that you are single. You." Peri pointed at me, and I held my hands up as though I did nothing wrong.

"What's wrong with being single? I love it. I can go anywhere I want, do anything I want, and spend the day with a beautiful tourist." The charm was a bit thick, but I couldn't pull it back.

She held up a finger. "Number one. I'm not a tourist." She held up two fingers. "I think there's nothing wrong with your choices." A third finger joined the two. "And number three. Flattery will get you nowhere. Not with me. I don't care how beautiful and attentive you are to me. My business with Isabel is private." She threw her hands up in surrender, as if all along she knew what I was doing. I tamped down my anger and pasted on a smile.

"Whatever you think I'm doing, I'm not. I took you straight to Isabel. I showed you where she lives, and I asked around for you. I'm trying to help you find her. Nobody else here would."

She stared at me for five seconds before answering. "Mateo. Mateo would totally help me." Her eyes were my favorite part of her. She was beautiful and completely the opposite of what I was normally attracted to. My own thoughts and body betrayed me.

"He might. But he would definitely want something in return. We call him Casanova for a reason."

"Well, he could try, but he doesn't stand a chance. Not like... well, not like other people. Maybe he has a sister?"

"He has a cute cousin."

"That's something. Is Mateo dating anyone?" she asked.

I laughed because the idea of Mateo settling into a relationship seemed so unrealistic. "He's like me and probably won't settle down until he's forty. Everyone loves him. Especially Bisnonna." Fuck. Now why did I say that?

"Is that your grandmother?" she asked.

"Close. My great-grandmother. My grandmother is Nonna, and my great-grandmother is Bisnonna. They are both very much alive and are very active in my life."

"Family is important here. I wish I had more family. I'm an only child. One day I'm going to have to be some kid's fake aunt because my parents stopped after having me," Peri said.

"My dad always says they stopped having children after me because they reached perfection." Plus, my mother didn't want any more children. Three were enough, and as soon as I, the girl, came along, that was the end of their baby-making days.

"Oh, I like that reasoning. I'll have to use it sometime." Peri looked at her watch after stifling a yawn. "I'm sorry, but I have to go back to the B&B. It's late for me, and I still have work to do."

Just when I thought we were getting somewhere. "Okay. No problem. I'll drive you back." I threw money on the table and waved the waitress over. Peri waited for the leftovers. Did her place even have a microwave? I didn't care, I reminded myself. How was I going to get her tomorrow? "How do you feel about motorcycles?"

"Motorcycles? I don't really have an opinion. I see a lot of them and electric bikes here, but I never thought to rent one. I'm not that adventurous."

I couldn't tell if she was being serious. I went for it anyway. "How about tomorrow I pick you up on my motorcycle for coffee, like we did today, and we try Isabel's apartment again, if she's not there, maybe we can branch out and ask around in town? Somebody is bound to know something."

"I like the idea of asking around if she's still not home, but I don't know how excited I am to ride on the back of a motorcycle."

I didn't want her to be afraid. I'd been riding one for twelve years and had only wrecked once. "I really am the best driver. I've been riding bikes for years, since I was a young teenager."

"How many times have you had passengers?"

Good point. I shaved off the numbers to give her a reasonable one. "Maybe five? Most of my dates are too afraid, but I don't think you are."

"What's the weather like tomorrow?" she asked.

I pulled up my weather app. "Same beautiful weather as today. Come on. It's so hard to say no to spending the day on a motorcycle in Italy on a warm summer's day."

"You're making this very difficult for me," she said.

"Then let me choose for you. Just say yes. Maybe you will smile more than you did today." I enjoyed teasing her.

"I guess it couldn't hurt, but I really have to try harder tomorrow to find her."

I nodded because, even though I'd be able to push her away from Isabel's place, the truth might come out. Luke lived in Bisnonna's old apartment and would be out of town for a few more days. I could only hope Peri didn't extend her stay and that she gave up before the truth came out.

"You owe me big-time," Mateo said.

"I know. Whatever you want. I'll pay you back." I kissed his cheek and returned his truck keys to him. "I even filled the tank."

"This is a bad idea." He shook his head at me even as he reached for my keys to the store. "And you need to tell your mother what the plan is. I know she doesn't mind that I fill in for you, but she will be curious why I'm running the store two days in a row."

I finished pulling my hair back and straightening my lipstick. Even though it was supposed to be warm today, I grabbed my tight leather jacket and my extra helmet. "I'll take care of informing the family that you're filling in for me."

"Where are you taking her today?"

I didn't tell him that Peri was looking for Bisnonna because I knew he'd immediately take Peri to her, believing her intentions were good because she was pretty. "I was thinking the town square, then drive down by the water."

"Has she been to the winery and the groves? You could spend days just walking the property and telling her about the history of the Rossini family. And you can make it romantic. Take a picnic. Set it up by the big tree that overlooks the vineyard and the groves."

That meant exposing her to my family, our business, and Bisnonna. That was a resounding no. "Maybe. Depends on her schedule. I know she's going home soon, so it might not be an all-day event." She'd only agreed to morning and lunch.

"You should bring her by the shop," Mateo said. He gave me a once-over and made the okay symbol with his fingers. "You look great. Have fun and text me if you decide to stop by." He kissed my cheek and left to open Isabel's Oils early because he hated to be late to anything.

"Camila, why are you still here?" My mother swooped into the room to pour coffee in her travel mug. "And why was Mateo running the store yesterday?"

"And today, too. I'm giving an American a tour of the area."

My mom put her coffee down and looked pointedly at me. "Camila, who is this person?" Apparently, I looked guilty. My mother could always read me. "What are you up to?" She knew me too well.

I shot her a look that hopefully was a mix between innocence and boredom. "Nothing. Just trying to be nice. That's all."

"How did you meet this American?"

"She was at the fair on Saturday and came to our beach party Sunday night."

"Who is she?"

I shrugged. "Just a woman visiting. She's leaving in a few days, and I thought I would be nice and show her around."

My mother didn't look convinced. "Bring her by the winery. Most people like that tour. Is she alone?"

I nodded and poured myself a cup of coffee, even though I was going to grab a cup with Peri. I needed to keep my hands busy, or my mother would know something was up.

"She sounds brave. It's a good thing she found you. Does she speak Italian?" she asked.

"No. She's been using an app on her phone to communicate with most people."

"Then it's a really good thing she found you. Be nice and have a great day."

She kissed my cheek and headed out the door. I dumped the coffee into the sink and waited until her car rolled by the window. If she knew I was taking Peri on my motorcycle, she would have insisted I take her car, and I didn't want that much quiet, alone time. I turned the key, smiling when my bike purred to life. It was going to be a beautiful day for a ride.

"Good morning."

I found Peri inside the café staring at the menu. I approved of her riding outfit of form-fitting jeans, Converse high tops, and a black T-shirt that advertised a television show I knew about but had never seen. Her blond hair was pulled back in a French braid and hung halfway down her back.

"Good morning. Hopefully this works." She held out her arms and motioned her hands up and down so that I had no choice but to look her over. Her T-shirt showed off curves I didn't notice yesterday.

"It's perfect. I have a light jacket you can wear for added protection."

"My wardrobe is severely limited here." She shrugged.

"You look fine. Let's grab coffee and see if Isabel is home, yes?" I liked the way she tugged on the end of her braid and looked at the menu as if she could read it. "What do you like back home? I can order whatever you prefer."

"I like cream and sugar. More cream than sugar," she said.

I nodded. "I know exactly what you want." I ordered for both of us again, and we sat at the same table as before while we waited. "How was your night?" I wanted to know if she found out anything. I didn't think there was anybody named Isabel Rastelli in Sequina, but knowing my luck, there probably was, and she probably knew my bisnonna.

She stifled a yawn. "I've been here almost a week and am finally getting into a normal sleep schedule. I didn't think jet lag would get to me as much as it did."

"Were you able to work at all?" I wanted to know if she had other cases that needed her attention.

"I had some emails to answer. Nothing pressing."

Peri was vague, and I was surprised to realize I wanted to know more about her job and her life back in Connecticut. I googled where she lived in relation to Dallas. It was about the same distance from Naples, Italy to Finland. A very long way. "So, what has been your most exciting case?"

"This one." Her eyes were fierce.

"Tell me about one that isn't this one. Tell me more about you. You know all about me, and I only know a few things about you."

"My job takes up most of my time, but trust me. What I do is more exciting on television than in real life." She downplayed her job, but I still heard the pride in her voice and the slight tilt of her chin as if in defiance.

"I sell olive oil, so no matter how boring you think your job is, I win hands down. I sit by myself in a store five days a week. I can't even make it exciting. People don't browse the store. They come in specifically for the oil."

"I love good olive oil. Remind me to pick some up before I leave. My mother wants a bottle of wine, but I think she would appreciate the oil more. If we have time, can we swing by the store?"

I'd told her too much. I should have kept my life vague, but something about her made me want to share. I was sabotaging my own goal. "We're going in the opposite direction, but maybe we can swing by or I can just bring you a bottle if I see you after today. When is your flight again?"

"I have a red-eye flight a few minutes after midnight tomorrow. So today really is the last day I can spend looking for her. I hope Isabel is home. Shall we go?" Peri looked at her watch.

I had to give her credit. She was trying hard to be cordial, but the nervous energy coming off her was palpable.

"Definitely," I said.

I pointed to my bike on the way up to Isabel's. "That's our ride for later."

Peri stopped and touched the handlebars. "She's beautiful and smaller than I pictured."

I stopped and looked at it through her eyes. "She's old, but she's reliable."

"A true classic," Peri said.

I rang the bell again several times, knowing full well nobody was going to answer. I sounded resigned. "Well, I guess she's not back yet."

Peri threw her hands up in frustration. "How is this possible? I'm so close, yet so far. And I can't stay here until she returns because we don't know when that will be." She sat on the stoop and dropped her head to rest in her hands.

"I know you're going to say no, but I can be your agent and give it to Isabel whenever she returns. I'll sign whatever papers you want saying that I will ensure Isabel gets whatever memento you have. I can even record the exchange." If it would hurt Bisnonna in any way, I could easily find someone to pose as Isabel. Peri would be none the wiser. I frowned when she snorted.

"Thanks for the offer, but this is personal, and I have to do it myself."

"I understand. Let me know if you change your mind. We should probably get going, but we'll definitely finish the day here."

Peri held back. "Maybe I should just stick around here today. Her neighbor said maybe she would be back yesterday, so if I hang out here, maybe I'll catch her."

I reached into my purse and pulled out a tiny notepad and pen. "Here. Write down your contact information, and we'll leave a note saying who you are and why you're looking for her. I'll even put my phone number and vouch for you, if that would make you feel more comfortable. We can tape it to her door. I'm sure I can get Leo to open the main door for us."

I almost squealed when she took the notepad and wrote down her name, phone number, email address, and where she was staying for the next thirty-six hours. I wrote a note explaining her situation, knowing full well the note would be tossed. "I'll see if Leo is in the back. He can tape it to her door."

"How do you know Leo?"

Shit. I never really explained how I knew him. "He's a regular customer in the store."

"Your olive oil store?"

"Yes." I didn't remember telling her about the winery. That would have been a dead giveaway. "Repeat customers always come into the store and hang out and chat. You get to know them well." I put away my notepad and pen and waved the piece of paper. "Let me ring Leo." I hit the button and waited.

"Maybe he's out back," Peri said.

We walked to the backyard and found him digging in the dirt. "Leo." I called out.

"Ciao." He waved the trowel at us and carefully pushed himself to a standing position.

I flipped to Italian and asked that he didn't laugh but appear somber and nod a lot. I gave him a quick explanation, handed him the note, and told him to throw it away the moment we left. He held the privately folded note close to his heart and nodded at Peri. I'd known Leo since I was a little girl. He used to make pasta for me and Bisnonna before she moved back into the villa. I knew he would help me out, but this was more than I could have hoped for.

"Do you feel better now?" I nudged her back down the drive, away from Leo and a note that could come back to haunt me unless he destroyed it like I asked.

"That's the best I can do. I'll check my emails later this afternoon. Maybe I'll get a nibble from Intellenet. Who knows?"

I pushed my panic down. Would she get information before she left? "Hopefully. In the meantime, let's get on the bike and let me take your mind off things while showing you beautiful places. Are you hungry? Was the coffee enough? Lunch won't be for another three or so hours." I stood in front of her and touched her hands carefully. Peri looked like having a few hours of fun would destroy her. "And we can come back early and check again and again." She seemed to be teetering between staying and waiting or letting go and having a little bit of fun with me. "Besides, why sit here in the heat when you can at least feel a breeze and get to experience a little more of Italy?"

CHAPTER SEVEN

THE TRUTH—PERI

What the actual fuck was I thinking? I didn't know Camila Rossini, and I sure as hell didn't trust her. Her pendulum swayed from happy to angry entirely too fast and too often for my taste. One minute she was overly helpful and the next seemed like she resented me. She was extremely pretty, though, and I was guilty of saying yes to women for all the wrong reasons. Also, I was in a different country, and things weren't the same here as they were back home. So, against my better judgment, I agreed to go on a quick sightseeing tour. Mostly to get her to quit pushing, but also maybe to have an excuse to be close to her for a few hours on the back of her bike.

"You can either hold the metal bar back here, or you can put your hands around my waist. Your feet go here." Camila pointed to two bars on either side of the back wheel. She hopped on the bike and patted the small seat behind her.

I saddled up, hoping I looked comfortable and at ease, even though my stomach was quivering out of fear and something to do with her nearness. I waited until she started the bike and leaned with her when she merged into traffic.

"You're a natural at this," she yelled.

I moved my hands from the back handle to her waist when the road narrowed and the cars on the other side were closer than normal. Ignoring her hard abdomen and the way her muscles flexed under my touch as she maneuvered the motorcycle in traffic was impossible, so I gave in and enjoyed the ride. My new position scooted me closer to her, and I clenched my jaw at how I physically responded to her. She felt warm and smelled like berries and cream.

I tapped her shoulder. "Don't you think you're driving too fast?"

She laughed and slowed down. She was so confidently sexy, and I hated that I didn't trust her. She said we could ask around in town if they had seen or knew Isabel's family, but I sensed that she wasn't going to push it. She was doing everything she could to make me enjoy Italy, but I wasn't feeling it. Amma gave me money to find somebody, and here I was traipsing around Italy with a beautiful woman instead.

"Even though this building is old, it's actually our library," she said after she parked. She waited until I slid off the back before climbing off.

"Wow. This is a beautiful building," I said.

"I thought maybe we could do some investigation on Isabel. The building is hundreds of years old, but the collection and technology is somewhat up to date. Plus, it has a lot of historical records of the town and people. Maybe we can find Isabel's family."

I was suddenly excited. "This is such a great idea. Thank you so much for bringing me here." The outside was impressive, but the inside took my breath away. High stained-glass windows let in the sunlight and painted the room in rich reds, royal blues, and bright yellows. "This is gorgeous." For a moment, Camila's smile made me forget why I was here.

"Follow me," she said.

She walked up to the information desk and asked for something in Italian. I understood only the name Rastelli out of everything she said. Camila was gathering what she could for us to review. I took a moment and quietly made my way through the rows of books in a language I couldn't read. There were plenty of recent books, but I took the time to run my fingers over books that I knew were older and had been handled by generations before mine. I loved books. I always said I would have tons of bookshelves in my own house—whenever I made enough money to own a larger house than the bungalow I lived in now. I was probably going to break even on this job, if I was lucky. Not that the money mattered. Finishing the job was the least I could do for Amma.

"Well, here are a few books we can look through, but the librarian suggested we browse the microfiche."

"Wait. They don't have it digitized yet? How is that even possible?"

Camila shrugged. "Unfortunately, no. Most of the old newspapers and even annual school-classroom photos are on microfiche. Do you know how to use a microfiche machine?" Camila asked.

"No, but it can't be that hard."

"Neither do I, but we can divide and conquer. We'll search the database and divide the microfiche. Surely we can find other names associated with hers. Engagement announcements, birth announcements, divorces, and anything. Is she young or old?"

I couldn't remember if I gave Camila an approximate age range, but if she said she knew her, she would know that. I wasn't sure, but if Amma passed at one hundred, then Isabel would be about the same. "I think in her mid to late nineties."

She lifted her head. "Okay. I can start looking in the nineteen forties. Around the war. There's sure to be a lot of information from old newspapers and magazines. It might be easier for you to look at the school photos. Fewer words to read and understand."

"That's a good start." I followed Camila's example and pulled out a microfiche, slid it under the glass, and looked at the screen. It took me a while to figure out how to work it, but I found a rhythm and was able to find the school photos and school newspapers that mentioned Rastelli. I scribbled down a few names that might be worth checking out tonight.

"How are you doing? Do you feel like taking a break?" Camila asked.

We'd been scrolling for two hours. Scanning for her name and not knowing the language was exhausting. My eyes hurt, and a tiny headache was starting to poke at the back of my brain. I stretched my arms out and cracked my neck for comfort. "Wow. I can't believe it's after noon."

"How about some lunch? Are you hungry? There's a little café just down the street."

"I could use a sandwich or something."

"Let's turn these in and talk about what we found over lunch."

I watched as she returned the boxes of microfiche to the information desk. The librarian was completely charmed by her. Maybe Camila really was trying to help. Who else would take the time out of their week to dig through dusty microfiche with me? "Did you find anything important?"

"I wrote down a few names that were promising," she said. Her voice picked up as she grabbed her bag. "I'm hungry, too. It's not far away. We should walk since it's such a beautiful day."

I slipped on my sunglasses and followed her out the door. I couldn't decide if I liked her better in a sundress or decked out in tight jeans, a sleeveless button-down top, and motorcycle boots. She'd pulled her hair up while we were searching through the archives and never let it down. I found her to be a delightful distraction.

"I found where a Bianca Isabel Rastelli married a Giovanni Romano. Maybe that's her? She was born in 1920," Camila said as we descended down crooked steps to reach the café.

"But wouldn't she have taken his last name? Especially that long ago." Again, she held the door open and again, I stuttered. "Thank you."

"Maybe her husband died and she went back to her surname?" Camila said.

"Meh. Unlikely." I was tired of trying to find the name Isabel Rastelli in words that I couldn't understand. I needed to research the names I found and the ones Camila was willing to share with me. I knew everything was a long shot, but I would take any morsel of information I could.

"What looks good? Do you want a sandwich or a salad?" Camila asked.

"I need bread. I'll leave the rest up to you."

"Good choice." She ordered two Mozzarella di Bufala e Pomodoro sandwiches and two orange Fantas. I offered to pay, but she waved me off. I managed to keep my happy noises to myself as I devoured my delicious sandwich.

"This is probably my favorite thing I've eaten here. Well, this and the gelato."

"It's just mozzarella and tomato. Don't you have this in Connecticut?" She pointed to her chin, and I quickly wiped mine off.

"I'm sure we do, but I'm not adventurous with food. I just eat whatever's easy."

"You work too hard, don't you? Food should be enjoyed. You probably grab something on the go, right?"

I hated that she pegged me so quickly. I shrugged. "I hang out with my family a lot so I eat with them, and then my mother sends me home with leftovers."

"Do you live close to your family?"

"About ten minutes away. The town I live in is small."

"Small like Sequina?"

"Bigger and not as charming. I have to say, the little bit of Italy I've seen, it's beautiful."

"You leave tomorrow, right?"

She played with the empty bottle, rolling it against her hand with her fingers. She was graceful doing the simplest things.

"I do, but the flight is a few minutes after midnight. That doesn't give me a lot of time to search for names. I should probably get back to my room and see if I can narrow down things. Maybe I still have a small chance of finding her before I leave."

Camila tore off her notes and handed me the two pieces of paper. "There's not a lot there, but they're worth checking out."

"Thanks for your help the last few days. You've taken time out of your busy week to help me. Even if I never find her, I appreciate all your efforts."

"It's no problem. I hope you find her."

❖

I spent my afternoon researching all the leads I'd generated with Camila. All of them led me nowhere. As a last-ditch effort, I rang Isabel's bell one more time. I wasn't expecting anyone to answer, so I was shocked when a nice-looking man with dark brown eyes and a killer smile opened the door.

"Isabel?" Shit. I completely forgot every word in Italian.

"No."

"Shit. Um, hello. I'm looking…Isabel?" My words weren't making sense.

He crossed his arms in front of him and leaned against the doorjamb. He wasn't making this easy for me. "Oh, you're looking for Isabel?"

"You speak English!" I refrained from reaching out to squeeze his muscular forearms in excitement.

"I do. Why are you looking for her?"

I tried to be professional, but this was the break I needed. "I'm Peri Logan, a private investigator from Connecticut. I have a client who has asked me to find Isabel and deliver a small package to her." I braced myself for another no or get out of here, but when he spoke, I got weak-kneed.

"She used to live here, but not anymore. Good news. I'm on my way to the family villa now to have dinner, and she'll be there."

My mouth fell open and I stared at him. Before I could ask the obvious, he extended an invitation. "You are more than welcome to follow me there or catch a ride with me. I'm Luke Barnes, by the way."

"You have no idea how nice it is to meet you, Luke. I've been searching for Isabel for six days and was about ready to give up and fly home."

"Let me grab my keys and we can go."

I waited for him on the sidewalk, trying hard not to whoop with delight or cry happy tears. I took a few deep breaths and smiled at him when he pointed to his car and told me the villa wasn't far away. Because I didn't know where we were going, the drive felt like it was taking forever, when it had been only six minutes. He turned onto a windy road flanked by grapevines and drove up to the light-colored giant stone house that took my breath away. It was magnificent. I parked on the cobblestone driveway behind him, allowing both of us space.

"Come on in," Luke said.

He was very trusting. I could be a murderer or rob them at gunpoint. "Thank you again." I grabbed my bag and stepped into the most beautiful house I'd ever seen. Impressive wasn't the right word, but it was close.

"Isabel doesn't get a lot of visitors. I'm sure she'll be happy to see you." He opened the door for me, and I almost stopped when I crossed the threshold. The decor was rustic, with large stones, wood beams overhead, and plants everywhere. It was gorgeous. So very different from the large houses back home. "I'm guessing she's in the courtyard," he said.

I knew I looked a mess. Loose hairs from my windblown braid feathered out to give me a fuzzy look. I tried to smooth them with my hand but knew I was failing. Amma wanted me to find this woman, and I was coming in hot without a pause to freshen up. "Thank you again for being so nice, Luke. I really appreciate it."

"Looks like we're both surprising people. My family isn't expecting me until the weekend."

I slowed down. "Are you sure this is okay?" What if this guy wasn't family, and he was the murderer or the robber? That was silly. He seemed to know exactly where he was going, and his body language was relaxed, so I went with it.

He laughed. "I grew up here. I'm sure we'll run into somebody soon."

A high-pitched shriek followed us, and we both turned around. "Signore Luke! You're home!"

He looked at me and winked. "I told you." He returned his attention to the woman who walked quickly toward us. "Hello, Sophia. It's good to see you, too, but I was only gone a few weeks."

Sophia, a woman who looked to be in her early fifties with a sprinkle of graying hair at her temples, clasped her hands together to stop herself from reaching out to him. Their relationship was close, but not that close. "You're always missed." She looked at me and cocked her head as though waiting for an introduction.

I had no idea so many people spoke English in Italy. I held out my hand. "Hi. I'm Peri."

"Hello, signorina. Welcome to the winery."

"It's beautiful."

"Peri is here to see Isabel. Is she in the courtyard?"

Sophia nodded. "Everyone is out there eating and drinking. I'm headed down to the cellar for more wine. They will be happy to see you back home so soon." This time she patted his arm and touched mine as well.

"I have a feeling I'm going to like your family," I said. Eating and drinking at four in the afternoon sounded relaxing, and truthfully, I was going to need a glass of wine to steady my nerves. I was about to be face-to-face with the woman Amma wanted me to find. I heard laughter and general noise of a happy family spending time together as we rounded the corner.

"Luke! You're home early."

He held his arms open, and a beautiful woman fell into his embrace. I smiled at them until I realized everyone's attention had moved from him to me.

"This is Peri, and she's here to visit Isabel." He walked over to a frail woman sitting at the head of the table and motioned me over. "Bisnonna, you have a visitor."

"Sì. I do?"

Luke pointed at me, and I stepped closer so she could see me. "Hi, Isabel." I stretched my hand out to properly introduce myself.

She put her hand on her heart. After a few awkward moments of me standing there with my hand out, she reached out to me. She clutched my fingers and pulled me closer. "Hilde. You've finally returned to me."

CHAPTER EIGHT

DAMAGE CONTROL—CAMILA

"What is she doing here?" Anger flooded my senses hard and fast. I placed the plates on the table with a clatter and folded my arms. From the harsh looks every single member of my family shot me, I knew immediately I'd approached the situation wrong.

"Camila! Where are your manners?" My mother apologized to Peri. "I'm so sorry for my daughter's outburst."

"Yeah, sis. Calm down. Peri showed up at the apartment looking for Bisnonna, so I brought her here," Luke said.

I was fuming, but I had to keep my emotions in check. Everyone was watching me. I pasted on a smile and sat down, staring daggers at Peri.

"You knew. All this time," Peri said. A fake smile that resembled mine quickly replaced her initial expression of shock. She was pissed.

"Isabel Rossini, meet Peri Logan. Apparently, she has something very important to give you." I snarkily tilted my wineglass at Peri and took a long swallow. This was going to be a long night. My heart, fueled by anger, pounded and then melted when I saw tears in Bisnonna's eyes. After briefly assessing the moment, I realized she wasn't angry or threatened. Her body language showed she was very comfortable with Peri. I shook my head. I could kill Luke. Had he just stayed away for another twenty-four hours, we all would have gone back to our lives, and Bisnonna would be happy and unaware. Honestly, though, she looked happy to see Peri. Perhaps I'd been too overprotective.

"Is there somewhere private we can speak?" Peri asked.

"No. We'll leave," my mother said, standing. "Come on, everyone. Let's give them privacy." She herded everyone out and placed her hand on Peri's shoulder. "Please let me know if you need anything."

"Thank you for your hospitality. I promise not to overwhelm her," she said.

"Camila?" My mom gently pressed my arm.

I shook my head. "I'm staying right here."

"It's okay that Camila stays. Maybe now she'll understand," Peri said. My mother nodded and left the courtyard. Peri took Bisnonna's hand. "You called me Hilde. I'm Peri, but Hilde was my great-grandmother."

She touched Peri's face. "You look just like your beautiful great-grandmother."

"We called her Amma." Peri pulled out a small velvet satchel. "She hired me to find you and give you this."

I figured Bisnonna would have problems with the small bow so, at Peri's nod, I untied it for her and shook out a gold locket. I placed it in the palm of her hand.

"Open it," Peri said.

It housed photos of two beautiful women. One I recognized immediately as my bisnonna. The other woman looked very similar to Peri. I watched as Bisnonna brought it closer to her face. So many emotions crossed her features, and I felt like I'd just lived the memories with her. It dawned on me that she was in love with the woman in the photo. My heart crashed, and I put my hand on Bisnonna's shoulder. "She's beautiful."

"That's my great-grandmother," Peri said.

"You look just like her," I said. For the first time since arriving at the villa, Peri looked like she didn't want to murder me.

"She was always a classy woman. She dressed up every single day and fixed her hair and put on makeup. Looking good made her feel good."

"Was?" I asked. Oh, shit. She passed. Grief fell across Bisnonna's face, and I rubbed her back in a soothing way.

Peri held Bisnonna's hand. "Hilde passed away a few months ago, but the very last thing she wanted to do on this earth was find you. I'm sorry we didn't get to you sooner."

I wiped away the tear that perched in the corner of my eye before it could fall onto my cheek. When Bisnonna started sobbing, I dropped to my knees and held her close. "I'm so sorry. You loved her, and she obviously loved you." My face was only inches from Peri's. She looked at me in confusion. I lifted my eyebrow at her and whispered, "Why else would your great-grandmother hold onto a locket with those two pictures for decades before asking you to find the other woman?" I tried to keep the anger out of my voice because the obvious wasn't obvious to Peri.

Peri leaned back in the chair as though all the oxygen had left her. Obviously everything finally fell into place for her, and I couldn't tell if she was okay with it or not. It wasn't my place to console her, nor did I want to. Maybe now she understood why I was protective of Bisnonna. Not everyone needed to know everything. Not after living an entirely different life than she was allowed to.

"What happened to her?" Bisnonna reached out for Peri, who immediately sat forward and cupped her hands.

"She was perfectly healthy. She just didn't wake up one morning. No pain, nothing bad, no long illness. She just didn't wake up," Peri said. She stroked Bisnonna's hand as though she'd known her forever. "She had a good life. A family who loved her. She had the nicest friends and even drove a car until she was eighty-five."

Bisnonna smiled softly. "She was always a daredevil. I hope that you have a little bit of her spirit."

"I would love to hear more about her, if you are willing to tell me," Peri said.

"Oh, yes." Bisnonna's smile grew until only a tinge of sadness remained.

"How about we give Isabel a break? Bisnonna, would you like to lie down for a bit? I know this has been overwhelming."

"Yes, bella." I helped her into her wheelchair. She didn't necessarily need it, but when she wanted to get somewhere fast, it was easier for everyone. She stopped me before I wheeled her away from the table. "Peri, please stay for dinner. I want to hear more about Hilde and her life."

Peri nodded and smiled but didn't say anything. I didn't know her, but I could tell she was fighting tears, as was I. What a horrible mess. I was angry, but so sad. I put myself in Bisnonna's place and knew I would want to know about my great love. But I also didn't want her to be so upset. I was worried for her health. A broken heart, especially one that was ninety-six years old, was hard to repair.

"I'll be right back." My voice came out harsher than I intended. I nodded to Peri and rolled Bisnonna to her room. She was still crying, although not as hard as before. Bisnonna clutched the locket in her hand as I helped her into her bed. My mother followed us into the room.

"What's going on?"

I stopped in front of her and pasted on a smile. "Nothing. Bisnonna wanted to rest for a bit."

"Why is she crying? Did that woman upset her?"

Even though I wasn't a fan of Peri, I didn't want my mother to think she purposely upset Bisnonna. "No, Mom. Not intentionally. I'll explain later. She's staying for dinner, so maybe everybody can go back and chat with her." I doubted Peri would tell anybody. It wasn't her story to tell.

Bisnonna grabbed my hand. "Come back for me in a few hours. I want to hear all about Hilde and her great-granddaughter. They look so much alike, Camila. It's like seeing her again after almost seventy-five years."

I kissed her forehead and promised to collect her before dinner. I wanted to hear the story now, too. I made sure she was comfortable before I quietly slipped out of her room and marched back to the courtyard. My energy level was ramping up, but I wasn't sure if I was angry or frustrated or excited for the truth. Remembering my mother's words from earlier, I took a deep breath before I sat in front of Peri.

"I know you're angry I lied to you, but I was protecting her. She's not a strong person, and I had no idea why you were looking for her."

"Do I look like somebody who would purposely go around hurting other people? Everything I said was true. Confidentiality is a thing, even if you don't think it applies to you," Peri said.

"Can somebody please tell me what's going on?" Luke asked. He poured six glasses of wine and handed them out to everyone at the table.

I sighed. I needed to 'fess up. "I met Peri at the art fair last weekend. She saw my sketch of Bisnonna and demanded that I take her to her immediately."

"I don't think I demanded anything," Peri said. Her cheeks were flushed, and tears still clung to her blond eyelashes.

"Okay, maybe not demanded, but begged." I smirked. I had no idea why I was being such a jerk after we'd shared such a tender moment just a few minutes ago.

"She said she would take me to meet Isabel but then ghosted me," Peri said.

"What do you mean ghosted?" The anger in my mother's question was unmistakable. I shook my head. I knew she wasn't going to side with me.

"It means she disappeared. She probably promised to meet Peri somewhere and never showed up." Luke wasn't going to be on my side tonight either.

"That's exactly what happened. But then I stumbled on her little beach party Sunday afternoon, and she agreed to help me out. Her friends seemed really nice. Mateo was super friendly. I hear he's very close with your family."

Smiles broke out around the table as my family nodded and started talking about Mateo.

"He's going to be here for dinner. I invited him since your brother showed up earlier than we expected." My mother loved Mateo like one of her sons.

"Can we get back to the story of why Camila was horrible to this very nice woman?" Ethan, my oldest brother, asked. He had been quiet during the entire visit but was obviously chomping at the bit to find out why I was such an ass. I shot him a look, and he grinned at me. We all knew our parents weren't going to be pleased with me.

"She took me everywhere in town but here. We even spent hours at the library looking through old newspapers and town photos for an Isabel Rastelli, who was not the same Isabel I was looking for," Peri said.

I cringed. None of this sounded good. My mother put her glass on the table and folded her arms in front of her chest. "Camila Isabel Rossini Barnes. You walked away from your responsibilities at the shop so you could take this poor woman on a goose chase? We raised you better than that." She turned to Peri. "I'm so sorry Camila did this to you. That's not who she is, and I apologize that she wasted so much of your time. When do you leave?"

Peri looked embarrassed for me, which was the exact opposite of what I expected. "Tomorrow around midnight. I'm just happy Luke was at the apartment and was able to bring me here so I could finish my job."

"Nothing like last-minute. Somebody fill her glass. Sounds like after a lot of time with our sister, she deserves some excellent wine," Luke said.

This was bad, but it wasn't awful. "Can I just say one thing?"

Both my brothers booed, and one even threw a cracker at me and was promptly scolded by my mother. At my mother's nod, I continued. "I'm sorry I duped you, Peri. And I'm sorry for disappointing everyone. I know this is hard to believe, but I really was protecting her. You showed up at my booth with an old photo of my bisnonna. I don't know you, and you weren't telling me anything substantial enough to make you trustworthy. You seem nice, but plenty of nice, beautiful women are criminals." I could have gone on, but my dad gave me a silent nod and I slowly sat down.

"I understand. I think you judged me unfairly, but I can't say I blame you. I'm just glad I found her after all."

"What did you give her?" Ethan asked.

I stepped in before Peri could answer. I knew she wouldn't tell, and I didn't want her to be in an awkward position. "Bisnonna will tell everyone when she's ready. In the meantime, give her space and be nice to her."

Two grapes were thrown at me this time.

"Boys," my dad said. They stopped immediately.

Peri smiled at me and nodded. I gave her a small smile in return, still uneasy about the entire experience.

"Tell us about yourself, Peri," Mom said. "And help yourself to anything on the table. We're just snacking until dinner."

She gave my mother the sweetest, softest smile and thanked her again for her hospitality. I hated that I looked like the jerk. Not that Peri was either, but I wanted my family to rally around me, to be proud that I was protecting us even though Peri clearly wasn't a threat.

"I'm from Connecticut. I own a private investigating firm."

"That's so cool," Luke said.

Peri smiled. "It's a lot of hard work for very little reward."

"Peri used to be a forensic scientist." I wanted to add to the conversation because I felt left out.

"Oh, wow. That's impressive. What made you switch careers? If I'm not being too nosy." My mom loved science. She was responsible for subtle changes in our wines using math and science. I liked what pleased my senses. I knew what tasted delicious and smelled delightful and rich, but my mother had a scientific system. I wasn't complaining.

"I just wanted to broaden my horizons and get out from beneath the microscope."

"Both jobs sound like fun. Your parents must be proud." Mom was so obvious.

"I'm the only child, so even though they are proud of me, I'm sure they wanted me to continue with science and become a doctor." Peri didn't sound dejected or disappointed. She was matter-of-fact, and I could tell she was comfortable with her decision.

"I'm sure they are proud of you. Apart from our daughter's interference, how have you been enjoying Italy?" my father asked.

Peri's smile was tight as she seemed to think about her trip thus far. "It's beautiful here. The sea, the people, the houses. Your villa is amazing. I wish I had more time to enjoy Sequina."

"We are happy to have roots here. We are the fifth generation of winemakers. And thanks to Isabel, who started our olive grove, we have a small business of different olive oils," Mom said.

"So, there were some truths in your story." Peri didn't back down, not even in front of my family.

"It's a good job, but I'm waiting for the opportunity to work the winery," I said.

"You're too young. Your palate is barely developed." Ethan grinned.

I was getting really frustrated with my brothers and how they couldn't stop embarrassing me tonight. Not in front of Peri. Not after everything. I felt beat up, and I needed a break. My dad must've sensed my mood.

"Camila is going to be great at selling wine when it's her turn."

"I think she's a great artist. I was impressed with her oils and sketches. If it wasn't for her sketch, I would have never recognized Isabel," Peri said.

Wait. Peri was coming to my defense? After everything we'd been through? Everything I did to her?

"It's a nice hobby." My dad winked at me as though we shared a secret. He wasn't being supportive, and that irked me.

"Oh, I think it could be more than a hobby. Have you seen her paintings? They're beautiful."

I could feel my mom looking at me, then at her, then back to me. I could almost see the wheels turning.

"Peri! What are you doing here?" Mateo and his stupid timing. He kissed my mom, shook hands with my dad and my brothers, kissed my cheek, and hugged Peri. "I'm so excited that you're still in Italy."

"Mateo. It's good to see you."

"Where's Isabel? I have something for her." He clutched a small bouquet of flowers that I know he'd picked from some neighbor's garden on his way here. It was a shame his family didn't appreciate him as much as we did.

"She's resting now, but we're supposed to get her for dinner in about an hour," I said.

The features on his face pinched with concern. "Is she okay?"

I nodded. "She's fine. We'll see her in a bit."

He relaxed in the chair next to Peri. "Have you tried the wine? It's excellent. It's what I was drinking on the beach the other day."

"It's lovely." Peri took a sip to prove her point, and Mateo smiled hard at her. As much as I wanted to watch him crash and burn with Peri, I didn't want to out her, too. Mateo would find out soon enough.

"Peri was just telling us about her life in the United States." I was positive Mateo didn't know where Connecticut was on the map. I only knew because I googled it.

"She's a private investigator like Veronica Mars or Sherlock Holmes. How exciting is that?" Mateo remembered our conversation on the beach.

Peri shrugged. "It sounds cooler than it is, although I do get to travel."

"Can you tell us about some of your cases?" he asked.

"Mateo, that's inappropriate," I said, suddenly defending Peri's privacy. I even rolled my eyes at my own hypocrisy.

"No. It's okay. I can keep it general. A few weeks ago, a woman who thought her husband was cheating hired me, so I followed him for three days until I was able to get photographic proof."

"Was he?" Mateo asked.

"Let's just say she's now filing for divorce."

"Ouch. That's got to be difficult—delivering bad news to people." My mom was always about decorum and rising above.

"It is, but you *are* helping someone make a decision to either move on or stick it out with somebody. I try to look at what I do as a good service to people. Honestly, most of the time I'm serving subpoenas or running background checks for businesses. It's quick, easy money and pays for the business and the staff."

The next hour was a blur. My family loved to talk about the winery, and Peri was extremely interested in the business. I was bored, but it gave me the opportunity to look at her, not as the American hell bent on finding my bisnonna, but as a woman traveling through Italy on business. She was pretty, and I found her long, blond hair fascinating. It was still in a braid, though riding on the back of my motorcycle managed to loosen it into a wispy and sexy, over-the-shoulder hairdo. Both Mateo and Ethan couldn't keep their eyes off her.

"Camila? Camila?"

My mother had been trying to get my attention. "Yes?"

"Will you please get Bisnonna? It's almost time for dinner."

I stood and nodded. I was eager to hear her story when she was ready to tell it. I doubted it would be over dinner in front of everyone. Even though Peri gave my bisnonna something that made her both extremely emotional and full of grief, I knew it was the right thing for her. I couldn't imagine loving somebody and never having the life I wanted with them.

Chapter Nine

The Villa—Peri

Aside from Camila mostly being a jerk, I really liked the Rossini-Barneses. Obviously, it helped that they all spoke English, but they seemed like genuine people who valued family above all. When was the last time my entire family sat down to eat a meal together? Amma's funeral? I told myself to try harder. Their family dynamic was beautiful. And the story of how Nerissa and Greg met? At a youth hostel? And fell in love the week he was traveling through Italy so he stayed? Their love was still obvious in the small touches and smiles that appeared when they spoke to one another. Respect. They had respect for one another. It was deeper than what my parents had. Maybe that was because they were running a successful wine empire or whatever the locals called it, but it showed, and it was genuine.

"Do you have dinner as a family every day?" I asked. It was a Tuesday. I could understand if it were a Sunday, but it was in the middle of the week. I was alone with Camila's family, and even though Camila and I weren't on the best of terms, I was starting to get nervous with her out of the room. With her gone, I was the center of attention.

"We try to. Sometimes during harvest, it's hard, but family is important to us. This way we can have face-to-face conversations and not through the phone." Nerissa pried Luke's phone from his hands and put it facedown on the table to emphasize her point. Even though she was born Italian, her English was good, her accent stronger than Camila's.

"Bisnonna is here. Sophia is bringing out dinner. I'm going to help her," Camila said.

She gently eased her great-grandmother back into her chair and left with the wheelchair. Isabel reached toward me, and I gladly accepted her hands. "Peri, tell me more about Hilde."

I could tell she'd made peace with the news of Amma's passing, but she was a long way from getting over it. Her eyes still had tears that threatened to spill out the corners, but she also had a sad, small smile.

"Who's Hilde?" Ethan asked.

I didn't want to force Isabel to share more than she wanted with her family. "She was my great-grandmother and friends with Isabel during the war." Isabel squeezed my hands, thanking me.

"That's really cool. We don't hear Bisnonna talk about her early life very often. How did you meet Peri's great-grandmother?" Ethan asked.

"On the beach. She was with the Red Cross. She was a nurse's assistant and helped the soldiers and workers who were repairing docked American ships. We became friends," Isabel said.

"Did you speak English back then?" Luke asked.

"No. Not well, but I wanted to learn, so Hilde and her coworkers spent a lot of their free time teaching me and my friends."

"Were you in school then? Did they teach it there, too, like they do now?"

"A war was going on, so attending school wasn't a priority. They certainly didn't teach English. We were fighting the British, after all. But one of our teachers spoke it, and she taught us some of the basics. It was like a secret club. We didn't want to get her into trouble," she said.

"Did you ever teach Hilde Italian?" It was weird calling Amma by her real name.

"Oh, yes, but most of it she picked up at her work. She was very proud of her job and very good at it, too."

Amma's main job was to report news back to headquarters, but everyone pitched in to help the wounded when things got heavy. "When she returned to the United States, she went to school and became a nurse. So did my grandmother and my mother. I'm the black sheep." I didn't care really. I don't think anybody did. Amma was proud of me and what I was doing, even if my parents were a bit disappointed that I didn't continue my medical education.

"I used to sneak out and take bottles of wine down to the beach, and we would drink under the moonlight and hang out until morning," Isabel said.

"I think we've all done that, too, Bisnonna," Camila said. She returned carrying a bowl of pasta, Sophia right behind her with soup.

"Was it safe to be on the beach during a war?" Nerissa asked.

"It was a lot safer after the war. Hilde was stationed here in 1945 and 1946. Most of the fun stuff happened the summer before she left." Isabel paused, and nobody pressed her. I quickly changed the subject before one of Camila's brothers could jump in to press her for more.

"What's the legal drinking age here?" I helped Isabel lay the napkin across her lap and did mine as well. The food smelled wonderful, even though I'd eaten the most filling and delicious sandwich only hours ago.

"Sixteen, but a soft sixteen. I mean, nobody's going to give wine to a baby, but at most restaurants, you have to be sixteen," Camila said.

"That blows my mind. In the States, you have to be twenty-one, and they definitely card you."

"Things are more relaxed in Europe," Luke said. He leaned back in his chair to make room for Nerissa to pass out the plates. "At least the last time we worked the ranch in Texas, we were old enough to drink, but barely."

"I heard about the ranch. Did you like it?"

Camila's brothers looked at one another. "No," they said in unison. Everybody laughed, including Isabel.

For being ninety-six, Isabel's hands were surprisingly nimble. She carefully twirled the pasta around her fork and got most of it in her mouth. I felt like an awkward child trying to mimic her and failed miserably. I mostly leaned over my plate and bit the noodles off that refused to cooperate. I ate pasta like an eight-year-old. Camila giggled at me, and I couldn't help but smile. I was supposed to be mad at her, but this wonderful place and the ease of her family life made it hard to stay angry. I rolled my eyes and quickly looked down at my plate, trying to ignore the flutter in my stomach.

"Peri, where are you staying?" Nerissa asked.

"At a small B&B down on Via Marconi."

"You should stay with us at the villa tonight. I'm sure Isabel would love to hear more about Hilde and her life," she said.

My first instinct was to run, but the pressure of Isabel's fingers on my arm made me pause.

"Please stay. I won't keep you up too late," she said.

"If it's not an imposition and you have room for me, that would be wonderful. Thank you," I said.

Camila stilled at my words. For a moment, I wanted to backpedal, because obviously she didn't welcome me, but then I remembered she'd been an ass to me and swallowed my words. It was only for a night. Plus, I could find out more about the relationship between our great-grandmothers. If Camila was right, then Amma had a secret she wanted me to know.

"We have the whole upstairs. Mom and Dad have the west wing, and Bisnonna's living quarters are on the east side, off the kitchen," Camila said.

"I didn't mean to impose. It's hard to say no to your mother." I took my suitcase from Camila and placed it beside the dresser. "This is a beautiful place."

"Privacy is iffy. Mateo will bust in without so much as a knock."

I looked at the doorknob and pointed at the old-fashioned metal key sticking out of the lock just below it.

"It works, but why should I have to lock my door in my own house? Even my brothers give me privacy and at least knock."

She slid her hands into the back pockets of her jeans. "We'll be downstairs. Just follow the noise, and you'll find us. Let me know if you need anything else."

"I'm just going to freshen up, and then I'll be down."

Camila nodded and closed the door behind her.

This guest room was beautiful and spacious. With the en suite bathroom, it seemed bigger than my place. I pulled out the only fresh clothes left and decided to shower. The bathroom was stocked with scented soaps and high-end shampoos and conditioners. This was a dream home. No wonder Camila still lived here. Of course, she didn't have a car, and her motorcycle was a hand-me-down, so I was confused about her situation. Perhaps I would never know.

A half an hour later, I joined the family, feeling invigorated. "Where's Isabel?" I had my iPad with me to show her some photos. I'd correctly assumed Granny had left the photo albums all out on the dining-room table. When I asked her to snap some photos with her phone, she responded immediately.

"Isabel's in the kitchen getting tea. Feel free to join her. It sounds like you have a lot to talk about," Nerissa said.

I found her sitting in a comfortable chair in the family room off the kitchen that overlooked the vineyards sipping a hot tea. "May I join you?"

"Yes." She patted the cushion of the chair next to her. "With your hair down, you look more like Hilde."

I blushed. Amma was beautiful, and I never thought I looked like her. I saw similarities, but nobody ever made a fuss until today. "That's sweet of you to say. Thank you."

"Tell me everything about her, you, your family."

"I have something you'll like even more." I unlocked my iPad and pulled up a folder marked family. "I had Sandra, Hilde's daughter, snap photos with her phone and send them to me. Photos from years ago when maybe you knew her." I didn't tell her how I almost lost my shit trying to explain to Granny how to snap a picture and text it to me. Most weren't in focus, but eventually she figured it out, and I was rewarded with twenty-four photos of our family, as well as the more recent ones I had in my phone.

Isabel covered her mouth with her hand. "Oh, my goodness."

She touched Amma's face on every single photo she was in. "She looks so happy."

I treaded lightly because I still didn't have enough detail about their relationship. "Hilde had a good life. She loved her family and friends. She was always kind to everyone and volunteered for a lot of projects in our town." I was quiet after that because watching the emotions that crossed Isabel's face told a story. Their story. Camila was right. Our great-grandmothers had history. I watched as she pulled out the locket and handed it to me.

"Can you open this for me?"

I carefully pried it open and placed it back in her hand. "Will you tell me your story?"

Isabel waved me off. I lowered my voice. Maybe her family didn't know. Maybe she was embarrassed to tell me. I tried a different approach. "When I was sixteen, Amma caught me and my girlfriend kissing in her car. Amma had a pristine 1957 Studebaker Golden Hawk that was parked in the garage. It was black with white fins and had a giant backseat. I'm sure you can guess where this is going." Isabel smiled and nodded for me to continue. My story wasn't that exciting, but the look on Isabel's weathered face made me embellish just enough to bring a sweet blush to her cheeks. "She knocked on the window and offered us lemonade and told us not to spill any on the seats."

"You must have been so embarrassed," Isabel said.

"I was mortified. I mean, my great-grandmother caught me with a girl, and we were barely dressed. My parents didn't even know I was a lesbian. They didn't figure that out until college, when I brought my girlfriend home for Thanksgiving."

"Are you the only child?"

"Yes. Just me. My parents have always been supportive. They didn't care. Even my Granny didn't care." I softened my voice. "It's a different time now. People are more accepting. Women are independent and can have careers, and they don't need a man to support them." We sat in quiet as she scrolled through the family photos.

"What are you ladies doing?" Camila slipped into the kitchen and sat beside Isabel, kissing her on the cheek. It was such a natural move, and my heart constricted. I couldn't do that to Amma ever again.

"We're just looking at photos of my family," I said.

"Do you mind if I see them, too?"

At my nod, she scooted her chair next to Isabel and leaned in.

"Your hair is so blond in these photos," Camila said. She zoomed in on it. "Can you tell us who everyone in the photo is?"

It was a family Christmas photo from ten years ago. I didn't want to mention The Captain in front of Isabel, but Camila left me no choice. I listed everyone in the family and stalled when I got to Amma. "These are my parents, Mary and Bill, next to Amma and—" I stumbled. "And her husband. We called him The Captain."

Isabel nodded. "In the last letter she sent, she said he treated her well."

I silently sighed, relieved. Obviously, Amma married and had children, or else I wouldn't be here, but it was still hard to gauge how Isabel would react. "We lost The Captain not long after this picture was taken. He was a good man. Mom said he always showed up to her dance recitals and gave her candy when Granny wouldn't."

"How did they meet?" Camila asked me.

Before I had the chance to answer with the story that I'd heard for years, Isabel answered. "They met here in Italy. I introduced them."

Chapter Ten

Were They or Weren't They?—Camila

Peri and I looked at one another in confusion. So maybe Bisnonna and Hilde weren't lovers?

"You introduced an American to another American? Weren't they in the same place?" I asked.

Bisnonna nodded. "Yes, but a lot of people were there, and The Captain didn't arrive until the winter of 1945. He oversaw the workers who repaired ships."

I was going to have to delicately ask the obvious question and wasn't sure Bisnonna would answer. I was out and had been since I was a teenager. Surely she felt safe enough to tell me her story. Peri raised an eyebrow at me, and I gave a very slight shrug. "So, were you and Hilde close? I mean, she had a locket of the two of you. And you both looked so happy."

She touched my hand. "That's a conversation for tomorrow. It's getting late."

"Of course, Bisnonna. Do you want me to take you back to your room?" We were going to have to wait for more of their story.

"No. I can get there fine. You two stay here and get to know one another better."

I kissed her cheek, and Peri and I watched until she disappeared down the hallway.

"So, what do you think?" I asked, knowing full well that the news that Isabel introduced The Captain to Hilde also took Peri by surprise.

"I mean, it's possible they were just friends, but I think there was definitely more."

I rinsed out Bisnonna's cup and placed it in the sink. "But she introduced Hilde to her future husband. That doesn't fit."

"Yeah. I'm still trying to process if I remember Amma talking about women, or about Isabel. I was telling your bisnonna about how Amma caught me and my first girlfriend making out in her car, and she didn't bat an eye. I always knew she was amazing, but that confirmed it. She accepted my coming out more easily than the rest of my family did."

I held up a finger. "Can you hold on a moment? I'm going to check on her. I'll be right back." I retreated down the hall at Peri's nod and gently knocked on Bisnonna's ajar door. "Bisnonna? May I come in?"

"Of course."

I found her at her desk looking at a stack of letters tied together with a blue ribbon.

"Are those from Hilde?"

"Yes. We had a nice correspondence after she left. For about a year."

The stack looked thick for only a year's worth of letters. "Did you write each other every day? You must have fifty letters there."

"Some of them are ones that were returned to me for some reason or another. Mail wasn't very reliable after the war."

A shift of emotions worked their way across her unguarded face as she untied the ribbon that held pieces of her heart on tissue-thin paper.

"Why didn't you use your stationery?' I touched the delicate paper to feel their lightness and fragility.

"It was so expensive to send letters. The war hit the winery hard. It took years to make a profit, so money was tight," she said.

I made a mental note to quit complaining about simple things in life. Bisnonna's life and the path she was expected to take compared to the one she wanted made it clear how blessed I was.

"Would you like me to read the letters to you?" Her eyesight wasn't the greatest. Hell, I had a hard enough time reading the address on the air-mail envelope.

"Maybe tomorrow. Tonight, I need time to myself." She patted my shoulder. "Go spend some time with that beautiful young woman out there. I'm so happy our families got a chance to meet all these many years later."

Spending time with Peri didn't seem awful. She had to feel awkward around my family since she didn't know anybody, and she didn't strike me as an extrovert. "Okay. I'll go spend some time with our guest. I'm sorry I kept her from you, but I was only trying to protect you."

"I know, dear. That's why I love you so much. You're loyal to this family. We are lucky to have you."

I smiled and slipped out of the room. My heart ached for Bisnonna. I knew that she loved her husband, but I couldn't imagine marrying someone while loving somebody else.

I returned to the kitchen, but it was empty. Everyone was still in the courtyard so I checked there next. "Where's Peri?" I asked. "Did she go to her room?" I looked at the clock. It was still relatively early.

"Mateo took her out to the vineyards," Luke said.

"But it's almost dark out there. What's there to see this time of night?" Ethan asked with a smirk.

Mateo was going to make his move on her. Maybe Peri was bi or pan. Who was I to label her after one conversation about a couple of past relationships? I ignored the jealousy that crept into my throat, making it hard to swallow. Heat fanned out from my cheeks as I pretended not to care. I took a sip of wine to play it cool, but inside I was raging.

"We're in Italy. There's no place more romantic in the world," Luke said.

I shrugged like it was no big deal. Even though Peri was gullible, Mateo would behave. I pulled out my phone to scroll social media, but my mind kept drifting to them. What were they doing? Where were they?

"It's getting late. I'm going to head back to my place and crash. I'm pretty tired," Luke said. He kissed Mom and pulled my hair. "Maybe you should go find them."

"Go away," I grumbled.

"Get some sleep. Try not to think about the pretty girl asleep in the room next to yours," he said.

"Leave her alone, Luke. Be careful driving home." My mom stood and wished the rest of us good night. "Don't stay up too late, Camila. You have to open the shop in the morning. I don't think Mateo will work for you another day."

Ethan pushed the chair in and laughed. "Classic, Mom. I'm going, too. Tell your new friend that I hope she had a good time tonight."

"Ha ha. Go home, bro," I said. I loved my family, but they loved to tease me too much.

"What do you think of Peri?" Since we were the only ones left at the table, my dad moved from the head of the table to sit across from me.

"She seems nice," I said.

"So, how many days did you string her along?" he asked.

I knew he'd want to talk about it. I sighed. "Like three or four days, but it's not as bad as it sounds. She wouldn't tell me anything. She just yanked down Bisnonna's drawing and demanded to see her. That ruffled my feathers. I had no reason to trust her, and honestly, I don't know that I trust her now."

"Isabel seems okay with her, so whatever that locket was, she appreciated it."

"I think it was a keepsake from their relationship during the war." I wish I'd paid more attention in history class. With my mixed heritage, one would think I'd have concentrated more, but I never cared. Not until this week.

"She's a very nice woman. I don't think she's out to dupe us or Isabel."

"Should we look into her?" I asked.

"She's leaving tomorrow night. I don't think she's going to run off with the silver or the secrets to our wine. You need to relax more, Camila. I appreciate that you were cautious, but maybe just take a step back and be a friend to Peri. Isabel said she and Hilde wrote after the war. Maybe you two can start a pen-pal thing like them."

I stopped myself from snorting. If my dad only knew. "Nobody sends letters anymore, Dad. Maybe we'll be friends on social media. Her job is very interesting."

"See? That's a start. And she's obviously interested in the winery. Speaking of, why don't you take over the social media accounts? I don't think Ethan is doing a very good job, and you seem to have a pulse on that kind of communication."

I threw my hands up. "I've been saying that all along. That means I have to be on site, so I can't be at the oil store five days a week."

My dad cocked his head as though I was trying to get away with something. I gave him my most angelic, innocent look.

"I'm sure we can pick an afternoon one day a week when you can leave the shop early and finish out the day at the winery," he said.

I tried to be professional and give him a simple nod, but I was too excited. "Thank you so much. You won't regret it." This was the break I wanted. I put photos on my own Insta account, but having the business account? That was monumental. I was finally transitioning over to the winery.

"Your mother and I will talk about it, but I wanted to give you some good news. You aren't having the greatest day," he said.

I held my hands up. "It's the day from hell, and I'm looking forward to tomorrow."

"Go to bed early, and be nice to our guest."

He kissed my forehead and left me alone at the table. Normally I would love the quiet time, but my anxiety ramped up as time slowed down. Peri and Mateo had been gone for over half an hour. What were they doing? I rearranged the flowers, wiped down the already clean counters, and washed our wineglasses. By the time they returned, the entire kitchen was spotless.

"How was your evening?" I asked. Mateo's smile was enormous, and Peri looked relaxed and happy. Why?

"It was great. It was too dark to give Peri the proper tour, but maybe that can happen tomorrow morning. This place is too beautiful to leave without seeing it first." Mateo kissed the back of Peri's hand and thanked her for a wonderful stroll.

"Is everyone asleep? What time is it?" Peri asked.

He made a big production of checking his phone. "It's late. I should go, but I'll be back in the morning." He turned to me and smiled. "Don't worry about a thing. I'll take Peri around tomorrow. Maybe we can get Isabel to go with us since she's the reason you're here."

"That sounds great, if she's up to it. I don't want to push her," Peri said.

"She's seems to be feeling better today," he said.

I was trying not to let their good mood make mine slip down further. "She had a lot of information to process. Hopefully she gets a decent night's sleep."

"Ladies, have a wonderful night." Mateo took a sweeping bow and left us alone in the kitchen.

"He's so sweet. It's great that you've been best friends for twenty years. That's hard to find. My longest friendship is from high school, and honestly, we're not that close," Peri said.

She tapped her fingers lightly on the counter and sat in one of the high-back chairs tucked underneath. I slipped into the chair across from her. Any other day, with any other attractive woman, I would lay it on thick. I would tell her how beautiful her hair looked draped over her slender shoulder or how her eyes remind me of the water down at the beach when the sun is high in the sky. But she was leaving, and we had no time for flirting.

"I know I've apologized already, but I am sorry for stringing you along. It wasn't fair of me. The locket has obviously brought Bisnonna happiness."

Peri dropped her voice. "Do you really think they had some sort of affair when they were young?"

I thought about my words carefully because I didn't want to gossip, especially about my bisnonna. "Maybe they had a romance, but we won't know for sure until she tells us."

"When she said she introduced Amma to The Captain, I freaked out internally. Did that confuse you, too? I mean, were they together during the war or not?" Peri asked.

"Too many questions and not enough answers. Hopefully Bisnonna will share more of their story tomorrow. If not, at least you accomplished what you set out to do here." I still sounded like a jerk. "I mean, she has the locket. You might not have the answers you want, but at least you found her. That should give you some sort of peace. And you found her with no information other than a photo with Bisnonna's name and a date. That's impressive."

I could tell she was biting back the retort I deserved. She took a deep breath instead. "Thank you. It's because of your drawing. It was so precise and lifelike. Why do your parents think your art is just a hobby? Clearly, you have talent. Doesn't Italy have the best art schools? Why are you selling oils when you should be selling oil paintings?"

I waved her off like my art wasn't a big deal, but disappointment in myself and in my family's lack of support squeezed my heart. Ultimately it was my decision, but I was scared. I was good at family and good at our business, but I was bad at failure. "I don't think I'll ever be able to make a living at it. I'd love to, but my life is here."

"Why can't you have both?" She wasn't pushing me out of meanness, but she was making me answer questions I didn't want to face.

"I would have to leave and get formal training. Surprisingly, most of the best art schools are in the US or the UK. Not here." It was hard to have a normal chat with her. She unnerved me. The tension that radiated from her the last few days was gone. In front of me sat a confident woman who gave me her total attention.

"Wow. I would have thought Paris or Florence. But you know what that tells me?"

"No." I fiddled with my phone, popping the corner in and out of its case just to keep my hands busy.

"It tells me that it's crossed your mind. That you already know where the best art schools are." She took out her own phone and pulled up her search engine. "Wow. Two of the top hundred art schools are less than an hour from me."

"Which two?" I only knew about ones in California and in New York City.

"Rhode Island School of Design and Worcester Fine Arts Academy are in the Northeast. They both are about thirty minutes in opposite directions from where I live."

"It's a small world," I said.

"If you're ever interested, I could show you around. You know, extend the same courtesy you extended me." She folded her arms in front of her and smirked.

It was too perfect. I pursed my lips to keep from laughing but I couldn't stop the guffaw that bubbled out, and within seconds, she joined in. We couldn't stop. Our laughter was cathartic. The tension and our history washed away with the tears streaming down our faces.

"I'm really sorry, Peri. I was a real ass. It's been nice getting to know you. You are very delicate and respectful with Bisnonna, so thank you."

She blushed. "That's history. I'm not worried anymore. And your family is wonderful. It's nice that Isabel is sharing information about their relationship from so many decades ago. It sounded like even though a war was going on, they were able to have something sweet, regardless of their language barrier."

"Would you like a glass of wine to relax before bedtime? I'd offer you a different type of alcohol, but we stick to wine around here." At her nod, I opened a bottle of our 2017 merlot. "It's one of my favorites." I loved it so much, I had three cases in my section of the wine cellar.

"It's delicious."

"Hopefully, on your tour tomorrow, Mateo will show you the cellars. They are impressive."

"Everything about this villa is impressive. The architecture is so old and lovely. I get why you still live here. I don't know that I'd be able to move out either." Peri smelled the wine again. "It's too bad you have to work tomorrow. As much as I appreciate Mateo, I honestly wish you were giving me the tour. Maybe he can work for you tomorrow again. He knows the business, according to him."

Her confession threw me for a loop. I didn't think she was interested in me at all. I mean, she stood up for me with my parents about art, but most of the evening she was quiet around me. "He does, but my mother is already displeased with me for making Mateo work for me Monday and Tuesday. And I hate taking him away from his own work. He's working on another children's book."

"I understand. It just would've been nice to hang out for the rest of my time."

Was Peri flirting? I watched as she scraped her bottom lip with her upper teeth and broke eye contact. Maybe flirting was the wrong word. When her eyes met mine again, something stirred low inside me. A warm feeling ribboned in my veins and gave my heart a little squeeze. In any other situation, I would've made a move. "Maybe somebody can cover me for a few hours. I always tell my family that nobody's racing to buy olive oil at nine in the morning."

"I'd like that. I'm sure Mateo is an excellent tour guide, but you know…"

"How many times did he hit on you tonight?"

"Only twice, before I told him I'm gay, but he was extremely respectful after that. And then he said the tour would make more sense in the daylight." Peri laughed.

"I'm sure his heart was broken for about two minutes. Gemma, the pregnant woman who was at the beach with us, and I have decided he needs to write a romance. He would do so well."

"Maybe he can write a romance based on Amma and Isabel," Peri said.

I reached across the table and squeezed her hands. "That's the best idea ever."

CHAPTER ELEVEN

THE FIRST LETTER—PERI

S urprise."
 Camila was standing in the kitchen next to a plate of croissants and jellies. She poured me a cup of coffee and added more cream and sugar than I would have, but it was nice that she remembered how I liked it. I took a sip and hid my grimace at the overly sweet taste, forcing a smile instead.

"You found somebody to fill in for you? That's great."

Camila always looked refreshed. After sharing a bottle of wine with her last night, I fell into a fitful sleep, waking every hour on the hour until it was hard to ignore the sunshine. I had a lot to do today. I'd held back a pair of jeans I wore only once, a T-shirt, and Converse, but the rest of my suitcase was packed. I had to leave for the airport by seven tonight. I felt like a walking wreck compared to her.

"I did. My mother is going to work in my place, so I'm all yours." Camila cleared her throat as we both maneuvered around that innuendo.

"That's great. What did you have in mind?" Now my phrasing was just as awkward. "What's first on the agenda?"

"I thought we could have breakfast with Bisnonna, and hopefully she will tell us stories about her and Hilde. I know you're pressed for time, but I want to make sure we have enough time for a quick tour of the winery in the daylight."

"That sounds great," I said.

When Camila left to get Isabel, I quickly poured out half the coffee and added a splash of water.

"Good morning, Peri." Isabel slowly shuffled into the kitchen with a smile and a stack of letters held together by a blue ribbon. Her smile warmed my heart. Camila was right behind her, and hers warmed me in an entirely different way.

"Good morning, Isabel. How are you feeling?"

"I'm doing well. Did you sleep well, dear?" she asked.

"I'm afraid your tasty wine kept me up most of the night. But no worries. I can sleep on the plane home."

She slid over the stack of letters. "We've all had that problem before. I was hoping you could read these to me. To us."

I cleared my throat and took a sip of coffee, forgetting how awful it was. I coughed and swallowed hard. How could it be worse? Camila opened the refrigerator and handed me a Pellegrino. I wasn't fond of sparkling water but gladly accepted it. After a refreshing pull from the bottle, I carefully tugged the ribbon open and ran my fingertips over the stack of letters. I recognized the handwriting. My Amma wrote these letters decades ago. A wave of sadness washed over me as I realized I never knew this side of her, that her relationship was never recognized. How easy life was for me. I swallowed the lump in my throat and blinked back tears.

"Would you like me to read the first letter?" Camila asked.

I nodded and handed her the first letter. Her fingertips brushed my palm as she took it from my hand, and I ignored the thickening of my pulse and the warmth of the connection.

Camila pulled the tissue thin paper from the envelope. "Are you sure?"

Isabel reached for my hand and nodded. I grasped hers with the same conviction. "It's time for my family to know."

My free hand went up to my throat as my anxiety kicked up a notch when Camila unfolded the letter.

My dearest Isabel,

Do you remember the night we sneaked into the olive grove when it was just us under the biggest tree? A soft breeze rustled the small leaves around us, and we thought your brother had followed us, but no. It was just us. You pressed me up against the tree to hide me. You said the moonlight made my hair glow, and my eyes sparkled with something you couldn't quite identify. It was love, Izzy. In that moment, I knew I loved you. Our first kiss was the most amazing feeling of my life. I knew it was going to happen that night. I thought I was scared, but the moment I felt your lips on my cheek move down to my mouth, I knew it was meant to be. We were meant to be. It will forever be, in the history of my life, my favorite first kiss.

Camila stopped, I imagined, to watch how Isabel and I reacted. The lump in my throat grew, and I swallowed hard twice. Isabel dabbed her eyes. I squeezed her hand a little harder. Coming out was never easy, and at ninety-six, it had to be the hardest thing she had done, aside from walking away from her relationship with Hilde.

"Bisnonna, she sounded wonderful. How romantic. Do you remember this first kiss?"

"How could I forget something so powerful? Even though my mind isn't as sharp as it once was, my heart will always remember it."

"That's beautiful, Isabel," I said. I was overcome with such a rush of sadness and an overwhelming need to feel something that strong. I hadn't been that much in love and felt things so deeply yet, even though I foolishly thought I'd been in love before.

"Shall I continue?" Camila asked. She held it out to me. "Or would you like to read?"

She was truly being sincere, and although they were Amma's words, hearing them aloud seemed so personal and private. "Oh, please continue."

Camila nodded and picked up where she'd left off.

Being so far away from you is hard. Everywhere I go, something reminds me of you. Oh, Izzy would love this bakery or would love to dance to the song on the radio, or even take a walk with me in the fall. You would love Connecticut right now. The leaves are changing, and even though the sky is gray, the trees light up the sky with yellow

*and orange leaves that twirl like small fires on branches. It's cold
outside, but everything seems softer and easier with you in my heart.
I hate that you are so far away from me, my love, but what can we
do? I can feel your love from here even though an ocean separates
us. Please know that even though you are so far away, you are so
close to me that sometimes thinking about you takes my breath away.*

> *Always,*
> *Hilde*

None of us spoke while we let Amma's words sink in. Camila
poured Isabel tea, and I sipped my sparkling water. So many things
flashed in my mind. The definition of true love, beauty during a war,
a love that could never happen. They must have been so torn inside.

"Isabel, what would have happened if you and Hilde were
caught?"

Isabel wiped her nose on her handkerchief that she pulled
from under her sleeve. The gesture made me smile because Amma
did that, too. "We would have been kicked out of our families,
and worse. Here, the church told us we would be damned, and in
America, it was illegal to engage in such conduct. During the war,
many people would sleep with their friends, but then the war ended.
All those people like us returned home and married, as they were
supposed to. Honestly, Hilde and I didn't think it could ever be real
between us and couldn't last. I didn't know a single gay person. Not
until much later in life. And by then, we were both too old and too
embedded in our families to do anything about it."

I wanted to be angry at them for giving up and walking away
from such a deep love, but I had to remember that it wasn't that long
ago that LGBTQ people were given basic rights like marriage and the
ability to adopt children, although even Italy still didn't allow those
freedoms. "When was the last time you and Hilde communicated?"
I hated that I didn't know if they had phones in the 1940s or could
even call overseas. I was going to have to google that later.

"The last letter I received from Hilde was on her wedding day."

My heart broke right there in Italy at 10:16 in the morning. I
wanted to fall to the floor and cry for such romantic injustice, to

weep for a love that never had a chance. I looked at Camila, and her expression told me she felt the same.

"These are pretty revealing letters, even for the 1940s, Bisnonna. Were you afraid you would get caught? Did you hide them?" Camila asked.

"I was more worried for Hilde. Her family was very religious and strict. She could have been put in a mental institution. I sent her letters to a cousin who would ensure she received them, but I was still very careful," she said. She took the letter back from Camila and put it at the bottom of the stack, then handed her the next one. "Hilde didn't have to be as careful when she wrote me. My family gave me privacy and just assumed it was a very strong friendship. Hilde got me out of the house. I was so worried about the war, but she gave me hope, and my parents thanked her all the time for bringing me out of my shell."

"You were eighteen? Were your parents pushing you to get married?" I asked.

"I was almost twenty. We were trying to stay afloat, and they needed my help as much as I needed theirs. I was glad they didn't push me to marry the first man who gave me attention."

"You got married when you were twenty-three, right? Did you have a long engagement?" Camila asked.

"Back then, people just got married. We didn't have elaborate weddings and celebrations. Just our families and a few friends. And we weren't engaged for years. Lorenzo and I met in December 1947 and were married on Valentine's Day the following year."

"All this time I always thought it was so romantic that you were married on Valentine's Day," Camila said.

"You have Valentine's Day here?" I always thought it was American capitalism at its worst. It forced a make-believe holiday on us so we'd spend loads of money on chocolates, flowers, and cards.

"Sort of. Of course, it's overdone, and people go overboard."

I grunted with understanding.

"How are my great-granddaughter and Hilde's great-granddaughter so negative about love? A few moments ago, you were both so sad, and now you're rolling your eyes at love," Isabel said.

"It's not that—" Camila promptly interrupted me.

"We're not negative. We just love love on our own terms, and we don't want to be told how to show it, right?"

For once we were on the same team. "Exactly that. Love is beautiful when people don't expect things."

Isabel waved her hand at us as though shooing a fly away. "I don't believe you. You are both too much like me and Hilde. You are just too stubborn to admit that it's nice when somebody gives you something to show that they care for you."

"But not something so ridiculous as chocolate. I get enough calories from the wine," Camila said.

"I can always tell when you are lying, Camila. Your eye twitches," Isabel said. I giggled. Isabel turned to me. "And you are a part of Hilde, so I know you enjoy romantic things, too. You aren't fooling me either."

It was Camila's turn to smirk at me.

"I mean attention is nice, but I like different things. Not necessarily chocolate, but other romantic things." I started fidgeting with my phone when I realized Camila was studying me.

"Like what?" Camila asked.

I squirmed under her scrutiny and started to brush her off, but I didn't want to upset Isabel. "Like something handmade or even a beautiful letter like Amma wrote."

Isabel pointed at me. "See? You are a romantic."

"What about you, Camila? What do you like?" I asked.

"To give or receive?" She stared boldly at me.

I blushed at her words. Camila was beautiful and confident. A flash of her topping me crossed my mind, and I tamped it down. I didn't need any complications. "Both. How would you make somebody feel special? And wine doesn't count." I wagged my finger at her.

She playfully huffed. "Fine. No wine. Obviously, I would draw something that she liked. Maybe even a sketch of her naked, sleeping in my bed."

My jaw dropped at how open she was in front of Isabel. As cool as Amma was with me, I wouldn't think of saying something that inappropriate. "After everything we've heard today, that's what you say? In front of your bisnonna?" I liked the way it sounded coming out of my mouth. My accent sounded authentic, but Camila smirked again and then shrugged as she returned her focus to the conversation.

"It's fine, Peri. Camila likes attention. I'm used to it."

"You've seen my art. You know what I'm capable of."

"Wow. This is a whole new level of confidence." I did a double take when I noticed Isabel was smiling. I could totally see why Amma and she had a connection.

"What do you like to receive?" I asked. "Giving is the easy part."

"Whatever they want to give me." She leaned on the counter with her hip and studied her nails as though she was bored, but I could tell by the slight constant movement of her foot that she was nervous. That, as well as Isabel's wink, gave me confidence.

"Can you be more specific?" I didn't want to know, but I refused to back down now. Or maybe part of me did want to know.

"Something that reminds me of our date. Like a shell from the beach, or maybe dessert from the restaurant we had dinner at. For me, it's all about her."

A control freak. That's who I was dealing with. "Maybe she wants to do something for you. Don't assume all women take and take and never want to give."

Camila frowned and stepped back. "I don't. I mean, women have given me things before to show their appreciation."

"Show their appreciation? That's sounds like you're selling them something or providing a service."

"I do provide a service. A very intimate one." Camila lifted her eyebrow, and that smirk showed up again. A part of me wanted to wipe it off her face, and another part, much to my dismay, wanted to kiss it away. I almost groaned. How was I attracted to her? She had the worst attitude about everything.

Isabel stepped in before I said something stupid. "Peri, she's playing with you. She just wants to get a rise out of you, and she shouldn't do that. You're my guest, and I thought for sure she learned her lesson yesterday, but I guess she needs a reminder."

"Sorry, Bisnonna."

"It's not me you need to apologize to."

The muscles in her jaw moved as she clenched her teeth. I smiled my cheesiest smile, which seemed to infuriate her even more. She didn't like to apologize, and I was going to enjoy every moment of it. I never thought I was annoying or unlikeable until this trip, and I childishly blamed Camila for my self-doubt.

"I'm sorry, Peri. My teasing went too far. Please forgive me?"

I hated that she sounded so sincere. I wanted to scoff, but Isabel looked so sweet and so hopeful that I simply nodded and forced the corners of my mouth into some semblance of a smile.

"Good. Now you girls go tour the vineyard before Peri has to leave. It's important that she have a better understanding of this place. We'll read more letters when you return. I'm going to rest in front of the television."

"Do you want to come with us, Bisnonna?"

"Oh, no. You two go and have a nice time. I want to hear all about it when you return." She tugged on Camila's shirt. "Be sure to show her the cellars."

Camila helped Isabel to the couch. Watching her gentleness with her was endearing, but I knew better than to lower my guard. Camila's tongue was barbed in a way I wasn't used to, and I wanted to avoid it at all costs.

"I will. And we'll take pictures." She kissed Isabel's cheek. "Here's your phone. You remember how to call, right?"

She waved us off. "Yes, I know how to make a phone call. Go. Have fun."

I smiled at her sassiness. I could understand why Amma loved her. I'd known her twenty-four hours, and I already loved her a little.

Chapter Twelve

The Cellars—Camila

W hat's your favorite wine?" I slipped behind the wheel of the ATV and motioned for Peri to hop in.

"I don't know a lot about wine, but the sweeter, the better," she said.

I smiled as she grabbed the small handle on the roof. She had a seat belt, but I didn't plan to drive fast. "You don't have to worry about my driving here. This vehicle is slow, and I don't want to crash into the vines. Grapes are too precious," I said. Peri visibly relaxed. I couldn't help but tease her. "But wait until we hit the olive grove. Then I'll kick it up a notch." I smiled and winked before slipping my sunglasses on.

"If you like, I can drive," she said.

I snorted. "But you don't know your way around, and you probably don't know how to drive a stick shift. Most Americans don't."

"Well, that's a dumb generalization. How many Americans do you know?"

"Half of my family is American. Besides, when Mateo worked at a car rental place by the airport, he complained that a lot of tourists whined when they didn't get automatics."

"Because only Americans visit Italy." She rolled her eyes at me.

I stopped the ATV and jumped out. "Feel free to drive if it means that much to you."

"Stupid challenge accepted," she said.

I walked around and waited until she slid over. Her legs were shorter so she struggled reaching the pedals. "There's a button on the side that moves the seat forward." I smirked.

She adjusted the seat accordingly until it was perfect. "Are you ready?"

"Let's go, hotshot."

With ease, she shifted into gear and drove up the hill to the main building where the tour would begin. Her Cheshire Cat smile should have annoyed me, but I laughed. "You always surprise me."

"Why? Because I can drive a car? Just so you know, I drive a manual Passat back home. I learned to drive on one and love it."

I looked her up and down through the privacy of my sunglasses. She wore jeans, a T-shirt, and her Converse sneakers. I could tell she was self-conscious, but I wasn't sure why. She was fresh and quietly charming. "Park over by the door. No tours run today, so we won't be in the way." I watched as she smoothed her shirt and patted down her hair. It was obvious that I made her nervous. "Bisnonna's right. The cellars are wonderful. You're really going to like them."

"Are your brothers around? It seems pretty quiet."

"The grapes won't be ready for months, so they're probably in the office making calls for future sales."

"I would think the competition in Italy is fierce," Peri said.

"It is, but the demand is so high that everybody in this region makes a profit. Here. Let's start at the main entrance. It's just a short walk away." I opened the door and almost ran into her when she stuttered and stopped in front of me. She'd done that several times. Did people not open the door back home for her?

"Is tourism big at your winery?"

"Yes, and we pay a lot to be on the bus tours' schedules. Fridays and the weekends are very busy, worse during harvest time, but tourists love to see the whole process. We sell more wine then." I couldn't hide the pride in my voice when we walked inside. "Welcome to Rossini Wines."

"This place is amazing," she said.

I looked at it from her perspective. Large stone walls held up wooden-beam ceilings. The rooms were small and connected by a series of arched hallways. "It was built over two hundred years ago. This is the original building, and we've added to it. Tourists can drink wine and eat a small lunch in this area. Some people like to sit and drink wine while their party goes on the actual tour." I pointed to a larger room off to the left. "And that's where they can buy bottles of all of our wines."

"Where's the tasting room?"

"The official one is upstairs on the balcony. I'm taking you to the private one down in the cellar. I think you'll like it." I opened an old door and flipped a switch, and a very dim lightbulb right above us provided a little light. Peri moved closer to me.

"Should we get a flashlight or something?" she asked.

"The electricity in here is old, but charming. Hold on. Let me turn on the other lights." I flipped the other light switch and watched her reaction as twin strands of white lights lit the hallway like fireflies on a warm summer evening. It was still dark, but the ambiance of the cellar changed. "Here. Take my hand." I locked her fingers with mine, and a hard rush of heat pushed against my skin at her contact. "Is this okay?" I held up our hands as if she couldn't already feel our connection. I tried to ignore how perfectly her hand fit in mine or how much I wanted it there. She nodded. Could she feel the flutters in my hands? She turned to me, her face inches from mine.

"This is kind of exciting. I've never been in a wine cellar before."

"Oh, you haven't even seen the best part yet." I turned on another light at the end of the hallway that opened to a large room full of wooden barrels with tiny spigots all marked with numbers and flavor profiles.

"Wow. This is amazing." She was impressed and rightfully so. The cellar was massive. Peri shivered in the cooler temperature.

"You'll be chilled for only a few minutes," I said. I led her to the back of the cellar to another door that required both of us to open. I turned on the lights. "It's so much warmer in here."

"Is this a speakeasy?" The genuine smile on Peri's face made my stomach drop and twirl. "This is officially my favorite place on the property. Wait. Italy probably didn't have Prohibition like the US did," she said.

"No, we didn't." I followed her down the three steps that led into the open floor plan. I had to admit that it was one of my favorite places, too. This room seemed so warm and vibrant. The walls were decorated with colorful artwork, including a few of my landscapes. Thick area rugs covered the wood floors, and floor lamps tucked in the corners added warm light to the room. "It's a place for the family and our friends to hang out when we can't hang out up at the villa. Sometimes people rent it for weddings."

"I bet a lot of people do. You're very lucky to live in such a beautiful place."

"I know. We can eat and drink and can be as loud as we want without disturbing the ceremony."

"I wonder if Amma came down here with Isabel?"

"This was a very popular place during the war because it was safe, underground, and could hide and support a lot of people. Maybe we'll find a picture of them over here." I pointed to the wall behind the bar. I'd seen the photos hundreds of times but never really looked at them. Each one had a year written on it, the earliest from 1890.

"This was a picture taken during the war, and the one next to it was a year later." I pressed the edges of the small photo flat against the glass so I could see it better.

"Why didn't people smile back then?" she asked.

"What was there to smile about? There was a war," I said.

"Isabel and Amma had a lot to smile about. And their pictures in the locket show beautiful, smiling faces. I guess I just don't know a lot about early photography."

"Look here. People are smiling in this shot," I said.

She moved into my personal space to get a better look. Heat radiated from her, and I felt her breath on my cheek when she turned to face me. I looked into her eyes, then down to her lips, which were remarkable. "So maybe in just those two photos they were told to be somber or something." What was wrong with me? My arms felt heavy, and I was leaning into her.

She took a step back. "Maybe since we're down here, we should sample some wine?" Peri asked. She smiled, knowing full well that, for a moment, I was under her spell. I almost groaned at how obvious I was about wanting a kiss.

"There's plenty to choose from," I said.

"What do you recommend?"

I walked to a rack of wine, pulled out a bottle, and handed it to her.

"Isabel. You have a wine named after your great-grandmother. Shouldn't you save this?" Peri gently handed it back with both hands as if afraid she'd drop and shatter it.

I wiped off the dust with a rag behind the bar and found a bottle opener. "I can't think of a better occasion for opening a bottle of Isabel wine. Besides, we have cases. This is a 2008 pinot noir and Bisnonna's favorite. She's into our wine, but her real passion is olive oil." I shook my head. "I don't even understand that."

"But your mother says it's lucrative, so that's positive," Peri said.

"I know. I just love the romance of wine. Nothing about oil is romantic," I said.

"Well, there is, but maybe not olive oil."

The way Peri's face lit up at her joke and her burst of laughter did funny things to my stomach. She sat on the high-back chair at the bar and playfully smacked the bar with her palm. "What's a girl gotta do to get a drink around here?"

I slipped into bartender mode and, after opening the bottle, poured a sip of wine into her glass. She looked at me expectantly.

"That's it?"

"This is a tasting. You're supposed to look at the wine and smell it. Then you taste it. If you like it, I'll pour you a full glass." I poured my own sip and tilted the glass. "Look at the color and viscosity." She tilted her glass like I had. "Now tell me what you smell in this wine."

She held the glass up to her nose and closed her eyes. "I'm really bad at this."

"Just try. Do you smell fruit? And don't say grapes."

She giggled into the glass. "Raspberry?"

I nodded. She sat up, suddenly encouraged that her nose wasn't as bad as she thought. "Something spicy. Like nutmeg maybe?"

"Very close. Cloves. You can taste it now if you want."

She sipped the wine. "I taste something fresh and floral but tangy."

"Hibiscus. It's Bisnonna's favorite flower."

"It makes perfect sense that her own wine would have hints of her favorite things," Peri said.

I filled her glass to an acceptable level. "Let's go sit down and enjoy this." I grabbed the bottle and followed her to a couch. She lifted her glass for a toast and turned so she was facing me. Her knee brushed my leg. She didn't move. I didn't move either. As tumultuous as our beginning had been, this was a nice truce. I held my glass against hers and waited.

"Here's to Isabel and Hilde. May they find one another in a different lifetime, because this one was too hard for them. They deserve it," she said.

I was never good at impromptu speeches, regardless of how small they were, but it seemed important to honor our great-grandmothers and their relationship. "Here's to two beautiful women who had the kind of love people dream about. Because of them, I'm here today getting to know you." I'm not sure why I added Peri to the toast, but our families were bonded because of Bisnonna's and Hilde's love. "Even though I fought so hard against it."

She waved me off like it wasn't a big deal, even though we both knew what I did was awful. "It's okay. The slate's clean. We're starting fresh right now."

"I'll drink to that," I said.

Her eyes never left mine while we chatted about the winery. I never pictured my week ending like this—down in a cellar drinking wine with her. I could tell she was nervous, but not enough to add space.

"Is it normally this quiet down here?" she asked.

"We're underground. It shuts out the outside world pretty effectively."

She held up her phone. "There's no reception down here either."

"There never is. But we should take a selfie for Bisnonna so she knows we had a good time."

Peri self-consciously patted down her hair, almost elbowing me in the process.

"You worry too much. You look adorable," I said. I held out my phone and tilted my head so it almost rested on her shoulder. Peri was my exact opposite. The phone showed a blush that feathered out on her cheeks and reddened her lips. Her blond hair seemed lighter, and her blue eyes sparkled. I snapped three pictures with my phone and promised to text them to Peri when we were above ground.

"Bisnonna's going to love this." I said. My head was still slightly resting on her shoulder as I edited the photo for Isabel. Peri sat quietly beside me and drank the wine. She did nothing to shift away from me. What was happening here? Yesterday, she didn't like me, but today we're both trying to figure out a way to keep a physical connection. We were so different. Our lives were different. Was I attracted to her? Hell, yes. I smiled. Was this how it was for Bisnonna? Were she and Hilde ever at each other's throats, or did they just slip into love like how I imagined love should be?

"There. I think she'll like this one."

I put the phone too close to Peri's face. She wrapped her fingers around mine and pushed the phone back so she could focus. I couldn't concentrate on what we were seeing. I could only feel the warmth of her hand and how her head was now on my shoulder. It hurt to breathe.

"It's a good one."

"I think it's great. We both look happy. I'll label it Isabel so that we'll always know we were drinking her wine." We finished our glasses, and it was becoming increasingly hard to not want to be closer to her. I needed distance. "Maybe we should take a walk." I stood and pulled her to her feet until she was flush against me.

She lifted her eyebrow. "Oh. Okay."

She licked her lips. My mouth suddenly went dry as I became hyper aware of her pressed against me.

I stepped back and held her hand as we walked toward the door. I pulled on the door, but it didn't budge. "Hmm. That's weird."

She leaned against the door, even though I was trying to open it. "What's weird?" I put my hands on her waist to gently move her to the side. "What are you doing?" She put her hands on mine.

"Moving you so I can open the door."

"Sorry." She blushed.

I tried the door again, but it still wouldn't open. "The handle won't turn."

"What's wrong with it?" She twisted it, but it didn't move. I liked seeing the definition in her arms as she struggled and wiggled the knob with no luck.

I tried it one last time before I threw my hands up. "Bad news."

"Bad news?" Peri took a step close to me.

"We're locked in."

"Is there a key in here? Can we call someone?" Peri immediately pulled out her phone, but she wouldn't have any more reception now than she did twenty minutes ago.

"Don't worry. We have an old landline behind the bar." It was an old rotary-style phone that my parents had to teach me how to use. It was reliable, though. I dialed Bisnonna first, because she was expecting us and I knew her phone number by heart. "Bisnonna, we're locked in down in the family room in the cellar. Can you send somebody down to open the door?"

"Oh, sure. Are you okay?"

"We're fine."

"I'll call your brothers and tell them to open the door. In the meantime, just relax and spend as much time together as you can. She's a special girl."

My heart clenched. She wasn't wrong. Peri was special, but unlike Bisnonna and Hilde, we weren't headed for epic romance. "She's sweet. We'll be up soon so we can finish reading letters, if you're still okay with sharing."

"Yes, bella. Go be a good hostess."

I placed the handset on the receiver. "We're saved. Maybe. Bisnonna is calling my brothers. Hopefully, one of them can rescue us in about twenty minutes." I sat next to her on the couch and realized my mistake immediately. We were too close.

"I'm fine. If I'm going to get stuck somewhere, this is the perfect place," Peri said.

I stood to create space again. I was drawn to her, but she was leaving in a matter of hours. Besides, she didn't even live in this country. Most of the time, that was the perfect scenario for me, but Peri was different. "I'm going to get us some water. We probably need to sober up before dinner."

"I think I'm okay, but water sounds great." She drank half of hers before setting it next to her wine glass. A tiny drop of water rested on her top lip and when her tongue flicked out to wipe it away, I made a noise. "I didn't realize how thirsty I was."

She was so obliviously sexy, and in that moment I realized I was frustrated because I couldn't have her. My emotions were all over the place, and we would always have this connection.

"I can't stop thinking about Isabel and Hilde. I mean, I want to know how Bisnonna introduced Hilde to The Captain. How can somebody do that? Hand over the love of your life to somebody else. I'm so thankful I live in a time when it's okay to be queer," she said.

I appreciated her passion about our great-grandmothers and felt mine rising as well. "I'm sure we'll hear more once we get out of here. I always thought Bisnonna married Bisnonno because they fell in love after the war. It never dawned on me that their story could be any different. They always seemed so fond of one another."

"Same with Amma and The Captain. They always appeared so close and respectful," Peri said. She wiped at the corner of her eye. "And that's not to say there wasn't love there. It evidently wasn't what they expected in life. I'm just grateful I was close with Amma when she was alive. And now I get to hear about a whole different life I never knew about."

She looked at me, and I melted at how heartbroken she seemed. I touched her cheek, she leaned into the palm of my hand, and without thinking I leaned forward and kissed her softly. It wasn't a first-date kind of kiss, where anticipation builds to a level of excitement. It was an impulse. The soft touch of my lips against hers took my breath away. I sat back. "I'm sorry. I didn't mean to do that." Her eyes dropped to my lips and stared as though she, too, couldn't believe what had just happened.

"Okay. No. It's okay. I just wasn't expecting it."

So many emotions were swirling around in those blue eyes that the need to kiss her again was strong. I sat back to break the spell. What was happening? "I wonder what's taking my brothers so long? I'm going to try calling them." Her fingers around my wrist stopped me.

"No, wait."

"What?" I answered quickly because, for the first time, I was nervous around another woman. I always controlled the relationship. It made no sense that the person I'd been pushing away since I met her was the one who got past my defenses so easily. She reached for my hand.

"I'm having a good time. Your brothers will be here soon enough."

She laced her fingers with mine and turned so we faced each other. "How many women have you brought down here? With a few lit candles and maybe some music, this is a real romantic hideaway."

"You won't believe me."

"Try me."

The look she gave me meant more than just literal words. I leaned closer so my mouth was mere inches from hers. "You're the first." I kissed her softly until her fingers threaded through my hair. Her mouth blossomed as my lips pressed against hers, and I moaned when I felt her tongue skim mine. She pulled me against her as our mouths found the perfect rhythm. I lost track of where I was, what time it was, and even why we were down here in the first place. I could only feel Peri in my arms—her warmth, her soft skin, her taste. I didn't even hear the door screech open. I thought the noise was the pounding in my chest.

"I'm here to save you both." Mateo found us entangled on the couch. "Oops. I'm so sorry."

Peri scrambled away and I silently cursed Mateo. "Thanks for the rescue, but your timing sucks," I said.

Peri scooped up our glasses and took them to the small sink behind the bar. She was obviously uncomfortable with Mateo busting in. When her back was to us, I scowled at him. He grinned and winked. "Cork the wine," I said to him. I walked over to Peri. "You don't have to do this."

She nervously wiped her hands on the towel. "It's all right. I don't mind. I'm just glad we're saved." She wouldn't look at me.

"Hey, are you embarrassed about what just happened?" I didn't know if I should be upset or consoling.

She took a small step forward. "No. Not at all. I'm just confused." She looked around until she found Mateo on the other side of the room very interested in bottles of wine that I'm sure he knew by heart. He was giving us space.

"Confused about what?"

She stepped back. So did I. "What are we doing? Did we just make out because of our situation or because we're attracted to one another?"

I cupped her chin until she looked at me. "I was attracted to you before I knew who you were. Before I knew our families had history." Her eyes darkened at my words. She knew what I was saying was true. She was into me, into the idea of us, even if it was just for an hour or two. I squeezed her hand and winked. "Mateo, remember when Gemma and I told you that you should write a romance?"

"I would be horrible at it. I'm not familiar with the genre at all. Besides, I'm already deep into my second book."

"You did a ton of research into children's books before you wrote *Luigi*. You'll do the same thing." I held Peri's hand and pulled her closer to me. "You will be wonderful, and I have the perfect story in mind." Peri squeezed my fingers, and she looked at me in alarm.

"Discretion is a must. I have to have your word that what I'm about to tell you is in private, and if anyone finds out, I will personally kick your ass."

"And even though I think you're wonderful, I, too, will kick your ass," Peri said.

Mateo held up his hands to defend himself. "Whoa. Wait a minute. I haven't done anything. Why are you ganging up on me?"

"You're right. It's not fair. Have a seat. We have a story to tell you."

He pointed to the now-ajar door. "Are you sure you don't want to go upstairs? How long have you been trapped down here?"

I grabbed his hand and pointed to a chair. "We're fine down here for now. Plus, it's private."

"Are we sure we can trust him? We don't know if Isabel wants the world to know," Peri said.

"It's time for their story to be told." My voice came out stronger than I intended, and I gave Peri an apologetic smile. "Besides, Mateo is a beautiful writer."

"What's going on? Will somebody please start talking?" Mateo took the cork out of the merlot he'd just sealed and poured himself a glass.

"I think Peri needs to start." I sat down on the couch and waited.

"I don't know where to begin," she said.

"Tell Mateo why you're here."

She nodded and told him about Hilde and how she gave Peri a job posthumously. During her story, I found out that it was actually her first assignment. I smiled, recalling how confident Peri was when we first met.

"Wait a minute. So, your great-grandmother and Isabel were lovers?" He sat back in the chair with a thud. The news had the same effect on him as it did on us. He took a deep breath and sighed loudly. "Who knows about this?"

"Right now, just the three of us and Bisnonna. I don't think she's told anyone."

"Oh, my God, Mateo. We only heard one letter, and it was amazing. I can't imagine Isabel not wanting their story to be told," Peri said.

"I wouldn't even know how to start recording this," he said.

"Why don't you come hang out with us and Bisnonna for a bit this afternoon," I said.

"Peri, aren't you leaving tonight?"

"That was the plan, but since it took me so long to find Isabel, maybe I should extend the trip. I'll need to check in with my office once we get to the villa and see if we're busy."

Everything inside me fluttered. She was staying. I could tell. Even if her job needed her, she was going to stay. Not because of me, but because she owed Hilde the time to hear her story.

"Let's go. I'll talk to Bisnonna and see if she's willing to share her story with Mateo, while Peri phones her office to see how long she can stay." I turned to face her. "And you are more than welcome to spend as much time here as you want. No strings attached. You won't be imposing. We both owe this to our families."

"Please, Bisnonna. This is so beautiful. I think Mateo would appreciate your story, too. We all have the utmost respect for you." I watched as emotions flashed across Bisnonna's face, but I didn't push. This was her moment. When she finally smiled at me, I knew she was all in.

"Okay, bella. Mateo can be a part of this."

I squeezed her hand. "Thank you, Bisnonna. You won't be sorry. It's our honor."

"What about Peri?"

"What do you mean?"

"Where is she? Is she going back home? I'd love for her to stay," she said.

"I'm staying for a bit. I want to hear more about your life with Amma." Peri entered the kitchen with a shy smile and hugged Bisnonna.

Bisnonna clapped her hands with delight. I smiled, knowing we had more time to get to know one another.

"Great. We can take your rental car back tonight if you want. That way you won't be hit with an extra charge."

Peri sat up in surprise. "I didn't even think about that. That'll save me a lot."

Even though he left an hour ago, I texted Mateo to come over for dinner and hang with Bisnonna while Peri and I returned her rental car. In true form, he arrived with flowers that I know he picked from the flowerbeds near the shop. I rolled my eyes at him, but Bisnonna oohed and ahhed over them.

"Camila, please get a vase for these beautiful flowers."

Mateo gave me the most innocent look. "I think there's one in the cabinet over the sink."

"You're here too much. Nobody should know that."

"Maybe if you brought Isabel flowers more, you would know where to find a vase in your own home," Mateo said.

"I'm going to run upstairs and grab my purse and keys so we can leave after dinner," Peri said.

"That's a good idea." I watched her walk away and scowled when I turned to find Mateo and Bisnonna grinning at me. "What?"

"Do I need to tell Isabel what happened in the cellar?" Mateo teased in that sing-songy voice I hated.

"What happened in the cellar, Camila?" she asked with a knowing smile.

I threw my hands up. "How could you possibly already know? I've been with you the whole time."

She shrugged and squeezed Mateo's hand. "I know how to text."

Chapter Thirteen

Feelings—Peri

Everything was different. The sun was setting, and I was riding on the back of a motorcycle with my arms around a beautiful woman whose kisses had rendered me speechless just a few hours ago. I wasn't even going to try to pretend that today didn't affect me. I was already emotionally spent, the last forty-eight hours a lot to process. My beautiful Amma was gay, or bi, or something that wasn't socially acceptable seventy-five years ago, and my heart broke for her. All this time. All this heartache.

Had she ever tried reaching out? Did she call Isabel when phones became common in households around the world? Obviously, Isabel has been in Italy at the family winery the whole time. Did Amma try googling when the internet and home computers became available? My parents had access to computers in college, so even twenty-five years ago they could have found one another. When I got home, I planned to rifle through all Amma's boxes. I'd asked my mother to keep everything until I had a chance to look for a secret stack of letters, too.

"I don't know why the traffic is bad, so I'm going to take a shortcut. Hang on," Camila said over her shoulder.

I tightened my grip on her waist and smiled when she squeezed my forearm before she accelerated. I trusted her. She seemed just as excited to get back to the villa as I was. "I hope Bisnonna doesn't tell Mateo anything we don't know," she said after I dropped off my rental car. "Let's go." I couldn't tell if she was excited that I was on the motorcycle with her again, or that we were going back to hear more of Isabel's story. Probably both. The rumble of the engine sent a jolt through me. I was already humming at Camila's nearness. She was tucked between my legs, and even though there was a gap between us, her accelerations were jerking me closer to her. My sensitive core pressed against her ass. By the time we reached the villa, I hummed all over with the need to release. I slid off the seat with wobbly legs and straightened my jeans. "Thanks for the ride. I appreciate it."

"You're welcome."

She took my helmet and strapped it to her bike. I excused myself for a moment to freshen up and give myself time to shake off the sexual tension. It would have taken too much time to go back to my room, which was on the other side of the villa, so I ducked into a small bathroom off the main hall and washed my hands and splashed cold water on my face.

"Ready?"

I was embarrassed that Camila was waiting for me. "Sorry. I was a little dusty from the trip."

"I know what you mean. I want to take a quick shower, but Bisnonna will go to bed soon, and I want to sit down with her and Mateo before she retires for the night."

"Your whole family is so nice to allow me to stay here. They don't even know me." My parents would have given any stranger that came to the door an inquisition and the address of the nearest hotel.

"Technically, you're Isabel's guest, and nobody fucks with her. You're also my friend, and believe it or not, that has weight, too, regardless of how much my brothers tease me about being worthless."

"They do like to tease you. A lot." I ignored the word friend. I think we crossed that line somewhere up on the hill in a cellar with a stubborn door.

"It's okay. I'm the baby of the family, and they like to remind me. I also get away with a lot that they never did," she said.

I couldn't imagine what life was like growing up with two older brothers who teased as much as they did Camila. No wonder she had thick skin and pretended not to care. "I guess that's a fair trade."

"My parents usually stop them, but not before they get their zingers in." She didn't sound upset, but more resigned that this was the way it was. "And don't worry. I fight back, too. I know it doesn't seem like it, but I do."

"Oh, I know you fight back when defending yourself." I'd witnessed it firsthand the night Luke brought me to dinner. I really enjoyed their family dynamics. I thought I was close with my family, but this was a whole different level. I was having fun. I'd always wanted siblings but ended up a spoiled only child.

We joined Isabel and Mateo in the kitchen. I think Isabel liked to spend her evenings there because not only was the view spectacular during the day, but the lighting was good, and her room wasn't too far away.

"Isabel, did you cook a lot when you were younger?" I asked.

"Si, but Nerissa is a better cook. And she's younger and can stand on her feet longer than I can."

"It skipped a generation with Camila, though," Mateo said.

Isabel and I laughed at her scowl in response. "Camila, where is your grandmother? Nonna, right?" I asked.

"On a cruise with the ladies from her church. She'll be back next week. You'll meet her then."

I knew that Camila's grandfather had passed a few years ago from lung cancer. She said her nonna was just as fierce as Bisnonna. I couldn't wait to meet her. "I'm looking forward to it." I slid into a seat opposite Mateo and smiled at how easily he fit in with this family.

"Isabel, I'm excited to hear about your wonderful story." Mateo took both her hands in his. "Thank you for trusting me."

Isabel turned her head and blushed.

"Mateo is family. He's always been supportive of me. We even have the same tastes in women. Don't be afraid, Bisnonna. This is a safe space," Camila said.

I loved that she always rubbed Isabel's back in tiny circles to comfort her.

"Can I read the next letter for us?" I asked. "Do you mind?" I waited for Isabel's permission before I reached for the stack. She nodded. It was the first time I'd touched them. I carefully pulled the next letter out of the envelope and took a deep breath.

Isabel,

I stare at your photograph every night. The ache inside my heart never lessens. It gets harder every day to be away from you. It's not fair to tell you that, but it's the truth. We always said we'd be honest with each other. I miss you, and I hope you are doing well. I've written you every day, but I don't want to complicate your life, so I send only every seventh letter. I can't decide if life is punishing me by crawling or flying by. It's already winter, and I felt like it's been decades since I'd held you. Yet sometimes it feels like you just left my arms. I'm so confused. I'm supposed to marry The Captain, but I don't know that I can. How am I supposed to say yes to forever with someone who doesn't have my heart? It's you, Izzy. It will always be you.

"She sent me a handkerchief with that letter. It was my early Christmas present. She embroidered my initials and a rose on a white lace handkerchief. It was beautiful," Isabel said.

"Do you still have it?" Camila asked.

"I lost it several years ago. I looked all over the villa and winery for it. I was devastated, but I can still picture it. It was so delicate and beautiful. She thought it was ugly and the stitches weren't perfect, but they were to me."

"But you still remember it, and that's what makes it special," I said. I continued reading at Isabel's nod.

As beautiful as your beaches are, I wish you could spend Christmas in New England with me. It's magical here when it snows. Sometimes we get snowed in and the only thing we do is sit by the fireplace and read or listen to the radio. It's very quiet and peaceful. When the snow stops, we shovel it off the driveway and sidewalks for us and the neighbors. I know you don't like the cold, but sometimes it makes you appreciate the fire more. The town square is decorated for the holiday, and everyone is in a good mood. Everyone has a lot of hope now that the war is over. I'm happy it is, too, but sad that it took me away from you. I hope this letter finds you well, and please know that I think of you every day and will for the rest of my life.

Always,
Hilde

"Isabel, how did you meet Hilde?" Mateo asked.

Isabel looked at Camila, who held up her hands. "It's not my story to tell. I wanted Mateo to hear everything from you," Camila said.

"We met on the beach one night. We were all supposed to stay close to our homes in case the bombing started again, but I would sneak out with my friends, and we would hang out at the beach."

"That was pretty risky," Mateo said. He scribbled some notes in a small pad.

"We were daredevils in our youth," Isabel said. She took a sip of warm tea that Camila poured for her. "We literally stumbled on Americans on the beach. We could hear them talking and laughing. We wanted to hang out with them. We had wine and they had music."

"On the beach? How was that possible?" I asked.

"One of the soldiers was an engineer. He was responsible for working on the navigation equipment on the ships or something and was always tinkering with something. He made a portable radio the size of a suitcase, but we could sometimes tune in and hear music."

"So, Hilde was with this group?"

"Oh, yes. She wasn't afraid to get up and dance. And she danced with everyone. Sometimes I would find her staring at me, and it always gave me such a rush. Here was a beautiful, popular American watching me," Isabel said.

"Huh. All this time I thought she was so prim and proper," I said.

"Oh, no. She was a pistol. She always had sweet biscuits that her friend in the kitchen sneaked her. They weren't great, but it was food and soaked up the wine. And she always had cigarettes, too. I think she was good at bargaining with her coworkers."

"Amma smoked?" She was so against it that nobody ever smoked in front of her. My whole life I feared cigarettes because of the wrath of Amma.

Isabel laughed. "Sometimes. I think it was just when she was partying. She never did it when the two of us were alone together."

"There's so much I never knew about Amma."

"Think about how much you hide from your family," Camila said.

I was fortunate and didn't have to hide a lot from my parents. I shrugged. "I was kind of a good kid."

"You never got grounded or your phone taken away?" Camila asked.

"Rarely."

"She's a good girl, Camila. Let her be," Isabel said. She looked back and forth between us. "It's as if Peri is more like me and you are more like Hilde."

We both smiled at her analogy. She wasn't wrong. Camila and I seemed to be opposites. She was inclined to jump in feet first, and I liked to dip my toe to feel the water.

"How long was Hilde here in Sequina? And how long were you together?" Mateo asked.

"She was stationed here for sixteen months—April 1945 until August 1946. I wanted her to stay, but that wasn't an option. We met in May, and in my heart, we're still together." She clasped Camila's hand. "I'm sorry, bella. Hilde was my first love. My true love. I loved your great-grandfather, too, but it was different. And we made an amazing family and life together." Her voice sounded strained from either exhaustion or emotional strain.

"I know, Bisnonna. Maybe we should finish the letters tomorrow. There's no rush. Peri's here for as long as she'd like to be. How about I take you to your room now?"

Isabel nodded. "That sounds good. I'll see you tomorrow."

I waited until Isabel and Camila were out of earshot. "What do you think?"

Mateo crossed his arms in front of his chest and leaned back in his chair. "I'm in shock. I feel so bad for her and your great-grandmother. Were you aware of this when you came here?" His voice wasn't accusatory.

"I had no idea. I just figured they were close friends from when Amma was stationed here. It never occurred to me that they were lovers." What seemed so obvious to me now hadn't been even a consideration when I first opened the locket.

"As amazing as their story is, I just don't think I can do it justice. How am I supposed to drum up emotions like that to write?" Mateo asked.

Camila walked back into the kitchen. "Oh, stop. You can make anything sound good. Mateo kicked my ass in composition class." She sat in Isabel's vacant seat.

"That's only because you skipped class."

"What?" I pretended to be surprised, even though I wasn't. Camila as a teenager screamed bad girl. As an adult, she wasn't far off.

She rolled her eyes. "I only skipped because I was working on something in art class. Writing was boring. It was much easier to create with paint or clay than with words."

"Mateo, didn't you illustrate your dolphin book?"

He brushed his fingers through his hair and smiled. "I did. Both Camila and I enjoy art. I prefer digital drawing. Camila likes painting."

"Both of you are excellent artists. I'm jealous. I don't have that skill."

He snorted. "So, when the apocalypse comes, she and I will die because we have no talents except for drawing and drinking wine. You will survive and probably come up with the cure. Here's to the scientist."

He toasted my water and drank the last sip of wine in his glass. His words brought a small smile to my lips. I'd never thought of that. I always had science to fall back on. "It's a bit rusty, but I could probably science the shit out of something."

"You and my mother both," Camila said.

With Isabel out of the room, I was hyper aware of Camila so close to me. I couldn't tell if I wanted Mateo to stay forever or leave right now. Did I want another kiss? Yes. Did I want an entanglement in a different country and to follow the same doomed path as Amma? No. Although it wouldn't be the same. And why was I even thinking about this? "Science is cool. Your mom rocks." That's what I said? I sounded like an idiot. I should go up to my room. Today had been an exhausting day.

"Okay, ladies. I'm leaving. It's been a long day. I'll open the store tomorrow. Maybe now you can show Peri where you work? Show her the other side of the business that isn't wine?"

"We didn't even get far on the winery tour because we got trapped."

"Yes, of course. You got trapped," Mateo said mischievously.

"We did." Camila sounded angry. "Do you think we locked ourselves in the cellar?"

"I never said you did."

Camila and I looked at each other, then back at Mateo. Who else could have possibly locked us in? "Mateo?" Camila's voice was dangerous.

"Well, the moon is full tonight, so maybe a quick tour by moonlight is in order." He winked at us, grabbed his keys, and whistled a nameless tune on his way out the door.

"He was joking, right?" I asked.

"He had to be." She didn't look like she believed that.

"Where's your family?" I looked at the time. "Holy crap. It's already eleven." I was nervous. We were alone, and things had happened the last time we were alone together. Things I was still processing.

"They go to bed early. We can save the tour for tomorrow. It's been quite the day." Her shaky laugh told me she was affected by today as much as I had been. Maybe for the same reasons. "Go ahead. I'll lock up. Let me know if you need anything."

"Thank you again for your hospitality. I'm happy that I met Isabel and know more about my own history." I hesitated before leaving. I was at that awkward stage where I didn't know if I should hug her or not. She didn't move, so I slowly turned and walked out of the kitchen. Now that I was staying, we had time.

CHAPTER FOURTEEN

MATEO'S IDEA—CAMILA

I have an idea."

I squinted in the morning light and groaned after looking at the alarm clock. "Mateo, it's not even eight. What are you doing?"

"I'm getting ready to do your job, but I have an idea of what we can do with Isabel and Hilde's story."

He rocked my hip back and forth until I angrily sat up. "Fine."

"I decided I do want to write their story, but as a historical romance. Maybe say this is based on a true story because I don't think I could do it justice as a biography. At the end, after the epilogue, we can have some of the letters they wrote to one another. Peri already said she's going to sort through all of Hilde's things when she returns."

"You've talked to Peri already?" What time did she get up? I tossed and turned all night long, kicking myself for not kissing her good night.

"Let's just say she doesn't wear pajamas and doesn't lock the door."

"Mateo!" I smacked his arm. "That's so rude. It's one thing to do it to me, but don't do it to our guests." I was furious with him. How dare he violate her space?

"Settle down. I'm teasing. I knocked."

I frowned at him until the anger left. "Why did you visit her first?"

He tucked a wild strand of hair behind my ear. I smacked his hand away. I was still upset. "I saw that you were sleeping and didn't want to wake you, but after my talk with Peri, I had to come in here. What do you think?"

"About what?" I slid back down and curled up with my pillow.

"About writing it as a romance based on a true story instead of a biography. I've been thinking about it all night." He lay beside me and stared at the ceiling. " Their story is so beautiful and so sad. How are you doing after finding this out about Isabel? Has it been hard?"

My great-grandfather was a nice man, from what I remembered. I was never close to him. He seemed so much older than Bisnonna, and we had nothing in common except the vineyards. And I was too young to be interested in the process of making wine. I was a child with a lot of energy, and somedays he never moved from his bench in the courtyard. I respected him only because he was family. I rolled over to face Mateo. "I can't believe she loved and lost so much at such a young age. She didn't have the option to love who she wanted. My heart aches for her."

"Would you rather have loved and lost or to never have been in love at all?"

I held his hand. That was such a heavy question. Did I want love? Yes. Did I think I would find it? How could I find something I was never looking for? "I'm too young to answer that."

"You're twenty-five. Every single woman in your family was married by your age."

"You're twenty-five, too, and I don't see you getting married."

"I don't need that connection yet. I'll get married when I'm forty and have four children." He laughed when I poked him. "I will embrace love when I find it—for real find it. Like what Isabel and Hilde had and what your parents have. Who wouldn't want that?"

We were both lost in thought when someone knocked on my door.

"Come in."

Peri slowly peeked into the room. "I followed the laughter."

I was torn between covering up and teasing her a bit. I ended up pulling the sheet so it covered my legs. My tank top showed more than it should, and I was rewarded with a blush that spread across her cheeks and down her neck.

"Come on in. Mateo was just telling me about his idea."

Peri sat on the very edge of the mattress and spent most of her time with her eyes on mine. I allowed myself to stare at her. Her long blond hair was pulled back in a ponytail and her blue eyes bright with excitement. She looked fresh and ready to go. Apparently, she'd slept.

"It's a great idea and should generate a lot of interest. Plus, you get more freedom writing a romance based on a true story rather than trying to fill in gaps in theirs," she said.

"We can use the locket with both of their pictures showing as the cover," I said.

"That's a great idea. Do you know any photographers?"

"Yes, me," I said. To see Peri's positive reaction made my heart sing. She believed in me. The two people who believed in me most were sitting on my bed.

Mateo squeezed my knee. "That sounds like a job for you after I write the book. I'm going to open the shop. Swing by later, and I'll give Peri a taste test of the best oils."

"Thanks for filling in for me." He kissed my cheek and hugged Peri on his way out the door.

"Hi. I'm waiting on laundry. Sophia was kind enough to show me the laundry room." Peri ran her finger across the window in my room and gazed out at the vineyard. She looked adorable in her shorts and pink polo shirt. "I've worn this twice."

"Let me guess. Sophia tried to do your laundry for you." She loved being needed. "But don't worry. Your outfit is perfect for the continuation of our tour." I was rewarded with a blush.

"I should have packed more, but I honestly didn't think I was going to stay this long."

"You are more than welcome to wear anything of mine. Plus, Ethan has a ton of T-shirts in his room."

"Thank you. Okay. I'm going downstairs to see if Isabel's there."

She gave me an awkward half wave before she pulled the door shut behind her. I jumped up and headed to the bathroom for a quick shower. I was excited to start our tour again and didn't want to miss out on any Bisnonna and Hilde news. My mother was still in the dark, but it wasn't my story to tell. I wasn't sure how much the family knew. If nothing else, my family was respectful of privacy, especially Bisnonna's.

I breezed into the kitchen twenty minutes later, wearing shorts and a button-down shirt. I kept it casual so Peri didn't feel out of place. I knew she wasn't going to borrow anything of mine. "How's everybody's morning?"

"Good morning, bella. How was your evening?"

Bisnonna kissed my cheek, and I sat next to Peri. Our elbows touched.

"We stayed up only a little longer than you did. Who wants coffee?"

"I had a cup, and Isabel already drank some tea," Peri said. She took a bite of a freshly baked roll smothered in my mother's homemade jelly. "I was going to wait, but I was too tempted with all this deliciousness here."

I grabbed a plate and a roll, too. "I don't blame you. We have a grueling schedule. Bisnonna, come with us. We're just going for a quick drive around the vineyard."

She laughed. "Maybe if we go to the olive grove, but I've seen you drive, Camila, and it's scary."

"What if I promise to drive carefully and slowly? We would love to take you back to these places if you'd like, especially the olive grove." I could tell Bisnonna was wavering. "We can just take a short ride."

"Okay. You win. I will go with you, but only for a little bit."

I lifted my hands and made a celebratory whoop. "That's amazing. Thank you." I nudged Peri and winked. I hope she knew this was an important moment. Bisnonna didn't leave the villa much.

"We should go before it gets too hot," Bisnonna said.

I nodded as I shoved a giant bite into my mouth. I reached for Peri's hand and pulled her up with me. "I'm going to need your help getting everything ready. Bisnonna, we'll be back in ten minutes." I didn't let go of Peri's warm hand as I led her outside. "She might not even need it, but I want to have the right wheelchair in case she wants to go into the grove, and I'm going to need your help. It takes two people to hook up the trailer to the ATV."

"I'm your girl." Peri blushed.

It was unbelievably easy to get her to blush. I wasn't even trying. I gave her fingers a squeeze. "Thank you so much for staying. She really needed this. I think she needed to tell someone."

"And now everyone will know their beautiful love story," Peri said.

I knew our great-grandmothers' story filled her heart because it filled mine. "Even if it doesn't go anywhere but our families, their love continues. If I have children, they will know, and I'm sure if you have children, you'll tell them."

"Do you want children?" she asked.

I had to unlock the garage, which forced me to let go of her hand. "Of course. At least two."

"I agree. Two is perfect. And not too far apart in age," she said.

"Well, you were an only child and wanted a sibling, and I have two who've made me feel like a third wheel. Two is perfect. They can play together and never be bored," I said. I unplugged Bisnonna's motorized wheelchair and drove it up into the small trailer. Peri helped me hook the trailer to the back of the ATV. She hopped on the seat beside me and closed the garage door behind us.

"I'm so glad Isabel is coming. I hope this is a healthy trip and her memories are good."

"It's too bad Mateo can't be here, but we can fill him in." I drove the ATV to the front of the house, where Bisnonna sat waiting on a bench. Peri hopped out and reached her first.

"Why are you out here in the sun?" Peri asked.

She carefully took Bisnonna's arm and led her gently to the ATV. With very little help, Bisnonna climbed into the front seat. I snapped the seat belt on her and winked at Peri, who slid in the back behind her. "Are we ready?" At their nods, I drove painfully slow through the vineyards and told Peri the history of our wines. Bisnonna interjected her own stories. When we reached the olive grove, I saw Bisnonna take a deep breath.

"I haven't been here in years," she said.

"We'll take it slow," I said. With Peri's help, I backed the wheelchair off the trailer. I attached the umbrella to block the sun and drove it to where she sat. "Your chariot awaits." It was harder for Bisnonna to climb out of the ATV than into it. Once she was situated, Peri and I walked beside her as she told us about the grove.

"This started out as a few trees when I was a little girl. I wanted something for me. Everyone else was so involved in the wine, and I wanted something of my own. My father bought me ten trees, but nobody thought I would stick with it. Now look at it." She swept the vista with her arm.

Peri took her hand. "It's beautiful."

It was wonderful to see Peri and Isabel holding hands and looking out at the grove. I was such an ass for thinking olive oil wasn't important. Seeing Bisnonna's happiness in something she started as a child made pride blossom in my chest. She was the driving force behind me taking over the oils because it was her gift to me. I swallowed a lump in my throat. "It sure is. You did a wonderful thing here."

"This is where Hilde and I had our first kiss."

"Her letter about it was perfect. I loved every word," Peri said.

"I'm so happy you found me," Bisnonna told her.

Peri crouched so she was eye to eye with her. "Can you tell us more about your time here with Hilde? Did she ever stay at the villa?"

"On the weekends she didn't work, she was here. Sometimes we would work at the vineyard, but we would always end our nights here."

"There's a lot of privacy. Did you have a favorite spot?" Peri asked.

She pointed to a tree up on the hill. "That tree right there. The trunk has twisted so much that it looks as if it's a heart."

"It does. Can we go up there? Can you make it okay?" Peri asked. She was so gentle. I knew Bisnonna didn't want the help from me unless she asked for it, but she sure was more than happy to receive Peri's help.

"You both might want to take a step back. That way I don't have to worry about running you over."

Peri laughed, but Bisnonna was serious. We followed her slowly until she reached the tree. I set the brakes and helped her out of the wheelchair. She went directly to the tree and ran her fingers over the trunk as though feeling for something. She set her mouth in a straight line as she traced something.

"Peri, what do you see here?"

Peri leaned in and ran her fingers over a rough heart. "Did you carve this? Wait. Are these initials?"

"I know it's silly, but yes. What can I say? We were young and in love."

I took out my phone and snapped a couple of photos. "It's adorable. Now be careful. Let's get you back to the wheelchair." I could tell the journey here was taxing. I handed her my water bottle and made her take a few sips. "How about we go back to the villa and you rest for a bit? It's almost lunch. We can eat, and Peri and I can continue while you take your nap."

She nodded. "This was a lot, but I'm so thankful you and Peri convinced me to come. My memories aren't so fuzzy after being up here again."

We drove back listening to stories of Hilde and Bisnonna sneaking away during the night for privacy. I didn't push for more information. She would tell us in her own time. Peri was being respectful, too, even though I knew it was killing her not to know everything at once. I also wanted Mateo to hear.

"Peri, after we eat, let's go into town. I want to show you the oil shop, and we can chat with Mateo." I hoped she understood that was code for updating him. He would love the photo of the carving.

"That sounds great."

By the time we got Bisnonna into the house, lunch was being served. Sophia fixed her a plate while we freshened up. "Your clothes are on your bed, Peri. I hope you don't mind that I finished it for you."

Peri groaned. "I totally forgot. I'm so sorry I made your job harder today."

"It's okay. I know you and Camila are busy with Isabel. I don't mind helping out," Sophia said.

"Thank you," Peri said.

I could tell she felt bad about leaving her laundry unattended. "Don't worry about it. At least now you have clean clothes," I said. She looked down at her dusty polo shirt and brushed away a few spots. Even though we were out in the sun for less than an hour, her arms and cheeks were pink. "Also, let's be sure to get you some sunscreen. You're obviously getting more sun than you're used to."

"Good point. Let me change my shirt and do something with my hair. I'll be done in a few minutes."

"I'm going to change my clothes, too." I followed her up the stairs and admired her shape the entire way. Her ass looked great in shorts, and she walked in a sexy way. Maybe she was confident, or maybe she knew I was watching her.

We stopped outside her room. "Again, if you need anything, don't be afraid to ask." I was stalling.

"I should be good."

She stood with her hand on the knob but didn't move. Her lips parted, and she looked down at my mouth. Encouraged, I stepped closer and reached up and touched the end of her ponytail. "I like it when you put your hair back in a braid. Like yesterday. It's so pretty." I ran my fingers over to her neck. Her skin was so soft and warm. When I leaned forward to press my lips against hers, she slid her arms around my waist. When I felt her body flush against mine, I moaned and deepened the kiss. She moved her hands from my waist up to my neck as our tongues found a rhythm that made me want to turn the knob to her door, walk her back to the bed, and make love to her in the middle of the day. It killed me to break apart. "As nice as this is, I think we're expected downstairs."

"I know. I'm sorry."

I cupped her chin. "Don't be sorry for wanting to kiss me. I want it just as much as you do. We can revisit this later tonight." I placed a small kiss on her lips and released her. "I'll wait for you downstairs." I slipped into my room and ripped off my clothes, eager to wear something sexy and not practical. I settled on a sundress and comfortable sandals, twisted my hair up, and put on mascara. In less than ten minutes, I was downstairs waiting for Peri. She didn't disappoint. Wearing a sleeveless linen shirt and a skirt that hit above her knee, she took my breath away. "You look amazing."

"Thank you. So do you."

She nervously looked around to make sure we were alone before kissing me softly. I quickly squeezed her firm waist and walked with her into the courtyard. Bisnonna smiled at us as though she knew our secret.

"How was your morning?" my father asked.

"Bisnonna, Peri, and I went to the olive grove."

"Isabel, you went out? That's great," he said.

"We had a very nice time," I said.

"What's this I hear? Isabel had a journey this morning? That's amazing." My mom breezed into the courtyard on her lunch break and kissed each of us on the cheek. "Peri, I'm glad you're here keeping my favorite women company."

"It's been an absolute pleasure. There's so much history here, and this place is beautiful," Peri said.

She was quietly charming. I wondered what she was like back in her town, in her environment. Mateo and my family adored her, and it was obvious that we had a connection. Something was happening here. I didn't want to compare us to Bisnonna and Hilde because our situations were completely different, but I was drawn to Peri in a way I couldn't explain, and I wasn't going to let her go until I found out.

CHAPTER FIFTEEN

THE KISS IN THE GROVE—PERI

"Ladies, you made it." Mateo greeted us with hugs and pointed to a tray containing pieces of bread and different oils to taste. I didn't hesitate.

"Which is your favorite?" I asked him.

"The extra-virgin is my favorite because it's simple, but the garlic-infused oil is delicious and a blend the tourists love. Try this."

He pointed to a tiny cup with extra-virgin olive oil, garlic, and spices that he rattled off, but I didn't pay attention to his list because the sample was delectable, and I gave it my full attention.

"This is so smooth and spicy. If I lived here, I'd learn so many wonderful things to cook," I said.

"How was your morning?" he asked.

"We took Bisnonna to the olive grove, and she showed us her and Hilde's tree." Camila pulled her phone out and showed him the photo of the carving.

"That's so adorable," he said.

Camila told him about the trip to the grove and the stories Isabel had shared with us on the way.

"Do you want me to come over to read more letters tonight?" Mateo asked. "Peri, I do hope you're able to find letters from Isabel to Hilde. That would really help tell their story completely."

"Trust me. If Connecticut was closer, I would have already flown home and torn apart Amma's room and all the boxes in the attic, the garage, security-deposit boxes—anywhere she could have hidden letters." I already had a mental checklist of places to look the moment I touched down.

"Good. Hilde must have kept them somewhere safe."

Camila took my hand. "I'm going to show Peri the wine shop, and then we'll drive through the vineyards. Come by after you close. Tomorrow I'll open, and maybe you and Peri can have a nice day with Bisnonna." She held my hand as we crossed into the other store. Ethan was ringing up a customer and had two more in line. As adorable as Isabel's Oils was, I could understand why Camila felt trapped. It was boring. Even with the door between the shops open, most of the action was in the wine store.

"So, why do you want to sell wine? Your brother doesn't seem to be doing anything but smiling, taking money, and moving on to the next customer. It's really no different than the oils."

Camila sighed. "Since spending time with Bisnonna yesterday, I finally understand why she loves the grove so much. I think she's the reason the family is pushing me that way, and I get it. It's Bisnonna's gift to me. It was hers and she's passing it down to me."

"But she understands that you have bigger dreams, right? That you'd much rather be an artist, and she supports that." I knew that Isabel was very proud of Camila and how artistically talented she was. "Maybe she just doesn't understand that you can make a living with your art and thinks the oil business will give you financial freedom."

"I never talked to her about it. She has always been supportive of my art. I just never thought of the olive oil business the way you put it, but it makes sense."

"Who makes the oils for you?"

"We do everything at the villa. On the other side of the grove, which we didn't get to earlier today, we have a small processing plant."

"So, you could still be in charge of that and draw and paint, right? I mean, the olives need time to grow and mature, so you aren't needed there every day. Like the grapes. Your brothers work every day, but they aren't needed here every day, right?"

"There's always something to do with the wines, but you're right. I don't need to babysit olives."

"Maybe Isabel did this on purpose. Did you ever think about that?" I lifted an eyebrow at her.

"Peri, it's good to see you. I take it you're staying for a bit longer." Ethan slipped out from behind the counter to give us hugs after the last customer left the shop. Camila's cousin called in sick so Ethan had volunteered to run the store.

"I am. It's such a beautiful place, and getting to know your bisnonna has been wonderful," I said.

"So, what are all your secret chats with her about?"

Camila lifted her chin. "If she wanted you to know, she would tell you."

"Are we ever going to find out?"

Because she knew something her brothers were dying to know, she smugly took her time answering. I turned my head to hide my smile. "Eventually, yes. But you don't need to know right now."

"Then what's Mateo doing there?"

"Unlike you, Mateo understands women."

Ethan rolled his eyes. "Whatever. I'll find out. Now get out of my store." He winked to let us know he was joking and left to help a new customer.

"Is there competition between Mateo and your brothers? With the ladies, I mean?"

"You know how attentive Mateo is. My brothers have that American confidence that Italian women can stand for only so long. Mateo is the exact opposite."

"Your father seems so different from your brothers." I studied Ethan, in his short-sleeve black polo shirt that was tight across his muscular chest. He wore faded jeans and square-toed cowboy boots. Obviously, the ranch had rubbed off on them. "So, Italian women love cowboys, huh?" Camila's brothers were fit, tanned, and charming. While they were obviously attractive, Camila was beautiful on a whole different level.

"Apparently. My mother got tired of them bringing women to the villa, so she kicked them out. But before that, she definitely gave them an earful about respecting women and how she didn't want grandchildren until they got married. Very old school, but I think they took it to heart."

"What about you? Do you bring a lot of women to the villa?" Our situation was different, but I braced myself for her answer. My ego had been bruised a lot on this trip.

"Honestly? No. I'm too busy for a relationship. I don't like being tied down. Does that make sense?"

I nodded. "Oh, definitely. I already told you about my last girlfriend. She tried very hard to change me, and naturally, I fought her. My motto now is love me for me, not for somebody I'm not."

"Speaking of love." She paused and gave me a full look-over. Something popped inside my chest when her eyes met mine again. "Let's get back to the villa and chat with Bisnonna."

I rolled my eyes at her.

"What?" She laughed but knew full well the effect she had on me. She grabbed my hand, and we walked to the villa with our fingers entwined. I never stopped smiling.

"You mentioned that you introduced Hilde to The Captain. Can we talk about that?" I asked. It was almost seven in the evening, and we were gathered around the kitchen table drinking tea and eating cookies. I wasn't sure how far to push it, but Isabel couldn't expect me not to ask. That point was pivotal to their story and my existence.

"Yes. I suppose I should tell you about that night."

Mateo looked up from scribbling in a small notebook. Ever since he had a new scope for their story, he was always around when we sat with Isabel. I didn't know him well, but I trusted his passion for capturing the story once he committed to it.

Camila and I stared at one another in alarm. Her tone didn't sound good, but I was guilty of always thinking the worst. "Sounds like it was pretty important." I willed my brain to stop filling my head with awful scenarios.

"We were at a club near the beach. Hilde and I had been lovers for several months."

We had confirmation. Camila looked away. Mateo sat as still as possible, and I strangely felt relieved. We knew it, but this was the first time Isabel had called them lovers.

"It was a cool evening, and Hilde and I had built a small fire on the beach. Large rocks were behind us, and we thought we were secluded enough. We had a blanket draped across our shoulders and were talking about what life would be like if we could be together. Right before she kissed me, a group of young men came out of the darkness from behind the rocks and surprised us."

Oh, fuck. I assumed they were sexually assaulted. The hollow pit in my stomach ached with every second that slowly ticked in the silence between us. No. Not Amma, not Isabel. "What happened then?"

"Thankfully, I knew two of the men. One of them, Guido Lazzo, was a childhood friend. The other was an American soldier Guido had introduced me to earlier in the day. His name was Captain Nicholas Bennett. He was tall, handsome, and very polite. He was also older than the rest of the young men on the beach. He apologized for interrupting us and immediately grabbed the others and walked away."

"Thank God," I said. I didn't want to hear that anything bad had happened. What could have was bad enough.

"We didn't know if we were more scared of getting caught or what would have occurred had I not known Guido and The Captain. We quickly put out the fire, grabbed our things, and raced to the villa. We never went to the beach alone again."

"So, that's how you introduced Amma to The Captain?" I asked. I wanted more.

"Not then. The whole exchange was only a few minutes. Not the place to introduce people. That night was too unpredictable. Too unsafe. It was a few days later when we saw them in town that I introduced them."

"I would have been so scared," I said.

"It was different when we saw them in the park. The sun was shining. People were happy, and we weren't alone. The Captain was very respectful. He was nice looking—a clean-cut, all-American soldier. He had eyes for Hilde."

"That had to piss you off," Camila said.

Isabel shrugged. "I was jealous, but I knew he would be able to give her a life I couldn't. I pushed the relationship."

I snorted, knowing full well Amma fought her. She was too fiery not to speak her mind, even in her youth. "Let me guess. She said no."

"It was more like hell no, but we knew her time here was limited. As much as I wanted her to be with me, it just wasn't the right time. The war was over, and my family needed me, and her family would never let her stay."

I blew out a deep breath. Women were so fortunate today. We had rights, independence, money to travel, technology that kept us in front of people, and the ability to make our own choices. Today Camila held my hand in town, and neither of us thought we were in danger. "At least The Captain was good to Amma."

"She didn't like to talk about him when I was around. She mentioned him in letters." Isabel tapped her shaky finger on the letters on the table between us. I wanted to read through them all at once, but this wasn't my story, and we had time.

"Do you mind if I read the next letter?" Mateo asked. At Isabel's nod, he opened it and read aloud. With every word, it was obvious that their love had grown. It was refreshing to hear true love on the page. Letter after letter, word after word, found their way into my hardened heart. I had never been that free or open in any relationship before and found that I craved it.

When Isabel started nodding off, Camila helped her into her room and into bed. Mateo and I talked about everything we'd learned. I was eager to find any letters Amma had to see if they would fill the gaps. Phone calls to both Granny and Mom gave me nothing. They hadn't found any letters in Amma's desk or her personal belongings, but my mother reminded me the attic was untouched and all mine to dig through.

"Today was long for Bisnonna. Maybe tomorrow we'll take it easy on her."

Camila sat in the chair beside me and reached for a cookie. "I don't know about you two, but I'm exhausted."

"Right? I feel like I could sleep for days," I said.

Camila stood and reached for my hand. "Let's go for a walk. We could use some fresh air."

"You two go ahead. I'm going to stay here and take notes." Mateo waved us off.

"You weren't invited," Camila said dryly.

I walked with her through the courtyard and down the first row of grapes. "What do they taste like?"

"The grapes? Here. Try this." She plucked a ripening grape from the vine and handed it to me. "Be careful. They have seeds."

I popped the grape into my mouth and grimaced at the sour explosion in my mouth. "Ugh. These are awful."

Camila laughed at my expression. "They're not ripe. And not the kind you snack on."

"Well, why did you tell me to eat it then? Jerk," I said. When she reached for my hand again, I smiled, and she noticed. "It's such a beautiful night, and we have enough moonlight for a nice walk. And a chance to clear our heads from Isabel and Hilde's story," she said.

"You know what I want to do?" I stopped, and Camila turned to face me. She came toward me without slowing down and kissed me hard. I wrapped my arms around her neck and clutched her to me. I kissed her with the same amount of passion she gave me. She molded herself against me, and I moaned. She was soft and hard and bold. When she pulled away, I was breathless. She tried hard to seem unaffected, but I could tell our kiss had moved her by the way her hands shook slightly and how her chest heaved and her nostrils flared as she tried to calm her breathing. "I was going to say visit the olive tree, but that was a nice surprise," I said.

She touched my braid and gently pulled me closer. "Your lips are wonderful."

I blushed under the summer moonlight. Her compliment warmed me. I had come to Italy to find someone and, in a roundabout way, ended up reliving my Amma's life. I wasn't in love with Camila, but we had an emotional connection that turned physical the moment her lips touched mine.

"And I think going to their tree is a wonderful idea. Hearing their story has made me rethink relationships. We're very fortunate to have options. I couldn't imagine loving somebody so deeply and not having them in my life."

"I'm sure it happens more than we know. Do you remember the first time you were in love?" I asked.

"I've never been in love."

I should have been surprised, but after meeting Isabel, I realized that I'd never been in love before either. High school was a hot mess, and college was experimental. My ex, Jasmine, wasn't somebody I respected. She bullied her way into my life, and I allowed her to because I was tired of looking for a relationship. "Me either."

I liked the way she pulled me closer as we walked to the olive grove in the semi-dark. She pointed out dips in the dirt road, but after the second time I stumbled, she turned on her phone flashlight. "I don't want you to break any bones or scratch your beautiful skin."

I looked at her to see if she was teasing me about having beautiful skin, but the only thing I saw was a genuine smile. "Thank you. The sun doesn't like it. I bet after a weekend on the beach, you get a nice tan."

"Living on a beach has its perks."

"You're living in paradise. The villa, the vineyards, the grove. This is the stuff dreams are made of."

"I'm spoiled. I know it."

I pulled her closer. "But you really appreciate it. And you wouldn't stay if you didn't have to, but you're fulfilling a deep family obligation. I know you have other dreams."

She stopped and sighed heavily. "I love it here. I really do, but my passion is art. I wish I could do both."

"You can! I'm sure your family will understand if you want to go to art school. It's not like you won't be back. Your brothers are taking over the winery, and we know the olive grove takes care of itself. Have you talked to them about it on a serious level? They seem like reasonable parents." I'd known them for only a few days, but I didn't get the kill-your-dreams kind of vibe from them.

"I don't want to break their hearts. The business is everything to them. Also, look where we are." Camila grabbed a low branch and swung herself closer to me. "It's the special tree."

I put my hand on the thin, twisting trunk near the initials and leaned in so we touched from head to toe. The bold move surprised her, and using that momentum, I kissed her. There was nothing gentle about how our lips met or how her arm tightened around my waist. Her mouth was hot and demanding, and her hunger for me made my skin tingle. I had never felt so alive as I did when I was in Camila's arms. I'd experienced passion before, but not the kind that burned me from the inside out. When her fingers slipped under my shirt and brushed my bare skin, I shivered with delight and want.

She broke the kiss long enough to ask, "Is this okay?"

I vaguely remember nodding and pulling her back into my arms. My senses were reeling. Her skin was the softest I'd ever felt. She smelled like warm vanilla. Every soft moan and noise from her lips ignited a passion foreign to me. It was hard to pull away, but we went from holding hands to almost shedding our clothes within minutes.

I pulled back. I didn't want to make a mistake and tumble into regret. I touched her swollen lips. "We should probably go back."

She took a deep breath and nodded. "You're right. I'm sorry. That shouldn't have happened."

"Oh, don't be sorry. Kissing a beautiful Italian woman in an olive grove is something I can check off my bucket list." Humor wasn't my strong suit, and my attempt at it fell flat. We were quiet on the way home. Even though we were holding hands, I felt sad. Our connection had calmed. She turned on the flashlight until we were close enough to the villa's lights. At the stairs, she tugged my hand.

"I'm going to lock up. I'll see you tomorrow. I hope you sleep well."

When she played with the tip of my braid, I knew she was going to kiss me again. This one was sweet and unassuming. I put my hand on her shoulder and ran my thumb along her jawline. "Thank you for a special night."

Upstairs, I slipped into pajamas and crawled into bed but couldn't find sleep. I kept tossing and turning. What was I really doing here? I had completed Amma's job. I knew about their history. We were almost done reading the letters. I had maybe three more days before I became a freeloader. Logically, I knew I should go and not take advantage of the Rossini-Barnes's hospitality, but something heavy was pressing on my chest. My time here wasn't over, and I needed to find out why.

Chapter Sixteen

Family Secrets—Camila

"Don't you think it's time to let me in on what's going on here?" my mother asked.

"Mom, it's not really my place to tell you, but I'm sure you can guess."

Mom sat next to Bisnonna, who had fallen asleep in the courtyard under the large oscillating fans. The early afternoon breeze was nice and relaxing. Peri was upstairs checking emails, and Mateo was working the morning shift at the store. He would come here when my cousin and aunt covered for the afternoon.

"We all have our secrets." She nodded and gently straightened Bisnonna's collar while she slept. "I always knew she had a certain sadness. When you were a little girl, she would wander the olive groves for hours. It wasn't because she wanted her pulse on the business, so I figured she needed alone time. It wasn't obvious to most, but sometimes she would get lost in thought. But I never questioned what was happening."

I wanted my parents to know about Bisnonna and what we were doing. They deserved to understand why the four of us met every night after dinner and why Peri was our guest. I was torn between privacy and truth. "Life was different for Bisnonna when she was young. She didn't have options like I do." That was my way of telling her without actually outing Bisnonna.

"So, Peri's great-grandmother and Isabel were in a relationship?" She didn't sound surprised. She was looking for confirmation.

I nodded and shrugged. "Life was different back then. They would have never been able to be together."

"That's very sad," she said. She lifted the locket that Bisnonna wore around her neck and studied it carefully. "This is a beautiful piece. Somebody spent a lot of money." She opened it and smiled when she saw the photos. "Bisnonna was beautiful. And Hilde? Peri looks just like her. It's amazing how much."

I smiled. "She doesn't think so."

"Same cheekbones, same lips, same smile. She's a pretty girl."

Without hesitation, I agreed. "And she doesn't know it. She's very self-conscious."

"I don't know why. She's smart, adventurous, beautiful, and personable. I've enjoyed getting to know her. Not as much as you have, but she seems like a good-hearted young woman."

"She makes me aware of my flaws. I can't believe I was such an ass to her." I shook my head, recalling how we met and how I compared her to a lost puppy. "I wasn't fair to her."

"Lesson learned, I hope. I'm just glad she forgave you. Isabel is so much happier with Peri in our lives."

I found that I was, too. What had started out as a bad joke on my part had become a really nice thing. Peri was the first woman I had ever felt more than lust for. I respected her. "When Peri joins us this evening, you should stay when we chat. I mean, the family is going to know soon enough. Plus, it might be good to have you on our side when Nonna returns from her trip. You are on our side, right?"

"Of course I am. After raising two devilish boys and a girl who likes to live on the edge, nothing surprises me. I can't promise Nonna will be as open, but I think she'll understand."

"I'm worried." I wouldn't say that Nonna was conservative, but when I came out, she was shocked and angry. She didn't talk to me for days. I tried to explain, but she didn't want to hear. I gave her time to process. Once she understood that I wasn't doing it to piss people off or for attention, she came around. I wasn't as close to her as my brothers were, but that was probably my fault.

My stubbornness got in the way of long-lasting relationships. If somebody didn't accept me the way I was, I held them at arm's length for my own emotional protection.

My mom patted my knee. "Whatever happens, Isabel has you and me. And if it goes in a direction we don't want it to, I'll take Nonna into another room."

"The last thing Bisnonna needs is her own daughter judging her." I was getting so worked up over something that hadn't even happened, I didn't hear Peri enter the courtyard.

"Oh, Isabel's still sleeping." Peri covered her mouth and sat in the wicker chair next to me. "Hello, Nerissa. How was work?" Her whisper was a little too loud, but Isabel obviously didn't hear anything. We were used to her falling asleep in the middle of chatting. If she wasn't doing the talking, she would nod off.

"The store is busy. The weekend always brings more business to town and to the winery."

"I guess I've noticed more traffic, but the villa is far enough away that you can't really hear the busses," Peri said.

"Since it's the weekend, how about you, me, and Mateo go for a night on the town? Do you like to dance?" I asked.

I think Peri blushed because my mother was sitting with us, and that embarrassed her. "Um, sure. I haven't danced in a long time." She nervously twirled a piece of hair around her finger. It was adorable, but truthfully, I would be nervous around her parents, too.

"Just don't drive," Mom said.

I stopped myself from rolling my eyes. I'd never driven under the influence, and my mother knew this. Growing up on a winery, you learned to respect alcohol.

"You have Uber or Lyft here?" Peri asked.

"We have a rideshare app called itTaxi. It's the same thing, basically. A friend of mine drives for them. We'll probably just call her," I said. Peri tensed up. She probably assumed I'd slept with the friend, which was not the case. "It's a girl we went to school with. Maria. She's married now and has twins. I can't even imagine."

"Her husband is really great. He works during the day, and Maria picks up shifts at night. It gives her a chance to make some money and get a small break from the babies." I loved that my mother jumped in to explain the situation to Peri.

"Twins. Wow. That just sounds like a lot of work," Peri said.

I saw Bisnonna blink and look around. "Bisnonna, you're awake." I leaned over and placed my hand on her knee in case she was disoriented. She patted my hand.

"Did I sleep long?"

"A few hours. Mom is home, and Peri is done with her work, so you woke up at the perfect time. Can I get you anything?"

"You can help me stand. I need to freshen up."

"I'll get the chair." My mother grabbed the wheelchair parked in the corner of the patio. "You and Peri sit and relax. Plan your evening." She leaned closer to me. "I'm going to ask her if I can stay tonight and be a part of the conversation."

I nodded. "See you soon," I said as Mom wheeled Bisnonna by us. I turned to Peri. "Everything okay with work? Can they continue to spare you?"

"Yes. I was able to do a few background checks and send the reports off. Very boring, I know. I'm still tempted to fly home, search through all Amma's things, find matching correspondence, and race back. It would be so nice to have matching letters and read what Isabel wrote back."

"Maybe she didn't save them. Maybe it was too hard for Hilde. I couldn't do it." I didn't save trinkets, but my relationships were superficial. Plus, nobody wrote letters for me to have saved. The only time I wrote anything was on a card, and most of the time it was just a signature. Because of my great-grandmother and her secret love, I was now a fan of handwritten letters. Hilde's penmanship was beautiful and her messages heart-wrenching. I understood why Bisnonna treasured them.

"That's true. I don't think I could either," Peri said.

"Maybe it's because we've never been in love before."

"We're young."

"They were younger," I said.

"A war was going on. Life was unpredictable. Love was the one thing people could grasp and hang onto," she said.

"Love has been in existence since the beginning of time. We're just selfish." I held my hands up in surrender. "Okay. This is getting too philosophical. Let's not overthink love letters."

"You're right." She paused and changed the subject. "Tell me about this place you want to take me to. What's it like?"

"Loud music, alcohol, dancing. You have clubs like that where you live, right?" I asked.

"Yes, but not as close as I would like. What kind of music do you like?"

"Music with a beat. I listen to it all, really."

"Then we'll have a good time no matter what," Peri said. She looked at her jeans and shirt. "I don't really have anything to wear."

"You can borrow something of mine. I have plenty of clothes." I held her hand and smiled. "Some you would look really sexy in."

Another blush. Peri had kissed me with wild abandon last night. For a few moments, she allowed herself to let go and just feel the passion of the moment. Maybe it was too much at once, and we both knew it. She couldn't be a one-night stand. We were always going to have a connection because of the people in our lives, even if we couldn't have one ourselves.

Mom wheeled Bisnonna back into the room. She looked refreshed. "We're back with a stack of letters I'm excited to hear. Isabel has allowed me to sit in and listen to words your great-grandmother wrote her years ago." Mom nodded at Peri, and I sighed with relief. Finally, somebody else in the family knew.

"You good, Bisnonna?" I asked.

"Yes, bella. I'm good. Are we waiting for Mateo, or should we start without him?"

"Why don't we sit around and talk girl stuff until he gets here?" I sent him a message and he responded immediately. "Which will be in about twenty minutes."

"I can spare the next hour or so. Plus, it'll be nice to get to know Peri better. What do you do back home besides work so hard?" Mom asked.

"Starting a new business is nonstop. I probably bit off more than I could chew, but it's nice to be my own boss. In the last year, I just haven't had the opportunity for other things besides work."

"That makes sense. Now's the time to find out what you like in life and what you don't."

I almost choked at my mother's advice. Everyone else got that courtesy, but it didn't apply to me. Out of the corner of my eye, I saw Peri look at me. I silently pleaded with her to let it go. I wanted a pleasant afternoon, and Bisnonna didn't need the added stress of my dreams on top of her lost ones.

"Maybe this is for me, or maybe it's not. I'm not worried. I'll always be able to get a job. I have a great degree and can apply it anywhere," Peri said.

"This is true. The applications of a science-based degree are broad. We have a chemist here on staff. I use him quite a bit when we work on new wines."

I hated science in school. At first, I thought they were punishing me by keeping me from the winery because so much science was involved, but now I realized I wasn't being kept from something. I was being given a beautiful gift and planned to do my best to make the business thrive.

"How about for the olive oils? What chemistry is involved in that side of the business?" Peri asked.

"You haven't been to the processing plant yet? Camila, what have you been doing the last few days? I thought you were giving Peri a tour?"

We both blushed at my mother's questioning. Thankfully, Bisnonna stepped in.

"Oh, I've been keeping them busy enough. They've been so kind listening to my stories and reading letters to me. And don't forget, we did a small tour of the grove. It's been wonderful." Bisnonna held her handkerchief to her mouth and coughed a little.

"Are you okay?" Peri asked.

Bisnonna waved her off. "I'm fine."

"We can turn off the fans," I said.

"It's fine, bella. I'm just clearing my throat."

Mateo swept into the room. "I'm a lucky man to be surrounded by all these beautiful women." He hugged everyone at the table and gave Bisnonna and Mom each a handful of flowers that I just knew I would have to run inside and get vases for. He held out a single pink rose to Peri. "A pretty flower for a pretty woman."

"Thank you, Mateo. It's lovely," Peri said. She sniffed it and smiled sweetly at him.

I rolled my eyes at him. "Where's mine?"

"My friendship is enough. Besides, you always tell me how stupid it is to give the women I adore flowers, so I know you won't appreciate the gesture."

The only flower he bought was Peri's. The rest came from planters outside shops in town. The shop owners knew but humored him anyway. His giving flowers was sweet, even though I hated to admit it.

"So, Mom is going to hang out with us while we read the letters," I said.

Mateo lifted his eyebrow, and I gave him a short nod. He smiled. "That's great. I have my notebook here ready to take notes." He shimmied a chair between me and Peri just to be a shit. I jabbed him with my elbow and smiled at his soft grunt.

"You smell nice," Peri said to him.

He blushed. Mateo was dressed and ready for our night out.

"Now that Mateo is here, maybe we can talk about the letters." My mother wasn't super patient, but we were all too nervous to start.

I knew Bisnonna wasn't going to just blurt it out, so I decided to jump in. "Well, during the war, Bisnonna met Hildegarde Brown, who was a nurse's assistant for the Red Cross." I treaded lightly and told the truth. "They had a deep friendship that grew into more. Hilde was Bisnonna's first love."

Mateo froze beside me, watching my mother's reaction, not knowing I'd already kind of told her. This was confirmation.

She nodded slowly. "We all have first loves." She turned to Peri. "And your great-grandmother is Hilde."

"Yes. I was given a locket with a note to find the mystery woman. Hearing their story has been a true blessing. It makes me understand Amma's life a little better," Peri said.

My mother squeezed Bisnonna's hand. "You have nothing to be ashamed of or embarrassed about. Love is love, and I'm sorry that it couldn't have played out the way you wanted."

Bisnonna dabbed her eyes again. "I never cry this much. Now look at me." She gave a small laugh that broke the tension in the room. "And I loved Lorenzo. He was a good man to me and to our family."

"Without a doubt," my mother said.

Before I read the next letter, we filled my mom in on a few of the things Hilde had written about, including their first kiss, their time on the beach, and how Bisnonna introduced Hilde to her husband. That surprised her, but she didn't say a word. I picked up the next letter. We were getting close to the end. The original light-blue envelope had crept higher up the stack.

Dear Izzy,

Soon I will be Mrs. Nicholas Bennett. I can only imagine my social obligations when I become The Captain's wife. The women I've met in his circle of friends are incredibly attentive to their husbands. I told The Captain he'd better not expect that from me. He just laughed and said he liked my sass.

I can't wait to finish the nursing program. The local hospital is in desperate need of help. Hopefully, we won't have to move for his job. I'd hate to start a career, only to have it cut short because the military stations him somewhere else. I know I'll be able to help wherever I go, but I hate the idea of building a community like we had and being forced to abandon it again. I need to stay busy. I felt so valuable in Italy by my work, my peers, and by you.

I made a list of things I love about you because I don't know how much longer we'll be able to write one another. The Captain already thinks I write you too often, and I realize it's not fair to either of us if we keep writing. I want you to have a beautiful life in Italy.

I love the way you look at me as though I'm the most important person in the world. I love how soft and full your lips are against mine. I love how you feel in my arms. You're the perfect fit for me. I love how huge your heart is for everything in this world. I love your dedication to your family and your business. Maybe one day we'll be together again, but just know that until that time comes, you will forever be my everything.

Always,
Hilde

I looked at my mom, whose expression had softened after hearing Hilde's sweet words. "They're all so beautiful, Mom. Every single one."

She nodded. "They're lovely and precious. How many are there?"

"Around fifty or sixty," I said. I was sure Bisnonna knew how many, but she wasn't talking. Coming out to your family was hard, and everyone was watching my mother's reaction. I knew Mom didn't care. Thankfully, she was progressive. She never said anything negative about my community. I assumed the small worry line on her forehead was for Nonna's reaction. Not only was her mother Catholic, but opinionated. For the first time since finding out about Bisnonna, I was worried that someone she loved might not be as accepting as we all had been.

CHAPTER SEVENTEEN

A NIGHT OUT—PERI

"The car's here," Mateo shouted from downstairs.

I panicked. I was almost ready. I looked at the dress Camila had loaned me after I gave up protesting. She was taller than me, but the dress hit at a comfortable length right at my knee. It flowed out from the waist and made me feel free and sexy. I didn't wear red a lot but was rethinking my wardrobe after staring at myself in the mirror and liking what I saw. I looked good and felt even better. I left my hair down and slipped into my leather sandals that surprisingly worked with the dress. My heart jumped into my throat when I heard a soft knock at the door.

"Peri? Are you ready? No rush though, if you need more time." Camila's voice was sweet and gentle.

I opened the door. "I'm ready." Camila's mouth opened slightly, then clamped down, and opened again, but no words came out. I liked that I made her speechless. For a moment, I doubted my outfit until I saw hunger in her eyes. She pulled me to her and kissed me hard. I melted against her as though we'd been kissing for years. Chills raced across me and blossomed in areas that wanted her attention.

"Stop making out so we can go," Mateo yelled up at us again.

I sighed. "We should leave."

She kissed me again and released me right as I was ready to tell Mateo to go without us. "Okay. But only because Mateo is excited to get out, and I owe him for filling in for me this week."

"Yes. Remind me to buy him a drink."

"He won't let you. He's too chivalrous for that," Camila said.

We were greeted with a low whistle from Mateo. "I'm going to be so popular walking in with two beautiful women."

"Stop. You'll abandon us for the first available woman you see," Camila said.

"Thank you, Mateo. You're very sweet." I didn't have the relationship Camila did with Mateo, and what he said made me smile.

"I like Peri more," he said.

"I do, too," Camila flung back.

"There's plenty of me to go around. Are we all ready?"

"First a selfie before we get all sweaty and hot." Mateo held his phone out, and we squeezed together for the photo. It was hard not to go limp as Camila pressed against me and slipped her hand from my waist to my hip. "Peri, you need to smile."

How could I smile when Camila had her breasts pushed into my back and her hand near my ass? I was ready to feign a headache and race upstairs and wait for her to come to me. "Sorry." Trying to regroup, I gave a fake smile for the first photo and a calmer, genuine one for the second.

"Beautiful. Let's go."

He held the door open for Camila and me to crawl in the backseat. He sat up front with Maria, our driver for the evening. While they caught up, Camila and I shared small but powerful caresses in the backseat. When she touched my knee, it took all my strength not to pull her on top of me. The car ride was short, but it spiked my anticipation for the evening.

The club was already packed, and it was only ten. "This place is huge." I had to scream to be heard. Mateo marched us through the crowd to one of the bars.

"Shots?" he yelled over his shoulder.

We nodded. I needed release. It was time to let loose and let go of the energy building inside me. My own history had changed in the last week. I'd been in Italy for almost two weeks and wasn't going back home the same person.

"Here's to blowing off steam and living our dreams," Mateo said.

"Did you just make that up? Because it's horrible," Camila said. She tapped her glass with his and mine. "But it's true. Here's to new friends and old lovers."

I rolled my eyes even though I appreciated her sentiment. "How about just cheers?"

After the first shot, Mateo handed us a second. The first shot was to fire us up, and the second to calm us down.

Mateo leaned in so we could hear him better. "I'm going over to the other side. Are you going upstairs?"

Camila nodded.

"What's upstairs?" I pointed up in case she couldn't hear me.

"Let's go." She grabbed my hand and weaved through crowds of people and lines of them standing on the stairs looking down at the dance floor. "It's quieter up here, and it's the queer floor."

"How many floors are there?" I asked.

"Three, and this is the floor we want."

With rainbow flags and shiny things everywhere, not to mention the same-sex couples dancing, I would have figured it out sooner than later. "It's definitely quieter here."

"Different music, too. Downstairs is mainstream music, but their light show is amazing. This floor has incredible alternative music, but the dance floor isn't as big, and you can actually have a conversation up here."

"What's on the third floor?"

"A bar called Kinky. We can check it out if you want, but I think this floor is more us."

I was intrigued but not enough to want to visit. Spending time with Camila away from the villa was the true goal. "This is exactly where I want to be. Right here, with you, in this spot." I wanted to be flirty, but I forgot to add the filter, and what came out sounded raw and needy. I almost regretted it until I saw the look in her eyes. The hunger there sent chills over me and ignited a heat between my legs that made my clit throb.

"Camila!" Our moment was broken by somebody Camila wasn't happy to see. The woman looped her arm around Camila's shoulders, kissed her cheek, and turned her around. She was familiar enough with Camila to be in her personal space and was obviously drunk.

"Ciao, Katrina."

I shivered at the coldness in Camila's voice. They shared an exchange I couldn't understand, but body language was everything. Katrina was surprised to see Camila, and Camila wanted nothing to do with her. I sensed a story there but wasn't interested. I wanted her gone.

Camila took a step closer to me and reached for my hand. I gripped her fingers hard until she gave me a quick squeeze, reminding me to loosen my grip. Katrina looked me up and down and smirked. Whatever she said in Italian to Camila wasn't kind. Camila hissed out her response and led me away.

"So that happened?" I wanted more information about what Katrina said, but I didn't want to outright ask. It was obvious they'd once had some type of relationship.

"Just someone who didn't like the way things ended," Camila said.

I wasn't jealous, just curious. "How did they end?"

"Badly."

She offered no other explanation, and I didn't push. We owed each other nothing. For once I was enjoying spending time with a woman who didn't want a nasty entanglement. We both knew whatever we had was an in-the-moment thing. I was leaving soon. We were almost done with the letters and learning about Amma and Isabel. It didn't feel right to stay longer, even though I'd been invited to stay as long as I wanted. I had a new business to run, and doing it an ocean away wasn't working. Ginger had told me yesterday that Amma's lawyer had reached out to see if I'd completed the job. She said I would get back to him when I returned. I couldn't imagine Amma's estate wanting the money back if I didn't complete my mission.

"Do you want to dance?" Camila was already brimming with energy.

"Definitely." I was a better dancer when I was tipsy, or at least I didn't feel so clunky. Camila pulled me close, and even though the song was fast, we found a good, slow rhythm. She had her hands on me, and I allowed myself to enjoy the sexual tension between us instead of fighting it. It was liberating. And a massive turn-on. She was confident, beautiful in the way she took control of me, of us. Her lips brushed across mine whenever the crowd pushed us together or she held me against her. I was on fire, and judging by her slightly hooded look, she was, too. She pressed her lips against my ear.

"Let's get some air."

I nodded and followed her to a balcony. I was sweaty and hot but felt alive. I fanned my hand across the V-neck of the dress for some relief, but it didn't help. I pulled up my hair, hating that I was sweating and Camila could see. I closed my eyes and took a deep breath of cooler air. I kept them closed when I felt Camila's lips press against my neck. I moaned when she scraped her teeth across my shoulder and opened my mouth when her lips worked their way up to mine. It wasn't a gentle kiss. It pulled at every important part inside. My nipples hardened, my swollen clit throbbed, and something clawed inside my chest. It was an ache for her to touch me, to hear her whisper sweet words, to cling to her, but I didn't want to feel anything more than something physical. Emotions scared me.

"I can't stop touching you or kissing you or…"

She didn't finish her sentence. Instead, she brought me closer and kissed me again and again. The railing dug into my back, but I didn't care. I slipped my hands under her shirt and ran my fingertips up and down her back. She moved one of my hands to touch her hard stomach, and I shuddered at how soft her skin was. She looked into my eyes and moved my hand to cup one of her breasts. I gasped at how brazen she was but didn't hesitate to touch her. Her back was to the crowd on the balcony, and the excitement of touching her sent my pulse racing at a speed I didn't recognize.

"You're so beautiful," I said.

She inhaled sharply as my thumb grazed her nipple. Every other sound faded away except her aroused breathing and the pounding of my own heartbeat. She kissed me again, and I was ready to strip down on the balcony until a rowdy group of people trying to sneak in a smoke bumped into us. Camila turned and rattled off something that sounded really sexy but was probably a slew of curse words, judging by their reaction.

"Let's go downstairs and find Mateo. It's too crowded out here."

Her heated anger made me want her more, but I could wait. I couldn't find my voice, so I nodded and followed her. It wasn't hard to find Mateo. He was in the middle of the dance floor with three women and looked so happy. "We should join him."

Camila stared at me then back at Mateo. "And get in the middle of that?"

"Why not? We have a lot to celebrate." I pulled her to me and kissed her. "Let's go." I took the initiative and pushed us through the sweaty bodies to grab Mateo.

"Ladies!" He pulled us to him and kissed us both. He waved at the women around him. "These are my new friends." He pointed to us. "These are my best friends, Camila and Peri. They're a couple!"

"How much have you had to drink?" Camila asked.

I noticed she didn't correct him.

He shrugged and twirled her. "I don't know, and I don't care. Let's have fun."

Mateo was already high-energy, but alcohol fueled his exuberance. He was adorable and the main attraction on the dance floor.

"Is he always like this?" I yelled, even though Camila was right beside me.

"No. Never. He's the responsible one, but after a week like this, I can't blame him for wanting to let go. I'm surprised we haven't."

"I think we did."

"What?" Camila pointed to her ear.

"Let go." I wagged my finger between us and nodded. She grinned and shrugged one shoulder unapologetically. I smiled back at her. I didn't regret it either. My time here was ending, and whatever was happening here, I wasn't going to stop it until the moment I stepped on the plane.

❖

"I saw Katrina," Camila said.

Mateo sat slumped in the front seat, staring out the window while Maria drove us home. It was almost two, and I wasn't tired. I was hyper aware of Camila's hand on my knee and her arm pressed against mine.

"So did I," Mateo mumbled.

"Who is she? I thought maybe she was an ex-girlfriend or something." I looked at Camila.

"Not mine." Her eyes narrowed.

Secretly, I was relieved that she wasn't Camila's ex. She was pretty and sophisticated but had a certain bitchiness about her. "Wow. She must be a real asshat."

"She was horrible," Mateo said.

"She dated Luke. After three months, she told him she was pregnant and almost wiped out his savings buying new things for her place. My stupid brother just sat back and let it happen. He didn't question any of it. She even told him that she didn't want him to move in with her unless they got married."

"I bet Nerissa was pissed," I said.

"She said he was forbidden to marry her until they knew the baby was his. She even scheduled a pre-natal DNA test, and wouldn't you know it? The day Katrina was supposed to show up for the appointment, she told everyone she lost the baby."

"Did she?" It didn't dawn on me that my question could be insulting.

Camila frowned at me. "She never was pregnant. A mutual friend broke down and told me she never was, and it was just a way to manipulate Luke."

I whispered, "Why do I feel like something happened with her and Mateo?"

"She was just a total douche to him when he lost his mother. Told him to get over it. Said he wasn't a man because he always cried. Bisnonna told her she wasn't welcome at the villa anymore. She didn't care if Katrina was pregnant with Luke's baby."

"It's wonderful how protective Isabel is of Mateo," I said.

"I love how much you and Bisnonna connect. You see things similarly. Most people won't take time to spend with the elderly. I mean, I know it was your job at first, but it's nice that even after you did what you came here to do, you still want to visit with her."

"Isabel is wonderful. You're so fortunate to still have her around. She loves you so much, and your relationship is beautiful," I said.

We pulled up to the villa, and my heart did a reverse somersault with a forward twist into my stomach.

"Are you staying here, Mateo?" Camila asked.

He shook his head. "No. You all get up too early for me. Plus, if I get sick, I want to be home. I'll send you a message when I feel human again."

I climbed out of the car and kissed Mateo's cheek. "I hope you feel better. I had a great night."

He clumsily patted my cheek. "Good night, Peri. Sleep well, or don't sleep at all." He gave me a wink. I blushed at his innuendo.

"Go ahead upstairs. I need to lock up," Camila said.

She squeezed my hand and disappeared down the hallway. I was confused. Did that mean our evening was done or not? Either way, I needed a shower. I left the door to my room ajar and grabbed pajama shorts and a tank top. Not sexy, but the best I could do with my limited wardrobe. I was already going to have to wash clothes again.

In ten minutes, I was clean and sitting on my bed. Was I supposed to wait? Should I slip under the covers and grab my laptop like I was working? Scroll on my phone? After playing twenty questions with myself, I tiptoed out of my room and went across the hall to place my ear on Camila's door. Was she in there? Or was she still locking up? I stumbled back when she flung the door open. She, too, had showered.

"Were you going to knock?" she asked.

"No. I was just trying to eavesdrop with my ear against the door to see if you were asleep or—" I wasn't sure how to tell her what I wanted.

"Or what?"

I took a deep breath. I was tired of playing games. My time here was limited, and I didn't want to leave with regrets. "Or ready to act on this thing between us that makes every part of me want you."

Chapter Eighteen

A Morning In—Camila

Peri's words shouldn't have surprised me, but the rawness and honesty in her bright blue eyes took me aback. I pulled her inside my room, locking the door. "Are you sure about this?" She looked so sexy wearing tiny cotton shorts and a tank that left very little to the imagination. I was eager to touch her. I kissed her fingers and waited.

"Definitely."

That's all it took. I pulled her flush against me and kissed her while walking her over to the bed. Our lovemaking didn't even start soft. It began as a frenzied moment of tearing off clothes and crawling onto the bed. She was beautiful and shy in the brightness of the room. I turned off the light on the nightstand and stared at her, lit only by the moonlight. "You're lovely." Her sunburn had faded, and I kissed the tiny freckles that had popped up on her shoulders. She threaded her fingers through my hair and pulled me up to her mouth for a kiss that left me gasping. I nestled my hips into the sweet, soft spot between her legs, and we both moaned at the contact.

Her short nails dug into my lower back as she pushed me into her and started rocking her hips. I leaned up and bit my lower lip. "If you keep doing that, I won't last long." I'll never forget the smile she gave me—angelic but also sexy as fuck. I made some sort of growling noise and sank into her loveliness. I didn't want to rush, but time was precious. I moved down her neck, over her sweet breasts, and flicked her hard nipples with my tongue. She hissed when I grazed my teeth over them and squirmed underneath me. I stopped. "Is this okay?"

"Yes. It feels amazing. Please don't stop," Peri said.

I kissed and sucked both breasts and ran my hands up and down her, admiring her curves. I slid lower and placed a gentle kiss on her smooth mound. I held her hips down as I delved my tongue between her soft folds and found her swollen clit. I spread her apart and licked, pleased with her guttural moans and slightly thrusting hips. Her hand on the back of my neck encouraged me. I stopped only to spread her legs farther apart. She surprised me and held herself open.

"I need to feel you inside."

Her words melted me but also gave me a burst of sexual energy I didn't recognize. I slipped two fingers into her tight pussy and licked her clit as I waited for her to adjust. Because she was so wet, it took only a few moments, but it felt like forever. I moved my fingers when she was ready. She moaned loudly as she writhed, grasping my pillow, the sheets, and eventually my hair as she climbed to ecstasy. She was so beautiful as she let go. My past lovers were either super quiet or over-the-top loud. I always thought it was on purpose. Nothing about Peri or the way she engaged with me was fake. My stomach flopped at every moan and jumped at every gasp. I flattened my palm on her stomach and continued to slip two fingers in and out. When I sped up my thrusts, she dug her heels in the mattress and lifted her hips to meet my fingers. I went as deep as I could.

"Harder," Peri moaned.

"I can't tell you how fucking sexy you are." I desperately wanted to come, but I wanted to make her come more, so I continued stroking and sucking until she tensed and came hard and fast. She pressed her knees together and rolled to her side until the aftershocks subsided. I curled up behind her and kissed her shoulder and her neck. She was sweaty and slightly shaking, so I pulled the sheet over us and ran my fingers lightly up and down her arm. "Are you okay?"

She gave a small, weak laugh and turned so that she was facing me. She ran her fingers over my cheek and leaned in for a soft, long kiss. "That was amazing."

"More than amazing." I smiled because everything about tonight was just that. Incredible, unbelievable, and all-consuming.

"I'm not tired, even though I should be," she said. She leaned up to look at the clock. "It's almost four. How is that possible? We just got here."

I pulled her on top of me so that she was resting between my legs. She pressed into me, and a spark of lust ignited me. We were far from being done, and I was buzzing with need. I jerked when she pressed into me again.

"Hmm. I think I like this." She nipped at my bottom lip. I moaned at the sexiness of it. I'd figured Peri would be quiet and shy in bed, not this siren who was grinding into me.

"I think I like this, too," I said. I meant it. Normally, I didn't worry about my own needs, but I wanted Peri to kiss me and get to know me physically. I wanted her to touch me, taste me, and fuck me. Our time was limited, but we could at least have this one night together. She rolled her hips into mine, and I gritted my teeth to keep from coming.

In a move that had to have been calculated, Peri straddled me. I ran my fingers up and down her deliciously swollen slit and entered her swiftly. Even though my hand was at a bad angle, I refused to stop. The way she climbed to her next orgasm was the most beautiful thing I'd ever seen. "Just like that," I said. She leaned over me so her lips were inches from mine. When she came the second time, she kissed me hard and moaned against my mouth.

"I'm greedy," she said, but didn't apologize.

"I'm more than willing to give."

"You weren't kidding about giving." She stretched out across me. "But how are you about receiving?"

I smirked. "I one hundred percent support it."

She ran her fingertip across my sensitive mouth. "Good." She pulled off the sheet on her way down to the juncture of my thighs. "Because we aren't anywhere close to being done."

I fell back because the path of her mouth was making me weak. All my energy had pooled to my pussy. I grabbed the headboard and focused on stilling my hips. I couldn't help but move them a tiny bit as her mouth neared my clit. I was tired of wanting release and would orgasm quickly. When her tongue feathered against my pussy, I cried out but didn't come. Instead, I was relieved that I was finally getting the attention I wanted. She was eager and quickly pulled my orgasm out with her mouth. While I was recovering, she gifted me with another one. That had never happened before. I couldn't move a single muscle.

"Oh." That was the word I chose for back-to-back orgasms? "I mean, that was ah…well, incredible." Her mouth closed over mine before any more incoherent drivel could escape.

"Maybe we should try to get some sleep." Peri looked out the window and smiled. "Even though the sun is just starting to show herself."

I twirled a piece of her hair around my finger. "I always thought the sun was a he. All the mythology and folklore I read was misleading. Why she?"

"So much energy. It has to be a she," she said.

"Okay. Now we aren't making sense. Let's get some sleep," I said. We had lunch with the family in seven hours, and after dancing for hours and ending the night in each other's arms, we were going to be exhausted. I fell asleep with her in the crook of my arm and the amazing night stamped on my heart.

I woke to an empty bed and a sheet tucked around me. I squinted at the clock. It was almost noon. Even though I was tired and my muscles were sore, I jumped out of bed, excited to see Peri again. I grabbed a pair of shorts and a shirt and raced to my bathroom. Because I went to bed with my hair wet, the waves were disheveled. I threw it back in a bun, splashed water on my face, and brushed my teeth. It wasn't my best look, but my family would start looking for me if I didn't make an appearance. I walked in the kitchen and found my parents but no Peri or Bisnonna.

"There she is." My mother kissed my cheek and motioned for me to join the table. I wanted to find Peri and Bisnonna, but obligation forced me to sit in the closest chair. "How was your evening?"

Panic bubbled up, but I tamped it down. Nobody could've heard us because my room was on a different floor and on the other side of the house. "It was a fun night, for the most part."

"For the most part?" Mom asked.

"Mateo drank a lot, and we had the misfortune of running into Katrina." Both my parents rolled their eyes. "Yeah. I had the same reaction. She was all friendly and stuff. I can't believe she's still here. Go find some sugar daddy down in Sicily." Neither one of them corrected me or told me to be nice. "Where are Peri and Bisnonna? Are they together?"

"Bisnonna is napping, and Peri is on a walk. I think she wanted to take some photos before she leaves."

"Did she say when she might go?"

"She mentioned next weekend." My father flipped open the newspaper as though everything was fine, but everything seemed to be crashing around me.

I took a sip of the sparkling water my mother put in front of me and told myself I wasn't going to race out the door for at least five minutes. "Oh. Yeah. We're getting close to finishing the letters."

"Your mother told me about Isabel and Peri's history. I think it's really great that she's here and has given Isabel a chance to have closure on a very important part of her life," he said.

"I feel bad for Bisnonna. Learning about your first love passing away has to be incredibly hard." I kept my voice low in case she or Peri turned up and might hear me. My father kissed my mother's hand.

"I can't imagine letting go of my first love," he said.

My mom smiled sweetly at him. They had the real deal. They fell in love when they were young and never wavered. If I weren't a product of true love, I would never believe in it. Bisnonna and Hilde's story only cemented what my parents had shown me. Even my brothers were skeptical of love. I thought it was our generation and how independent we were, but really, we were just afraid. I was afraid I wouldn't find it, and after what happened to Luke, my brothers were afraid women were after them for the family money. I never got that vibe when I went out with women. Of course, I'd never been in a serious relationship like they had.

"Good afternoon." Peri stood in the doorway and smiled at me. She looked beautiful with her light hair braided back and her red lips still swollen. Those sweet lips had been all over me finding all my sensitive spots, even those I didn't know I had. I didn't realize I'd been holding my breath until I tried talking and ended up coughing.

"Are you okay?" My mom stood out of concern, but I waved her off.

"I'm good." I cleared my throat. "How was your morning, Peri?"

"Wonderful." She slipped into the chair beside me. "It was such a beautiful morning I decided to go for a walk."

"Did you get much sleep? I mean, we got in kind of late." I looked around the room to see if my parents would question us, but nothing registered on their faces. They didn't know.

"I don't need a lot of sleep and thought you were probably tired after our night," she said.

I shot her a look.

"I mean, we danced the whole night with Mateo, and you told me you always have a hard time waking up in the mornings."

"Oh, Camila is the worst to wake up. She could sleep through anything. Even alarms," Mom said.

"I believe you. I knocked on her door this morning, but she never answered," Peri said.

I stood. "Are you done with your walk, or do you want some company?"

"It's almost time to wake up Isabel and eat lunch, so stick around here." My mom picked up a section of the newspaper. Peri and I had a little bit of time to be alone.

"How about a quick walk in the courtyard?" I asked.

"Sounds perfect," Peri said.

"We'll be back in twenty minutes." I wanted to press her against me in a friendly hello kiss, just not in front of everyone.

Once we were away from my family, I pulled her into a small alcove and kissed her the way I wanted to. I wrapped my arms around her waist and slipped my tongue softly inside her mouth. She deepened the kiss until I thought I heard a noise and regretfully pulled away. "Good mor—" I stopped. "Good afternoon. Why didn't you wake me?" I kissed her fingers.

"I didn't lie back there. You're really hard to wake up." She smiled, and I touched her lips. I missed her mouth.

"I'm sorry. Did you get any sleep at all?"

"A few hours. I sneaked back to my room around eight but couldn't sleep, so I got up and started my day," she said. She wore a blue T-shirt and jeans that hugged her ass nicely. Her Converse were dusty from walking in the vineyards, and some of her hair had fallen out of the braid, giving her a sexy vibe.

Something stirred in my chest, but I chalked it up to her beauty and nothing else. I certainly didn't need to feel anything for Peri that wasn't friendship. "I'm sorry I'm so hard to wake up. I'd still be in bed if I hadn't wanted to find you." Did I just confess that I missed her? I was pathetic.

"It's okay. You deserved to sleep."

She slipped her hands under my shirt to stroke my stomach, and I made a soft sound of approval. "Don't leave me tonight."

Peri hitched her brow. "So that wasn't just a one-time deal?"

I probably should have left it alone. It should have been just one night, but now that I'd made love to her for hours, I needed to do it again. I was hooked. Was it because it had been a few months since the last time I had sex? No. I desired her. Sex was one thing, but I legitimately desired Peri.

"I mean, if you want it to be, then we can leave it that way." She kissed me back in a way that told me those were empty words and she either said them to convince herself or me.

"It's taking all of my will to not drag you back upstairs, lock the door, and have sex with you all afternoon," I said.

"Who says we have to go upstairs?"

Chapter Nineteen

The Secret Drawer—Peri

I couldn't stop thinking about her. It wasn't just about sex. I'd had casual sex before, and this wasn't it. My feelings were all over the place with Camila. I didn't like the way she'd played me at the beginning of this journey, and now I was trying to find a secret place to have sex. Camila had pulled me into the hallway and kissed me hard and fast, and I had to swallow my moan in case anybody was close enough to hear us.

"I guess we should wait until tonight. Too many people around and I need to wake up Isabel for lunch," she said. She dropped her arms from my waist after giving me a quick squeeze. I sighed when she took a step back, but I nodded. "I can be patient."

I tilted my head and raised my eyebrow. "Liar."

She shrugged and stepped closer for a quick brush of a kiss. "You're right. I can't stop kissing you. Maybe if you didn't have such full and deliciously red lips it wouldn't be so damn hard."

I playfully pushed her away and wagged my finger at her. "My lips are red only because they've been attached to you for the last twelve hours." My voice was a loud whisper. I looked around for any witnesses. Camila's phone dinged and she held up her finger.

"We've been asked to gather Isabel. She's awake and probably hungry." She put her phone back in her pocket. "It's amazing how much she can eat."

"Right? I thought maybe she was secretly working out when we weren't looking. That's a good sign though," I said.

She grabbed my hand and led me back toward the kitchen. "I'm glad she eats well. With all the medicine she takes, she needs to have food in her stomach. I do need to get her to drink more. And not wine. She's allowed only a few glasses a week. Don't believe her if she tells you different."

"I love how spunky she is," I said. Amma was the same way. She'd lived life to the fullest until her very last day. I knew she was old, but I always thought she was the exception to the rule, but then I met Isabel, who proved me wrong.

"She's always been feisty. She'll argue with you just to argue. That's the Italian in her."

I held her hand up. "Sounds familiar."

She pinched my side. "But Italians are passionate about everything."

"I love that you all are. Your brothers have your father's American chill. But you take after your mother. I bet when she gets angry at something, everyone backs down."

"Wait until you meet Nonna later today." Camila checked her watch. "My father's picking her up at eight tonight."

"Should I be worried about her? She might hate me for opening a door that's been closed for seventy-five years." For the first time, Camila looked worried.

"I get that it might be hard on her, but I'm going to make sure that I'm right by her side. Nonna can't accept me and not her own mother," she said.

"I say let's have a great afternoon with Isabel to keep her mind off things. We could take her somewhere. Or make her favorite dessert."

Camila paused outside Isabel's door. "We could ask her, but she hates to trouble people even if we want to be troubled."

I stood with my fists on my hips. "Then we'll make her understand that we want to do something for her. Even if it's making chocolate chip cookies or a cake." I wasn't the best cook, but I knew how to bake.

"You don't want to know what I like to eat?" She smirked.

I held up one finger. "One, this isn't about you, and two, I already know what you like to eat."

She broke into a full smile and laughed. "You," she said. She shook her head and softly knocked on the door. "Bisnonna? Are you awake?"

"Come in, bella."

Camila poked her head in. "Peri is here, too."

"She is more than welcome to come in."

I peeked my head in and gave her a small wave. "Hello, Isabel. How was your nap?" We had a cup of coffee early this morning, so I knew she'd had a good night's sleep.

"I feel very rested, thank you."

"Bisnonna, Peri and I want to do something for you this afternoon. Take you somewhere in town, go on a road trip, or Peri even thought about making you cookies or something from America."

"How about snickerdoodles?" I asked.

Camila turned to me. "Those are too easy."

I snorted. "Maybe we should have a bake-off, and Isabel can pick the winner." Isabel's smile warmed my soul. It was precious. I could tell she loved the idea, even if Camila hated it.

"Oh, it's on. After lunch, the three of us will take over the kitchen. What do you think, Bisnonna?"

"It sounds like a wonderful idea."

"Do you like snickerdoodles?" I asked.

"Of course. They pair well with wine."

Camila helped her into the wheelchair. "That doesn't mean you get to sneak an extra glass of wine today."

I put my hand on Isabel's before we left her room. "Speaking of which, I loved your wine. It was delicious, and Camila said I did a pretty good job of picking out the flavors."

"She's a natural." Camila winked at me.

"Should we get the letters?" Isabel asked. She looked back at the stack on her dresser.

"We can come back for them after lunch," Camila said.

"It smells wonderful," I said as we headed to the courtyard. I pushed aside the feelings of guilt for being at the villa even though the entire family invited me. The aroma also reminded me to call my mother. It had been several days since I'd seen her face, but we texted every day. "Will everyone be here?"

"Oh, one of my aunts and a cousin will be here later for dinner, but Ethan and Luke should be here now."

I leaned over so Isabel could hear me. "You have a beautiful family. Camila's brothers are so handsome."

"Hey. What about me?" Camila asked.

I bumped her with my hip. "You're handsome, too?"

She folded her arms in front of her. "That's not what I mean."

Without thinking, I leaned forward and gave her a small kiss on her lips. "You're beautiful." Her eyes went wide. Oh, shit. I looked at Isabel, whose hands covered her mouth, probably from shock, but also hiding a smile. "I'm so sorry."

Isabel grabbed my hand and squeezed. "Don't ever be sorry for telling a woman she's beautiful. And if your kiss is welcomed, kiss her as many times as you can."

Camila knelt to face Isabel. "Um, yeah. So, last night we went out and had a nice time with Mateo and danced, and I showed Peri what life is like here in Sequina."

"That's wonderful, bella. She is a special woman."

My heart bounced around as I processed what was happening. I fucked up. What was I thinking? Why did I kiss her? It was so natural, and she was so cute flirting with me. I looked at Camila. She didn't meet my eyes.

"Let's go. They are expecting us, Bisnonna." She was impossible to read. Her smile didn't reach her eyes. Was she mad or upset or shocked?

"I know I'm hungry," I said. The thought of food right now made my stomach turn, but I had to keep going as though the last minute of my life hadn't happened.

I was introduced to the rest of the family. I knew Camila's cousin from Isabel's Oils. After quick introductions, I sat beside Isabel and across from Camila. The tension between us was palpable. We needed a private moment to discuss what had just happened. Isabel must have sensed we needed that moment, too.

"Bella, Peri, will you go get me a handkerchief from my room?"

Everyone was too busy getting food to pay us any attention. I followed Camila down the hall, past Isabel's room, and out into the courtyard.

"I don't know why I did that. I'm so sorry. You just looked so cute, and you're so wonderful with Isabel that I got carried away. I'm sorry," I said. Camila stared at me for what felt like minutes but was probably only three seconds. To my surprise, she swooped in closer, took my face in her hands, and kissed me. I kissed her back with everything I had. I wasn't sorry we'd kissed in front of Isabel. I was only sorry if she regretted it. I pulled away to look in her eyes. "So, you're not mad at me?"

She shook her head. "Why would I be mad that a beautiful woman kissed me?"

I ran my fingertip along her collarbone and smiled. "You froze, and I thought maybe this was too new to share with anyone. Especially Isabel. Is it going to be too hard for her?"

She kissed the tip of my nose. "Mateo texted her that we kissed in the cellar. I think she's excited about us, but we might not want to tell anyone else until Nonna finds out why you're here. The entire family seems a bit worried about her return."

I swallowed hard. I wasn't one for confrontations, but I didn't run from them either. I was more level-headed than I was reactive. "Hopefully, she had a really good time, and we don't have to worry about a thing."

"Nonna is really weird. She's had the same core group of friends since Nonno died a few years ago."

"Does she have any long-term relationships? Any friends from when she retired, or was she involved in any clubs?"

Camila shook her head. "Nonno was everything to her. She lost a lot of childhood friends when she got married. And then she lost most of the friends they made as a couple when he passed away. So now she hangs out with a book club, and she doesn't like to read."

"Who doesn't like to read? I mean, I stay busy, but even I read. It's how I wind down."

"Nonna winds down with a glass of wine. But let's stop talking about her. She'll be here soon enough. Let's get back to lunch." She grabbed my hand and kissed it before letting it go. Walking back in holding hands would counteract the entire conversation we'd just had. "Oh, we better grab a handkerchief in case anybody asks." Camila opened Isabel's room, and we quietly entered as though we were disturbing the sanctity of it.

"Do you know where she keeps them?"

"Probably in the top drawer." She pointed to the antique dresser with an ornate jewelry box on top. Camila started counting the letters we had left without disturbing the pile.

I opened the top drawer and found papers. I quickly shut it as though I'd done something wrong. "Not there."

"Keep trying," she said.

I opened the second and found a collection of lovely Victorian hair pins but no handkerchiefs. The third drawer pulled completely out, and I had to grab it with both hands before it fell to the ground. "Holy crap. I wasn't ready for that." I looked at the drawer, then back at the dresser. Something was wrong with it. It was about three inches shorter than the other ones. "Camila, come here. Take a look at this." I handed her the shorter drawer while I picked up the stationery and pens that had dropped on the carpet. She set down the drawer and peered into the empty slot where the drawer fit.

"I think something's back here," Camila said. She shone her phone's flashlight into the cubbyhole. "No."

"No what?" Excitement and dread filled my heart.

She pulled out a smaller drawer. "Is this what I think it is?" Camila put the drawer on the top of the dresser. "It's a secret compartment." She carefully looked at the box that didn't seem to have an opening. She shook it gently and something inside rattled.

"Oh, be careful," I said. It was so hard not to rip it out of her hands and try to open it.

She stopped investigating and looked at me. "I don't think there's a bomb, but something's definitely here."

I gave her ten more seconds of patience before I held out my hand. "My turn."

She scowled at me but handed it over. I looked at it and, within ten seconds, saw a slight gap at one of the ends. I carefully slid the end cap over to get to what was hidden inside.

"Take it over to the bed," Camila said.

I carefully tipped it over, and a few items tumbled onto the comforter. I didn't know what to grab first.

Camila picked up a small but thick drawstring bag like the one that housed the locket I gave Isabel. She opened it. "This is a beautiful ring." She held out a small gold band with an emerald surrounded by five small pearls.

"Do you think this is Isabel's, and she forgot about it?"

"Probably. I've never seen it before."

"It's beautiful," I said. It was more ornate than anything I'd ever dared to wear. The yellow gold looked classic instead of outdated. It was lovely. I appreciated the craftsmanship and detail that went into making it.

"Look at these cool rocks." Camila dropped two smooth, heart-shaped rocks into my palm. "They probably found these on the beach. I bet all of this is theirs."

"Do you think this might be a keepsake box?" There wasn't anything special about the box itself except the contents.

"I think that's the idea. What else is in it?"

I put my hand on hers. "Wait a minute. Do you think Isabel would want us to snoop? I feel bad about this."

Camila sighed. "You're right. And I bet the letters aren't here only because that stack is too big for this box." She looked inside again. "There's something else inside. I mean, we've come this far. Don't you think we should at least finish? If not, we'll always wonder." She didn't wait for my response before she turned the box upside down and shook it.

"Okay. But we have to hurry. I feel like we've been gone for an hour." I looked at the time on my phone. It had been only five minutes.

"Whatever's in there is jammed." Camila found a knitting needle in a basket near Isabel's bed. She inserted it into the box and carefully pulled out something that stopped us both.

I put my hand on my chest. "Oh, my God. Camila, is that what I think it is?" I wanted to touch it, but were my eyes deceiving me? She picked up the delicate piece of linen and carefully unfolded it. We stared at it in disbelief.

"It's beautiful. Hilde did a wonderful job," she said.

It was the hand-embroidered handkerchief with initials and a rose that Amma made Isabel for Christmas that she had lost so many years ago.

CHAPTER TWENTY

THE HANDKERCHIEF—CAMILA

Lunch dragged. I couldn't concentrate on anything but what Peri and I had found in Bisnonna's room. We were going to be stuck at the table for at least another hour. We put everything back the way we found it, and I promised Peri we would show Bisnonna as soon as lunch was over. Peri was smiling at me so hard when we returned. She was good for the family.

During a lull in the conversation, my cousin decided to pump me for more information. "How did you and Peri meet?" she asked.

The only person who didn't jump in to talk about my relationship with Peri was Bisnonna. The noise level was so loud all at once that my mother stood up and said, "Hold on." She turned to my brothers and shushed them. She even pointed to my father who, in a rare moment of weakness, had joined the banter.

"We met at the street fair…" Roars of laughter drowned out the rest of my sentence.

"I saw her beautiful artwork and stopped to chat with the artist," Peri said.

I was curious why she didn't tell them she was looking for Bisnonna, but assumed she was doing it for discretion. It wasn't their business anyway.

"So now she's staying here?" my aunt asked.

"Peri is…" Bisonna started speaking, but the uproar was too loud for anyone to hear her.

I banged my hand down on the table to get their attention. The stinging slap felt good. "Bisnonna wants to say something." I softened my voice and even managed a small smile. The table quieted immediately.

"Thank you, bella. Peri is my guest, and I expect all of you to treat her with Rossini respect."

"Of course, Bisnonna." My aunt tipped her wineglass in our direction.

A low rumble of chatter started as people began different conversations until it was a normal lunch buzz. Pride burst in my chest as I smiled at Bisnonna. This was still her empire.

"I'm excited to sit down with you two after lunch," Isabel said. She smiled knowingly at us.

"We have a lot to talk about," I said.

She leaned over. "Maybe I should send them all home now. Tell them I'm not feeling well."

"Let's eat first, and then we can use that excuse."

"Good idea, bella. I want to hear all about your night," Bisnonna said.

"Some things we might leave out," Peri said.

I laughed. "You can hear us from across the table?"

She nodded. "I feel like we're talking in code anyway. Nobody's paying attention to us after that delivery. Thank you, Isabel, for coming to Peri's defense."

"I wouldn't have it any other way. At least tell me the start of the night."

"Maria picked us up. I don't know if you remember her. She worked at the winery the summer before college. Pretty girl with long black hair and, like, five brothers," I said.

"Oh, yes. She got married here, too, right? A few years ago."

I loved that Bisnonna's mind was still sharp. She was sometimes disoriented after naps but rarely forgetful. She always said it was her olive oils, and I was starting to believe her. "Yes. She and her husband had twins. She works some nights driving people around, like a taxi service."

"Is that safe? A woman alone in her car with strangers?"

"I don't think she's ever had an issue. That's pretty much how people make money now. They deliver food or take people places, such as to the airport or a show," I said.

"It's wonderful that women have so many options now," Bisnonna said. She paused to take a few bites. "Peri, what was your first job?"

"I volunteered at an animal shelter in middle school. It was for community service, but I had to be there three times a week like a real job. My first paying job was a shoe store."

"Right up Camila's alley. Have you seen her shoe collection?"

"No, but I've seen different sandals every day and motorcycle boots that are amazing. I have a passion for shoes, too, and I blame my first job. Imagine all the shoes you want at a discount," Peri said.

I loved that Peri was so open and engaging with Bisnonna. After twenty more minutes of waiting very impatiently for everyone to finish, we were able to escape the table, thanks to Bisnonna saying she wanted to rest. Her wink to me didn't go unnoticed, but nobody said anything. I helped her into her wheelchair, and Peri and I rolled her slowly into her room.

"Aren't we going to the courtyard?" she asked.

"Yes, but first we wanted to show you something." I quietly closed the door. "Remember when we brought you the handkerchief before lunch? Well, I wasn't sure what drawer they were in, so I just opened a few until I found them. Here's the thing. The third drawer down has a secret box. I wasn't snooping at all." I didn't want to put Peri in a predicament, so I took the blame.

"Oh, yes. I keep a few precious things in there. I'm not upset. I wanted to hide the letters inside, but there wasn't enough room."

Both Peri and I visibly relaxed. I wanted to ask about everything, but I knew one thing that was the most important. I pulled the delicate handkerchief from the top of the dresser and placed it in Bisnonna's hand. "We found this in the very bottom of it. It was stuck." Her mouth dropped open, and she clutched it to her chest as though it was the most precious thing to her.

"I thought I lost it all those years ago." I teared up at the sheer joy on her face. "Thank you, bella, for finding it," she said.

Peri and I sat on the edge of the bed and gave Bisnonna a moment. She showed us the rest of the items and explained that the ring was something she wanted to give Hilde, but Hilde wouldn't accept it. Not because she didn't want it, but because she didn't want to have to explain it and didn't want to hide something so beautiful.

"I ended up hiding it anyway." Bisnonna gave a small shrug.

"It's beautiful, Isabel," Peri said. She twisted the ring so the emerald caught the sunlight streaming into the room. "Did you get it for Hilde, or is it a Rossini heirloom?"

"It was my mother's, but I wanted Hilde to have it."

"You never wore it? Why not?" I took the ring from Peri and looked at it closely. It barely fit on my ring finger.

"We worked all the time, and I didn't want to lose it or misplace it."

We spent thirty minutes discussing everything in the secret drawer. The rocks were from the beach, just like I thought. I could tell how excited she was to have her handkerchief back. When we went into the kitchen for the bake-off, she tucked it inside her shirtsleeve. I was going to have to tell Sophia to always be on the lookout for it in the laundry.

"Are we really doing this?" Peri seemed surprised we were going ahead with her idea, but if this would distract Bisnonna, then I was happy to do it.

I pulled out basic ingredients from the pantry and put them on the counter. "Whatever else you'll need, you'll find in there."

"And while you're doing that, you'll have to tell me about your evening." Bisnonna looked mischievous. Obviously, she wasn't going to forget about the kiss. Nobody was in the kitchen, but I could still hear voices of people milling about.

I shrugged. "Not much to tell really. We danced, we drank a little, and Peri left my bedroom about eight this morning."

"Camila!" Peri covered her face with her hands. "Don't tell Isabel that." She peeked out from her hands and glared at me.

"What? She asked and I told the truth."

"It's okay. I remember what it was like to be young, in love, and have to sneak around."

I stiffened at her word choice. Peri, who was carefully measuring out flour, dropped the cup, and a puff of flour filled the space between us.

"Oops. Sorry about that. I'm so clumsy sometimes." She couldn't hide the nervousness in her voice. No more than I could act natural.

Bisnonna had it wrong. We weren't in love. I liked Peri, and we'd had a fantastic time last night, but love wasn't on my mind. Besides, she was going to leave in a matter of days. We were just enjoying one another's company and learning our families' histories. The kitchen was unnervingly quiet.

"Do you have a hand mixer?" Peri asked.

"What's wrong with using a spoon or just your hands?" I asked. I didn't need a recipe. I'd been making snickerdoodles my entire life. I started mixing the dry ingredients without measuring them.

Peri smiled smugly. "You're going to lose. Isabel, prepare yourself for the best cookies ever."

I switched to Italian partly to annoy Peri but also to ensure that Bisnonna had my back. "Don't forget who sneaks you wine around here."

"No cheating. English only during the bake-off," Peri said.

Bisnonna chuckled.

"There's no cheating in baking. I mean, who does that? Maybe a desperate person who knows she's going to lose. Hey, what are you doing?" I asked.

"Eyes on your own work," Peri said. She tilted herself between me and the bowl and continued mixing her butter and sugar on low speed. By the time I was done mixing ingredients and rolling my dough into little balls, she was just starting to add the dry ingredients.

"I'm going to beat you." I pulled out a cookie sheet.

"This isn't a timed event. It's a bake-off where Isabel will decide which one of us is the best baker," Peri said.

I dipped the dough into my mixture of sugar and cinnamon and placed my creations on the cookie sheet. "You continue to take your sweet time while I get cookies in front of Bisnonna."

Bisnonna waved her hands at us. "No. I will try both cookies at the same time."

I sighed theatrically. "I can't believe this is how I'm spending my afternoon."

"What? With a beautiful woman and your favorite great-grandmother?"

I looked at Peri and smiled. "You're right, Bisnonna. This is almost perfect." I leaned against the counter and watched as Peri carefully rolled the small balls into a generous amount of cinnamon sugar before placing them three inches apart on the cookie sheet.

"Those are pretty."

"Wait until you taste them," Peri said.

I must've made a noise because Peri's eyes widened, then narrowed with warning. I smiled in apology and glanced at Bisnonna. She was staring at her handkerchief, not paying any attention to us. "She didn't hear that."

Peri took a step closer and whispered, "I'm more of a behind-closed-doors kind of girl, and making out in front of family isn't my thing."

"Oh? You mean like earlier when you kissed me in front of her?"

"Yeah, well, that was a mistake. I'm usually more prudish when it comes to public displays of affection," she said.

I pulled her to me and kissed her. "But it's Bisnonna, and you already broke your rule. We can keep it private around the rest of the family, but I haven't seen her this excited about any relationship in forever."

Mateo slowly walked into the kitchen. "I need a tall glass of ice-cold water and maybe some aspirin." He winced when the ice cubes clanked in the glass. "Why is everything so loud?" He kissed both of us on our cheeks and sat next to Bisnonna. "What have I missed?" I was surprised Mateo didn't say anything about the lack of space between me and Peri. Maybe he didn't notice.

"Show him, Isabel," Peri said.

Bisnonna handed him the small linen handkerchief with the perfectly imperfect embroidered name and rose. He held it up gently on one corner and flipped it over.

"No. You found it? This is beautiful," he said.

"They found one of my secret hiding places, and this was stuck inside. All these years I thought I'd lost it."

"That's great. You must be so happy." He gently handed it back to her. "What's going on here? What smells delicious?"

"Those are my cookies. Peri and I are having a bake-off for reasons that escape me now. Nobody is going to know how to make this cookie better than me," I said.

"I'll be a judge."

I didn't like that idea. Mateo was too friendly with Peri and would probably side with her no matter what.

"That sounds great," Peri said.

"Since we're all here, should I get the letters?" I had five minutes left on the timer. At Bisnonna's nod, I retrieved the stack and placed them on the table. We had about a dozen left to read. I didn't want our sessions to end for so many reasons. I was learning so much about Bisnonna, and I had Peri in my life. When we were done with the letters, Peri would pack up and leave. She had a life and obligations back in Connecticut. Sadness pinged my heart as I realized I would miss her, and not just because we had sex, but because she was weaving her way into my life, letter by letter, day by day.

"Mateo, why don't you read one since the bakers are busy?"

He carefully untied the ribbon and pulled the first one off the stack. He cleared his throat, took a drink of water, and started reading.

Dearest Izzy,

I was so happy to receive your letter that I stopped everything I was doing and raced upstairs to read it in private. My heart skips when my cousin stops by the house or school. She usually puts your letters in books, and since she's going to nursing school, too, it's easy to hide them.

It was sweet how slowly Mateo read the letter and how Bisnonna smiled the entire time. The letters were all heartfelt and beautifully written, but truthfully, we were anxiously awaiting the last one, the one Hilde sent Bisnonna on her wedding day. My heart ached for that letter, but this was Bisnonna's story, and I was going to respect her pace even if not knowing was killing me. I was impatient. Oh, the things they could have done with today's technology. FaceTime, sending emails, texting, and God help me, sexting.

Mateo jotted down a few things in his notebook. "Do you know if her cousin ever graduated?"

"I don't know. We stopped sending letters a few months later."

Peri, who was finally putting her cookies into the oven, answered. "I think she quit because she got married and had a baby within a year's time."

"That happened everywhere. After the war, people were getting married and having babies. I waited as long as I could. I wanted a family, too," Bisnonna said.

Peri sat next to me and read the next letter. Hilde always told Bisnonna how much she missed her and thought about her in every letter, but she did it in a way that was creative and never the same. The honesty of her words hit my heart. They expressed her vulnerability, want, and unconditional love.

When the timer dinged, I followed Peri to the oven and looked at the cookies over her shoulder. They were beautiful, and my stomach rumbled just at the smell. I was going to lose, but I didn't care. "Hey. What's the bet?"

"What do you mean?" she asked. She popped the perfectly round cookies off the sheet and onto the cooling rack.

"What does the winner get?" I lifted my eyebrow at her until she got my hint.

"Oh. You mean, what do I want when you lose?"

I rolled my eyes. "Or what do you think I deserve when you lose."

She paused, but it didn't take long for her to come up with an answer. "Loser has to plan the perfect date."

"That's boring."

She looked at me pointedly and put her hands on her hips as though I'd offended her. "That includes the entire evening."

"I can get behind that," I said.

"I definitely can," she said.

Peri and I had spent only one night together, but her statement made me lift my eyebrows in surprise. I suppressed the shiver as my imagination conjured up several sexual scenarios with her behind me.

"Okay. Let's give the cookies a minute to cool down. May the better baker win," I said.

"I might as well plan my acceptance speech now."

For the first time ever in my life, I didn't mind losing.

CHAPTER TWENTY-ONE

FRANCESCA—PERI

Is the weather always perfect here?" I asked.

"Yes." Camila led me through the olive grove to a small hill that overlooked their land. She held a picnic basket in the crook of one arm and a blanket in the other, refusing to let me help her. When I tried to take the blanket again, she moved it out of my reach. "You won fair and square."

"I did, didn't I?" I smiled at how theatrical Mateo and Isabel were about my cookies. They knew exactly who baked what, and even though Camila's were good, mine were better. Camila was a good sport about it, which surprised me given how competitive she was. I bumped her shoulder with mine. "Where are you taking me?" It was almost sunset, and we'd skipped the evening meal to sneak away for a private picnic.

"You'll see. Just a little bit longer."

"I'm surprised you wanted to walk."

"I ate too many cookies and need to work off the calories. Walking seemed like the best way."

"One of the best ways." Where was this confidence coming from? I was acting and talking like a sex-starved teenager. I was never this flirty back home. Was it because I knew I was leaving and could get away with it? I frowned when I thought about leaving. It was inevitable, and I knew I was going to miss Camila and Isabel, even though I'd known them only a few short weeks. Camila was exactly the woman you wanted to have an affair with if you were on vacation somewhere for a short time. She was beautiful, sexy, confident, and not clingy. At the same time, she had layers, and I wanted to peel them back and get to the softness inside. I could easily see myself wanting a relationship with her. But that was impossible. I suddenly found it hard to breathe. I was trying to trick myself into thinking this was my life, at least until I left, but reality settled over me like a weighted blanket. It was uncomfortable and stifling.

"What are you thinking about?" she asked.

"What do you mean?" Guilt washed over me at being caught thinking such heavy thoughts.

"You suddenly looked sad. Is everything okay?" She rolled the blanket so it rested on top of the basket between the handles. I smiled when her fingers linked with mine.

I didn't want to lie to her, but I didn't want to confess anything either. The feelings swirling in my stomach were foreign, and I didn't want to assign them words that weren't true. "We're nearing the end of the stack of letters and our questions are getting answered. As much as I enjoy being here, I'm going to have to think about going home soon." My pulse quickened when the words slipped out of my mouth. I was trapped in my own fairy tale, and as much as I didn't want it to end, I had responsibilities back home. Who starts a new business and then leaves for weeks? This trip set me back professionally even though I got paid.

"I get it. I've enjoyed our time. Even in the beginning when I was a total asshole to you." She pulled me closer and put her arm around my shoulder. "I knew then you were special. I kept telling myself that if things were different, you would be somebody I would want to date."

"Different how?" Her sweet confession made my heart sing.

"When we first met, I thought you were trying to take advantage of my bisnonna, and even then I was attracted to you. Then I hated myself when I saw how wonderful you were with her, telling her news that was hard for her but also something she definitely wanted to hear. You've given her so much that we can never repay you for. You will always be welcomed here for as long as you like," Camila said.

I heard the passion in her voice and believed every word she said, but that wasn't who I was. I needed goals and direction. I couldn't stay here forever. "Thank you. That's very sweet of you. Really."

"Now, let's focus on the right now," she said.

"Good idea." It was easier said than done. By the time we reached our destination, I was wound tight, thinking about how in a week I would be in Connecticut, in my office that I barely knew, doing a job I wasn't sure I wanted anymore. "What's that?" I pointed to a tall, rolled-up canvas propped against a giant cypress tree.

"Since this tree offers a great view but very little shade, we keep a party tent up here. Have a seat while I set it up."

I sat on the rolled-up blanket while she snapped the tent into place in less than five minutes. "I'm worried about meeting your grandmother. She's going to wonder who I am, why I'm here, and what you and I are doing."

Camila pulled me up. "Help me put the blanket into the tent."

"Are you going to ignore my mini-crisis?" I asked.

She turned and kissed my pouting lips. "I'm going to cater to all of your whims once we're inside. But I need your help first."

I grabbed the corner of the blanket and helped spread it out. "You know, this is really nice." The tent had two of the four walls down to block out the setting sun, and two with nets to keep the bugs out. "We could probably sleep up here." I sat on the blanket and laughed when Camila playfully pounced on me and knocked me flat on my back.

"The thought had crossed my mind, but I like you in my soft bed with fluffy pillows and a bathroom with running water. At the moment, though, this is really nice."

I pushed my worries aside and gave in to this private moment. I'd learned from the letters that time was precious and to never take a second for granted. I enjoyed Camila and the time we spent together.

Her mouth was warm as her lips pressed against mine. She ran her fingertips over my cheek and stared into my eyes. Her meaning was clear, and the idea of us having sex again thickened my pulse. Every time this woman touched me, I felt like time stopped. I completely understood Amma's letters and how she said time sped up and stopped at the same time because of Isabel.

"You're tense. We're supposed to relax and enjoy the moment. We finally have privacy," she said. She kissed me softly again and again until I relaxed and blossomed under her. I felt safe with her. "Are you feeling any better?"

I smiled. "Definitely. Apparently, all I need in order to chill is a kiss."

"One kiss?" Her smile was confident and sexy as hell.

"Or like maybe a dozen. And if we're talking all over me, then at least a thousand," I said.

She kissed my neck softly. "One." Her lips moved down to my collarbone. "Two." She kissed my chin. "Three. You know, this could take a while."

"Let's see how high your count gets in the next hour," I said. I immediately got quiet when Camila unbuttoned my shirt and continued the count as she worked over my breasts and across my hard nipples. "Twenty-eight, twenty-nine," she said after an incredible mix of tongue, teeth, and lips on my breasts. She hit my stomach at thirty-four and stopped counting after she pulled down my shorts and panties. By then I didn't care about anything else other than her hands rubbing my skin and her hot mouth blazing a trail straight to the juncture of my thighs.

The ground was hard, and the blanket didn't offer much cushion, but I didn't care. I'd gotten wet the second we spread the blanket on the ground, and now I was soaked.

She swiftly slipped two fingers inside me, and I cried out at the overwhelming pleasure. She pulled all the way out and did it again and again until I begged her to go faster. I wanted that orgasm. I needed release, but Camila refused to rush anything. I knew she would build me up again and again until I was spent. Multiple orgasms were nice, but a giant explosion that shook me to my core was the best, and after last night, that's exactly what I wanted.

I took a deep breath and relaxed into her touch. When she spread me apart and I felt her hot breath on my clit, I whimpered, knowing what was about to happen and wanting it more than anything else I'd ever wanted. Camila wasn't just a good lover; she already knew what it took to please me, and that had never happened after only one night. Sex together was smooth, as though we'd been making love forever. She knew exactly how to build me up just by touching me and kissing me so deeply that I forgot about everything except her. This entire trip had been such an emotional ride. It was hard to connect with her on just a physical level. I was slipping into something emotional that was greater than myself.

Camila swirled her tongue around my swollen clit and pulled at it softly while her fingers found a rhythm that made my hips lift with her slow thrusts. It was such a smooth buildup that when my orgasm arrived, I leapt off the edge fully committed to enjoying every jolt and wave.

She crawled up me, and I tasted myself on her lips. "Four thousand and fourteen." A kiss on the other corner of my mouth. "Four thousand and fifteen."

My laugh was shaky. "Shut up. You didn't count the entire time." I reached up and kissed her because she looked so happy and beautiful.

"No. Did you?"

I ran my fingertips over her swollen mouth. "I lost track after thirty-four, but only because you were counting."

She shrugged. "Guess I'll have to start over."

I didn't stop her, but I forgot all about numbers and counting when her lips took another trip around my body.

We had sneaked upstairs and cleaned up before meeting Camila's nonna. I couldn't think when I'd ever been this nervous. Not for me, but what I represented to the family.

"Where's my granddaughter?"

I froze and slid a step behind Camila. We weren't even in view of the courtyard, and I was already panicking. "Maybe we don't have to tell her who I am," I whispered.

Camila stopped and turned. "What do you mean?"

"I can just be your friend from America. We don't have to bring up the real reason I'm here." Fear and doubt shredded my insides like a lion clawing his way to freedom. I put my hand on my stomach as if to calm it. "I'm so worried for Isabel."

"Okay. We can start with that, and once we have a conversation with Bisnonna, we can go from there," she said.

I nodded. "It's probably better to gauge her mood before we dump anything on her."

"Come on. Hopefully, her trip went well." Camila walked into the courtyard. "Nonna. Welcome back." She gave her grandmother a kiss and a hug and did the same with Isabel. Nonna stared at me. She was attractive, stately, but I detected a sour edge in the way she looked at me. "This is my friend Peri. She's from the United States. Peri, this is Francesca, my nonna."

"Hi, Francesca. It's so nice to meet you," I said. I sat in the chair across from Isabel and immediately took her hand. Francesca raised her eyebrow but said nothing.

"How was your trip?" Camila asked.

"It could have been better." Francesca leaned back in her chair, crossed her arms, and heavily sighed. She had a flair for the dramatic. Every single family member present rolled their eyes. This was expected.

I went ahead and took the bait. "It sounded like a wonderful cruise when Camila told me about it. Just you and your closest friends with unlimited food and wine. The ports you stopped in sounded like so much fun."

She stared at me for the longest time. I wanted to squirm in my chair under her continued scrutiny but kept eye contact and didn't move a muscle.

"Who are you again?" she asked.

"Mom, Peri is our guest. She's staying here for a bit," Nerissa said.

"Just a quick visit. I'll be out of here in a few days." It hurt to confess that, but it was the truth.

"I haven't seen you here before." She leaned forward as if to get a better look at me.

"I've never been here before, but the villa is lovely." I dialed up my charm only one notch. It was going to take time to win her over. Too much, too fast, and I would crash and burn.

"What's in the bag?" Camila asked. She opened the large brown bag that sat in front of Isabel. "Oh, this is pretty." She pulled out a beautiful silk scarf. "Who is this for?"

"It's gorgeous," I said.

Francesca was still hesitant, but she nodded. "For you, Camila. I thought you would enjoy the craftsmanship."

"It's beautiful, Nonna. Thank you." The gold, tan, and brown silk scarf was perfect for Camila's skin tone and hair color.

"The boys got Turkish delights, but I figured you should stay away from candy, so I got you the scarf instead," Francesca said.

I gasped but bit my tongue at her rudeness.

"Thank you, Nonna. That was considerate of you." Camila didn't show any emotion other than happiness.

I gave Isabel's hand a squeeze. She squeezed it back.

"Nonna brought me a pair of earrings," Nerissa said. She passed them down the table to Camila.

"They're lovely, but I didn't think your ears were pierced, Mom?" Camila looked at Nerissa in confusion.

"Oh. I suppose I forgot," Francesca said.

That told me everything I needed to know. Francesca was, for lack of a better word, a bitch. I felt sorry for all the women at the table.

"We should just switch gifts, Mom," Camila said. She kissed Francesca's cheek. "Thank you, Nonna. I appreciate the thought."

"It's been a long day of traveling. I'm happy I got to see you before I went to bed, Camila. I'm going to retire. I'll take Mom to her room."

"I'm going to stay up for a bit. I slept most of the afternoon," Isabel said.

"Okay. Then I'll see you all tomorrow. I've left my luggage in the washroom for Sophia. I'm glad to be home."

After well wishes of sweet dreams and kisses from her family, Francesca left the courtyard, and every single shoulder drooped with relief.

"That went better than expected," Nerissa said.

"That was better than expected?" I asked Isabel.

"She's always crabby when she returns from vacation. You would think she had the worst time, but she just hates change. It's a struggle to get her out of the villa and just as hard to get her back in. She'll be fine tomorrow after sleeping in her own bed again," Isabel said.

"It's getting late. Why don't we all head back inside," Nerissa said.

"Are you tired, Isabel?" I asked.

"We're so close to the end of the stack. I think I can stay up for a few letters. Is Mateo coming over?"

It was just after nine. I knew Camila was going to work the morning shift, so a late night was out of the question.

"I just texted him. He said he'll be over in ten minutes. He's excited to hear them, too," Camila said. She grabbed the wheelchair and helped Isabel into it. "Let's go inside where it's cooler and no mosquitoes."

By the time we got settled into the kitchen, Mateo busted in. This time he had a small bag of chocolates for Isabel. He kissed her cheek. "Don't tell anyone I gave this to you. You know how they get about sharing around here."

"Only one piece, Bisnonna. It's late." Camila shot Mateo a look. "I'm going to get the letters. I'll be right back."

"I wish I could make the letters last," Isabel said.

"They're beautiful to hear. Thank you so much for sharing with us," I said.

"I hate that you're going home soon. It's been such a delight getting to know you," she said.

"When are you leaving?" Mateo asked. He opened his notebook, ready to take notes.

"As soon as we're done with the letters. I have to get back to my business. This has been such a wonderful trip. I'm so grateful to have met Isabel and this whole family. And you, too, Mateo. I'll never forget it." It was easy to be honest without Camila there. My sinuses stung as tears fought to fall every time I thought of saying good-bye to her.

"It's been our honor," Mateo said.

"It's the best thing to happen to me since Hilde."

I smiled as Isabel ran her fingers over the once-lost handkerchief. "Amma would be so proud of you and what you've done with your life." I put my hand on her arm. "You're an amazing woman, Isabel."

"So are you, Peri. I miss her so much, but having you come into my life has been so wonderful and has reminded me that love is forever and always. Watching my great-granddaughter and hers fall in love in the same place we did has filled my heart."

I looked at Mateo and froze. He grinned at me. Wait. What? That couldn't be right. But it was. Just thinking about Camila made every part of my body swell. It was more than want and desire. It was deeper. Shit. How did I just now realize that I was in love with Camila?

Chapter Twenty-two

The Last Letter—Camila

It looks like we have only three more letters." I placed the stack in front of Peri and sat next to Mateo. Peri was pale and avoided eye contact. "What's going on?"

"Nothing. Just processing that only three letters are left." Mateo carefully pulled the letter on the top. He read it slowly, but I had a hard time concentrating on the words. Peri was obviously distressed about something.

"I remember she was so worried the closer she got to her wedding day," Isabel said. She touched Peri's hand affectionately. "Not because she was afraid of intimacy, but because she didn't want to hurt my feelings. It was hard trying to support her so far away."

"That had to have been hard for you," I said.

Bisnonna shrugged. "What could we do? What were our options? It never occurred to us that Hilde could stay here. The only thing we could do was live life the best we could."

Mateo finished the letter, and we sat in silence as the words cut deep.

"I love how she signed it 'always.' It's the perfect word," Peri said.

"Bisnonna, did you ever try to get in contact with her later after Bisnonno passed?"

"I was too old by then and was afraid of what I might find. People change in that amount of time. There's something romantic in not knowing and relying on your memories only. Plus, I'll always have letters and little mementos of her."

"And now you have Peri and the locket and all the photos to show that Hilde lived a full life. You gave her that gift by letting her go," Mateo said.

"Excuse me for a moment." Peri stood, gave a weak smile, and walked out of the kitchen.

"What's going on?" I asked. "Something happened when I left to get the letters. Somebody better start talking."

"You should go talk to her," Isabel said.

"Why?"

"Just go."

I held up my hands looking for guidance, but they stared at me blankly. "Fine. I'll go find her." I wasn't sure where to look for her, but the olive grove was a good start. I marched that way knowing every bump, every divot, but stopped short when I saw her sitting on the bench near the entrance to the grove. Her hair shone brightly in the moonlight. I smiled at how beautiful she was and how she didn't even know it. My smile faltered when I heard sniffles.

"Peri? Are you okay?" I sat next to her and took her hand.

She quickly wiped the tears off her cheeks and gave a small smile. "I'm okay."

"Seriously, what's happening? I know something happened, but nobody's talking to me."

"I'm just sad that I'm leaving—" She paused and took a deep breath. "That I'm leaving this place. It's almost magical. It's just been a really emotional time."

I put my arm around her shoulder and pulled her close. "I know. The last few weeks have been a roller coaster, huh?" I really didn't know what to say. I was pretending that it didn't matter that she was leaving, that the thrill of her in my world was just because she was different and brought so much happiness to Bisnonna. I melted when her head rested on my shoulder. "I don't even know what to think. You, Peri Logan, have certainly done something to me, and to our lives here. You've been so good for the Rossinis." I kissed the top of her head.

Her shoulders shook slightly, and I looked up at the night to keep my own tears from falling. I cared for her. My heart constricted and swelled so much that I had to quietly take several deep breaths. I refused to face my feelings. I was going to do that in the privacy of my room after Peri left. I couldn't show anything other than gratitude. It wasn't fair to tell her words I was unsure of, even though I'd never felt this way before.

"Knowing more about Amma comforts me a lot. I used to feel so empty thinking about her now that she's gone, but since meeting Isabel, I feel strong from within. Their story has empowered me, reminded me that we need to go for it. No regrets," she said.

I wasn't sure if she was specifically talking to me, but her words hit right in my heart. Was I ready to confess something I was still muddling through? I wanted to, but it wasn't fair to Peri. "I feel so much closer to Bisnonna knowing her story. And Hilde sounded like such an amazing woman. I hope when you go home, you can find the other half of the letters."

Peri took a deep breath and finally looked at me. "Speaking of which, we should probably go back and listen to the last two letters."

"Okay." I stood when she did and pulled her into my arms to hold her for a few minutes. She felt perfect, like she belonged there. "I wish we had more time."

Peri nodded and started back to the villa. I caught up with her and held her hand. She didn't pull away.

She slid into her seat in the kitchen and smiled at Bisnonna. "I'm sorry I left so quickly. I just needed some fresh air."

"We're happy to have you back. Mateo was just about to read the next letter." Bisnonna pointed to the stack, and Mateo plucked up the top envelope.

I braced myself for the words that were going to cut right through every part of me. Peri focused on the glass in front of her as we listened to the next to the last letter. We could hear the anxiety in Hilde's words as her marriage approached. Peri told me that she'd asked her grandmother why Hilde didn't smile much in her wedding photos, and her grandmother didn't have an answer. Now we knew. The letter was surprisingly short, and even though we knew what was coming, we all needed a moment to breathe before Mateo read the final letter. I was too emotionally invested to read it, and I knew Peri couldn't. Mateo didn't offer it to anyone because he must have known the three of us were only a few short words away from crying.

"Would anybody like anything to drink?" I meant shots of tequila or gin, but everyone settled for sparkling water. I cut lemon wedges and took my time on the presentation. I hated that all of this was coming to an end. Mateo held the last letter in his hands as though it was either going to explode or crumble like every single one of us at the table.

"Ready?" At our nods, he unfolded the paper.

My Dearest Isabel,

Today I'm wearing a wedding dress and marrying somebody who isn't you. You know you will be in my heart until the day I die. Thank you for loving me as completely and wonderfully as you have the last year. Such a short time in real life, but forever in my heart. I wish life was different for us.

I want you to have a beautiful life, Izzy. We survived a horrific war, and both of our countries will have to work hard to return to normal. The winery will survive and flourish, and I know that your olive oil business will do well in the years to come. I want you to listen to me, my love. I know this is hard to hear, but I want you to move on and find somebody who makes you happy. Have beautiful children who look just like you with big, brown, trusting eyes. I know you will be a wonderful mother. You are kind, considerate, and have the biggest heart of anyone I've ever met. Make lasting memories and fill your heart with love. As much as my heart is breaking, I know that I have to let you go in order for you to move on. This will be the last letter I write. I will treasure your letters and our memories forever. Promise me you will continue to live and love life with all your heart.

Always,
Hilde

Nobody spoke for a long time. Bisnonna dabbed her eyes with the handkerchief Hilde had made. Peri swallowed hard several times and never looked at us. She pressed her palms flat on the table and focused on the lemon wedge in her glass. Mateo stared at the wall behind me while the muscles in his jaws worked hard to keep his emotions in check. I walked to the window over the sink.

Their relationship was so unfair. I wanted to be angry at Bisnonna for not trying to find Hilde and vice versa. Bisnonna had lived in Sequina her whole life. She wasn't hard to find. Google, a phone call, an email. But that wasn't what the letter asked. Hilde had asked Bisnonna to move on and live her life fully, not to hope or wish for a different path, and that's exactly what she did. Even though she kept the letters and sweet keepsakes, she respected Hilde enough to let her go.

"Thank you, Bisnonna, for sharing this beautiful love story with us." I took a deep breath and turned to face the table.

"No, no. Thank you for allowing me to share it with you. And no sad faces. Most people never find what we had. We were lucky."

Fuck. My heart thudded with sadness, even though she smiled at us through her tears. "And you still remember after so much time."

"It's remarkable," Peri said. She sniffed and finally looked at me.

The overwhelming sadness in her eyes made me want to pull her into my arms and protect her forever. Double fuck. She had gotten through to me. This need to shield her from hurtful things and the way my heart detonated with every beat when I thought about kissing her could only mean one thing: I was in love. This was the real thing. My brain scrambled as I tried to understand what that meant. I looked at Bisnonna for guidance, and she nodded slightly, as if she understood. I unclenched my teeth and let out a deep breath. I relaxed into my newly found emotion. I needed to sit down.

"I could use a glass of wine." I grabbed a bottle from the rack and four glasses. "I think we all could use one." I poured and passed one to everyone, including Bisnonna. If anyone deserved a drink, she did.

"To true love," Bisnonna said.

I caught the sob before it escaped and swallowed it with the first sip. What seemed unfair to me was okay to her. I was so torn.

Thirty seconds ago I'd realized I was in love with Peri, but in a few days, I was going to watch her leave for good.

"It's time for me to retire," Bisnonna said.

"I'll walk you to your room." I needed a break and her strength.

"Good night, Isabel," Peri and Mateo said in unison.

I linked my arm with hers and shuffled at her pace. "You know, huh?" I didn't even have to explain it.

"We can call it family chemistry," she said. Even after the heartbreak of the last letter, she was smiling. "It's too late for us, but just the beginning for you two."

I took off her house slippers and helped her into her nightgown. "She lives a world away, and I don't know how she feels about me."

Bisnonna swatted my arm. "You know exactly how she feels about you. It's up to you to figure out what you want to do about it."

"Maybe it's not up to me. We have different lives and live thousands of miles apart. Maybe if she lived here or I lived there, we could go out on dates to see if we're compatible." Even I knew those words were lies. I was scared. "We're both young, too. By the time you were twenty-five, you were married and had a kid. But the world is different now, and I'm a naive, unworldly twenty-five-year-old."

"I can't believe you would lie to your bisnonna. You go talk to Peri right now before she packs up her things and leaves. At least tell her how you feel. Regret is the hardest thing on your heart. Trust me, I know."

I tucked her in and kissed her cheek. "I'll go talk to her now. Get some sleep." I closed the door and slowly walked into the kitchen. Peri was the only one at the table. "Where's Mateo?"

"He went home. Said he had an early start in the morning."

"Want to go upstairs?"

Peri nodded. "Are you going to lock up?"

"Yes. I'll see you up there." I always took my time locking up the villa, but tonight there was a different vibe. We knew our time was coming to an end. She was in the shower when I went upstairs, so I took a moment to wash off and slip into shorts and a T-shirt. It wasn't sexy, but I was going to be naked in a matter of minutes, and it didn't matter. Nothing mattered but tonight. I knocked on her door softly.

"Hi."

I entered when I heard her voice. She was sitting on the bed looking sad but also defeated. I sat next to her and pulled her close. "They had a great love story. You've done so much for her just by coming into her life." I was a chickenshit and didn't include myself, even though my life had drastically changed, too.

"I have to go home."

I tucked a piece of damp hair behind her ear. "Of course, but you know you can stay as long as you'd like."

She put her hand on my leg. "I love this place, but I just opened a business, and I have professional obligations. It's hard to be an investigator from here."

"I know. We'd like for you to stay, but I know you have to get back to your life and your responsibilities." What the fuck was I saying? Why was I pushing her away? It wasn't what I wanted. I was tired of talking. I was too afraid of my words, but I wasn't afraid of showing her how I felt. I kissed her softly, but sweet wasn't what she had in mind. She pulled me on top of her and pulled at my shirt until I ripped it off. Hers came off immediately after mine. "You're so beautiful."

Her lips claimed mine with a kiss that made me forget about everything other than her. I kissed and nipped at her skin on my way to the juncture of her thighs. I wasn't gentle. She pushed my shoulders to get me there faster, but I stopped. Peri was to be treasured. I didn't have a lot of time left with her, so I slowed when I settled between her legs. I placed soft kisses along her thighs. She relaxed when she realized I wasn't going to move fast. This was the first time I was making love to her. I pushed her thighs apart and softly licked her core. She was slick and swollen with need. I slipped two fingers inside and curled them up, moving slowly at first. She writhed under the pressure.

"More. Yes. Please."

Her encouragement fueled me. I added a third finger and waited to move my hand until I felt her pussy accept the added girth. I moved my fingers from side to side. She grabbed a pillow and yelled into it. Her legs were shaky, as though she'd already come, but I knew she had just started the climb. I tapped the small rough patch when I curled my fingers up and was rewarded with a moan that sounded like pure pleasure mixed with a sob.

Once my mouth found her clit, I didn't stop. I climbed with her on her journey, and when she tensed and finally came, it was the most beautiful thing I'd ever experienced. A pink flush colored her pale skin across her face, her neck, and her breasts. I climbed up her, my hand still inside, and lavished the hard, dusty pink peaks with my tongue. She pressed me harder against her, and after the third time of scraping my teeth across the sensitive areola, she came again. I was in awe of how she gave herself to me completely. She wasn't shy and didn't hold back. It was amazing. She reached for me, and I held her while she settled into sexual bliss.

"That was incredible," she said.

She felt hot and sweaty against me, so I rolled off her to give her air. She leaned up on one elbow and touched my face.

"You are flawless."

I blushed. When was the last time a woman made me blush? Or was this the first time? "My family will tell you that's not true, but I'm going to side with you." I wanted to make our night lighthearted even though it was anything but.

"I'm going to miss you," she said.

Her words stabbed my heart. Her blond hair was damp and wavy from the shower. It spilled over my pillow. Her big blue eyes that I could easily lose myself in made me want to remember this moment forever. I couldn't talk for fear that I would lose it. Instead, I focused on a tendril that stuck out from her temple and played with it for a solid ten seconds before I spoke.

"I'm going to miss you, too."

We made no promises tonight. We couldn't. I could tell that Peri felt the same way just by the way she touched me over and over again and the passion behind her kisses. It was there. Maybe it was always there, but we were on different journeys, and neither one of us was prepared for anything other than right here and right now.

CHAPTER TWENTY-THREE

BACK TO THE GRIND—PERI

I landed in a foul mood. I couldn't find the Lyft driver, and by the time I did, I had worked myself into a frenzied hot mess over nothing. He was exactly where he was supposed to be, but I had waited in the wrong spot. We drove thirty miles in complete silence. Even the soft music on the radio grated on my last nerve.

I sent Camila a message that I'd landed. I knew she was asleep but still unrealistically expected her to answer. I couldn't imagine she'd gotten a lot of sleep. Right before I left, Francesca found out why I was there. Nerissa got her out of the room, but it wasn't before she got a few jabs in on Isabel. It was almost enough to make me stay, but that was just an excuse. Isabel kissed my cheek and told me not to worry about her, but I was dying to know if they'd worked through things.

My mom called as I was unlocking my door. I looked around, thinking she was behind me because her timing was suspect. Did she know I was home? "Hi, Mom."

"Are you home yet, or do you need us to pick you up?"

"I just walked through the door, but I'm home safe. It was a good trip. Can I call you tomorrow?" I was going to be on pins and needles until I heard from somebody at the villa.

"Swing by and check on your Granny. She missed you."

Fuck. I hadn't talked to Granny in several days. Not since she texted me the family photos. "Okay. I'll stop by after I get settled." I hung up and plugged my phone in the charger while I unpacked. My mind was a whirlwind. I was dealing with feelings I had for Camila and developing an ulcer over Isabel and what had happened on my way out the door. I took a quick shower to wake up and threw on fresh clothes. It was nine, but Granny stayed up late, so I drove to her house. I needed to stay busy until I heard from Camila.

"Peri, you're home! How was it?"

I hugged Granny and handed her a small bottle of Isabel's Oils. "It was life-changing."

"I'm glad you were able to solve Mom's puzzle. I heard you were having a nice time. Tell me about the woman she hired you to find."

I hadn't given it a single thought before. I was going to have to tell Granny that her mother had been in love with a woman. "Let's have a seat." We sat at the kitchen table, and I pulled out my phone and showed her a photo of me and Isabel. "This is Isabel. She and Amma met in the war when Amma was working for the Red Cross."

"She's so sweet. She looks great for her age. How old is she?"

"Ninety-six, almost ninety-seven, and a wonderful person. That bottle of olive oil is from her business." I flipped through all the photos, careful not to show any private ones I had hidden of me and Camila. "This might be hard to hear, but Amma was close to Isabel."

"It was a hard time. I'm sure all friendships were important."

I held her hand. "Before Amma got married, while she was in Italy, she had a romantic relationship with Isabel." Please don't make me go into details, I thought.

"Oh." She paused, and I practically saw the wheels turning in her head. "Oh!" She looked at me, wide-eyed once the words sunk in. She reached for my hand.

"Their relationship had nothing to do with you. It was before she married The Captain. As a matter of fact, as strange as this sounds, she introduced them." I watched her face for emotions other than shock.

"So, my mom was gay?"

I shrugged. "I don't know. I would guess bisexual. She obviously loved her husband. You know how they were." They were sweet, from what I recalled.

"Dad loved her so much. You know, I always thought she was a little sad, but I just figured it was because she was stuck at home with me until I could attend school. She was a lot happier when she was at the hospital. I suppose keeping busy kept her mind off things." Granny was still processing, but she didn't seem upset.

"I'm sure it was a lot more. Amma loved being a mother. Before she got married, she wrote Isabel letters, and they were sweet. I have copies if, at some point, you want to read them," I said.

"I'm fine, Peri. I just feel sad for her. She never said anything. Did they even have a chance to at least try to get in contact with one another later in life? Dad passed away ten years ago. I wonder if Mom reached out then."

I shook my head. "No. They agreed to move on. I'm sure they never realized the world would be changing and become more accepting of same-sex relationships." I stood and paced the kitchen. "Back then, they didn't have any options. Not the kind we have now." I leaned up against the counter. "Granny, did you ever find any letters when you were packing Amma's things?"

"No. And by the way, I saved you a few boxes of personal items you might want to keep. I left them in her room."

My phone rang, and it was Camila, so I excused myself. I put my hand on my heart to keep it there as I answered the phone. "Camila."

"You made it home safely?"

Her sexy voice made my stomach tumble. "I did. I'm with Granny now. She's taking the news surprisingly well. How's Isabel? Did she and Francesca work through it?"

"Thankfully, yes. Once Nonna understood that it all happened before she married Bisnonno, she was more open. We didn't give her the details, just explained you were here to give Bisnonna the locket."

"Was she cruel to you or Isabel?"

"Not really. She gave Bisnonna a hug. Then my mother told us she had a girlfriend in college."

I heard the pride in Camila's voice. "No, really? That's great."

"It shut her down. She said she was meeting her friends and left. I can't tell if she's going to tell the world or keep it to herself."

"I'm glad she wasn't mean to Isabel. I was a wreck on the plane waiting to hear from you."

"I'm sorry I didn't get back to you sooner. I should have sent you a message, but honestly, it was exhausting. We were all on edge," Camila said.

"I'm just glad things are calm now."

"How are you? Tired yet?"

Her warm, caring voice washed over me, and I smiled at how it soothed me. "I'm tired, but happy now that I know Isabel's okay. How are you?"

"I'm tired, too, but I have to get up soon and open Isabel's Oils."

I figured out the time difference. "Oh, my gosh! Go get some sleep. It's not even five."

"I wanted to hear your voice."

Her voice was gravelly and choppy as she stretched. I pictured her T-shirt rising to expose her soft, tanned stomach and her long legs tangled in her sheets. "Now that you've heard it, go back to sleep and text me later. If you want to," I quickly added. I hoped I didn't sound as desperate as I felt.

"I'll give you a chance to sleep. I'll call you after lunch, okay?"

I disconnected the call, and my cheesy grin didn't go unnoticed by Granny.

"Is that the pretty girl in the photos? Camila, right?"

I blushed. "Yes. She's Isabel's great-granddaughter, and she's pretty remarkable." I spent a solid hour telling Granny about the villa and the winery, and about the cellars and Mateo.

"Honey, it's getting late. Go home and get some sleep. Are you working tomorrow?"

Oh, yes. I had a job. A new business that needed my attention. "I'll probably go in late. Why don't I stay here tonight, and we can have a nice breakfast at the café?" Guilt for being gone for so long and not checking in with her made me stay. Life was precious.

"That sounds wonderful."

She touched my cheek lovingly and promised to be quiet when she woke in the morning. I followed her down the hallway, kissed her good night, and slipped into the guest room that I considered mine. The last thing I remembered was crawling into bed fully clothed, holding my phone and hoping for a phone call from somebody who seemed a world away.

❖

"Thomas Peak is on line one for you."

Ginger's sunny disposition depressed me. What could Amma's lawyer want from me? Her estate was settled. I'd been avoiding him for weeks, since I had more pressing cases. "This is Peri. How can I help you?"

"Peri. Thomas Peak here. How are you?"

I rolled my eyes. I wasn't in the mood for small talk but forced a smile so he could hear it over the phone. "I'm well. How are you?"

"Great. Welcome back to town. I'm calling because I wanted to find out if you located the woman in the locket."

I cleared my throat. "Yes, I did."

"That's good to hear. I need you to swing by the office when you have time. I have more papers for you to sign."

"Let me check my schedule. Can you please hold?"

"Of course."

I hit the hold button and squeezed the bridge of my nose. The dull tapping of a headache was ramping up in the space behind my eyes. I'd slept like shit since I'd been home. Two weeks. I'd been home two weeks, and the ache in my heart hadn't lessened. I picked up the receiver and hit the button. "I can drop by at three today. Does that work for you?"

"Can you do it sooner? I have a meeting at three."

I hated that my schedule was empty. "Sure. Give me thirty minutes." I wasn't excited about having to drive into Hartford, but

I owed it to Amma to finish the paperwork. I used lukewarm coffee to swallow two ibuprofen capsules that I prayed would kick in soon. "Ginger, I'm out for a bit. Lock up if I don't get back to the office before you leave."

"Have a good afternoon," she said.

"I'll try." I waved to her on my way out. At least the sun was shining today. I slipped my aviators on and zipped onto the highway. Camila teased me about my *Top Gun* sunglasses, but I really liked them. She looked great wearing them. It was one of my favorite photos of her. I missed her. The time difference made it difficult to talk during the week. It was only a matter of time before she had things to do or I had things to do, and then the weekend calls would slip into every other week, until eventually we just stopped talking and only liked each other's posts on social media. I was my own worst enemy.

Thankfully, Thomas didn't make me wait at all. I walked into the lobby, and he made a beeline for me from the glass-walled conference room.

"It's good to see you again, Peri. Right this way."

He pointed toward the conference room he had exited and followed me in.

"Can I get you anything?"

I was so hungry, and as much as I wanted to say a club sandwich, a Coke, and a bag of salty chips, I shook my head. "No, thank you. Why am I here, Thomas?"

He slid a box and a thin stack of papers across the conference table. "Hildegarde said that if you found the woman in the locket, I was to give you this box upon your return. If you could sign the papers in front of you to confirm that you've received the box, that would be great." He handed me a pen before I had a chance to think about anything. I signed them and handed them back.

"What is this?" I looked at the box.

He stood. "I'll leave you alone to open it. Congratulations on closing Hildegarde's case. She would be so proud of you."

The lump in my throat prevented me from answering. I nodded as he closed the door. I carefully lifted the lid and tore it off when

I realized what I was seeing. I pulled out a stack of letters that I immediately knew were from Isabel. My hands shook as I untied the ribbon that held them together. Just as many letters from Isabel were here as Isabel had from Hilde. I also found a note and a cashier's check for fifty thousand dollars. In shock, I quickly opened the letter and skimmed it the first time, but settled down to read every word the second time.

Peri,

By now you know my truth. The woman in the locket is my true love, Isabel Rossini. When I was your age, a life with another woman wasn't possible. I hope you found her and she remembered me.

I'm sorry if you didn't find the mystery as exciting as some of the shows we watched while you were growing up. We had fun, didn't we? I'm sorry I got old before we could do more fun things together, like travel or go out to dinner or see a play. I looked forward to your visits every week. I always knew you would grow into an amazing person. I'm so proud of you. I hope Isabel's family accepted you and were kind. I can only imagine she raised wonderful children and they graciously made you part of their lives. Italy is a beautiful country. The beaches are amazing, and Isabel's vineyard is massive. I hope you were able to see it all.

The money is for your new business or for whatever makes you happy. Pride doesn't even begin to describe what I feel for you. You are taking a chance on your dreams. So many people are afraid to take the leap. I didn't have the opportunities you have, and I love that you have such ambition. Independence is more powerful than you know. I hope you find success in your job, your life, and your heart. I love you so much. Please be happy and follow your dreams.

Always,

Amma

I wasn't sure when I started crying, but I had to dig around in my purse for a tissue. What an amazing journey she had given me. As stressful as it was at the beginning, I, too, found love and happiness just like she did. Only I had the opportunity to do something about it. I gathered up the letters, the cashier's check, and the beautiful letter she wrote me. What did I really want to do with my life?

❖

I spent the weekend FaceTiming with Mateo and Camila, reading the letters to them. Sometimes Isabel sat in. It was overwhelming, but we didn't have the luxury of sitting around the kitchen table and reading a few at a time and waiting a day to read a few more. I scanned them and sent them to Mateo for his book. Amma had seventy letters from Isabel. We laughed at the funny parts and wept when Isabel's words shredded our hearts. English might have been her second language, but she had a way with words.

One night, before Camila went to bed, we were FaceTiming. It was afternoon for me, but I needed to see her face.

"Mateo would never say this, but he's really enjoying writing. Ever since you left, he's thrown himself into the story, and what he's written has been amazing."

"That's great. I'm excited to read it. This whole experience has been incredible," I said. I couldn't read her Amma's letter to me. Not yet. In time, I would, but I had to figure things out first.

"I never knew Bisnonna wrote such beautiful words. She always seemed so quiet and embarrassed by Hilde's words, even though hers were just as passionate," she said.

"How is she doing?"

"She misses you. So do I."

My heart skipped at her confession, and the soft spot between my legs throbbed. I didn't know how to tell her I missed her, too, without sounding pathetic. "I know." What a horrible thing to say. "I miss you, too." I felt awkward saying it. It was deeper than simply missing her. I felt hollow, like everything inside of me was a void. That was not a confession I was prepared to make, even though it bubbled up and threatened to push out. Amma's letter to me made me doubt all my life's choices. Why was I here and not in Italy?

"How's work? Are you getting new clients?"

"A few. What about Isabel's Oils?"

"We'll probably add a new line of herbed oils and try to market it. The tourists seem to like it, as does Bisnonna."

"Anything for her," I said. I sighed. I really missed life at the villa, which was a sliver of paradise. I wanted to tell her to look at the calendar and pick a week I could visit but didn't want to be clingy. When Camila had dropped me off at the airport, she'd gotten out of the car, pulled me into her arms, and kissed me hard. It wasn't a good-bye kiss, but an I'll-definitely-see-you-later kiss.

"When is harvest?"

"Grape harvest is in September, and right after that, it's olive time," Camila said.

"Well, maybe before then I can come out for a week or so." I tried to keep my voice casual, but the look of surprise and happiness on her face made me giddy.

"I'd love that. We all would."

"Okay. Pick out a week that works best for you, and I'll book my flight."

"Is next week too soon?"

My heart fluttered at the look she gave me.

Chapter Twenty-four

Find Her—Camila

Bella, I don't know why you're still here." Bisnonna held the letter in her hand and shook it at me. "This is everything."
Worchester Fine Arts Academy had accepted me as a transfer student for the fall semester. I'd sent my portfolio to them with my transcript from the handful of classes I'd attended at The Florence Academy of Art. Classes started mid-September, right at the beginning of harvest. As soon as I got the acceptance, Bisnonna paid the international tuition.

"I'm just so nervous. I'm going to miss harvest. I'm going to miss you."

"Don't worry about us or this place. You take care of yourself. This makes me so happy, and if anybody gives you a hard time, I'll remind them who really runs the show."

Bisnonna was so fiery. She definitely believed in true love. Peri and I had texted and video chatted for almost two months. We never said the word love, but I could see it in her face, and I was sure she could see it on mine.

I was too scared to tell Peri. Suddenly everything I ever doubted rushed to the front of my mind, knocking down my confidence. What if she didn't want me? How long could we go on with a week or two here and there over a course of a year? I had to do something. This was the best possible decision for me and for my relationship with her.

"Mom and Dad are going to be pissed." I sank down next to Bisnonna and held her hand. "Thank you so much for making this happen. And so quickly."

Bisnonna blushed. "I just want you to be happy, bella." How much money did Bisnonna have? I was completely oblivious to the family's finances. I knew my parents had enough, but it never occurred to me that Bisnonna had her own bank account. It made sense, since the oils and part of the winery were hers.

"I can't thank you enough."

"You don't need to thank me. You just need to do what you need to do."

I understood, but first I needed to have a conversation with my family, and honestly, I was dreading it. "I know. I'll tell Mom and Dad tonight at dinner." Shit. I was going to have to tell Mateo privately. I wasn't sure if he would swing by for dinner tonight, so I decided to go visit him. It was Saturday, so he was at the art fair. I was too nervous to think about anything like selling art. My stomach was tied in knots over everything. "I should go tell Mateo. Are you good here, or would you like me to take you to the courtyard?"

"The weather's too warm there. I'll just stay here and watch TV."

"Let's get you into the room." I helped her get situated and handed her the phone, the remote, a glass of sparkling water, and a small plate of cookies. "Don't eat all of them."

"Then why did you put so many on my plate?"

"Good point." I grabbed two before she could swat my hand away. "I love you. I'll see you this afternoon."

I loved watching Mateo interact with people. He was so friendly and open with strangers. It was no wonder he sold out every time he set up for a fair. He was signing books but waved when he saw me. I weaved my way through to his booth and handed him a fresh lemonade before kissing his cheek. "I'm here to help."

"Take their money or credit cards, and I'll keep signing." He handed me his phone with his mobile payment app and pointed to the box of stuffed dolphins. "Cash is in an envelope with them."

It was a solid two hours before he caught a break. My heart broke knowing I was leaving my best friend. Not forever, but probably at a time when he needed me the most.

"I like it when you help me, but then you aren't selling your own artwork."

"Well, I came here to talk to you before you came over for dinner."

The smile immediately disappeared, and he stared at me with a seriousness I hadn't seen before. "What's wrong?"

"Nothing's wrong. I'm fine. Everybody's fine." I handed him the letter from my back pocket. "Here. Just read this."

He snatched the letter from me, and I waited for the words to sink in. His jaw dropped open. "Oh, my God. This is wonderful." He wrapped his arms around me. "This is a dream come true. Oh, wait. Isn't this really close to where Peri lives?"

I shrugged one shoulder and smiled at him.

"No. Yes? You're going there to be with her?"

"And get a premier education in the process, but yes. To be with her. I just miss her, and I feel wonderful things when we talk but have been horribly sad since we've been apart."

He leaned closer as a new customer entered the booth. "Does this mean you're in love?"

I didn't hesitate. "Totally and completely."

"This is a big step for you. When do you leave?"

"Classes are in six weeks, so I need to get over there sooner rather than later. Also, don't say anything to Peri. I haven't decided how I'm going to tell her."

"You shouldn't tell her. How romantic would it be if you just showed up?"

The idea had merit. "Let me see how the family takes the news first. One hurdle at a time."

"I'm so happy for you. You deserve this. I'm going to miss you so much, but the book will keep me busy, and just knowing that my best friend's dreams are coming true is everything."

"Thank you, Mateo. That means so much coming from you."

"Plus, now when I go on my book tour, I can make your place my home base."

"You can visit any time."

Our conversation was cut short with customers piling in after grabbing lunch from the food vendors across the street. I stayed with Mateo until it was time to break down the booth and told him I would see him tonight for dinner. My stomach lurched just thinking about telling my family. I wasn't sure how they'd take the news.

❖

It took me two glasses of wine to settle my nerves, and by then, I didn't care what anyone said.

"You're doing what?" My mother was very calm.

"I'm moving to the States and attending art school in Massachusetts. It's time I take care of myself." That came out bitchier than I intended. "I just want to see what I can really do with my art."

"Does this have anything to do with Peri?" Ethan asked.

"It helps that she's close to school."

"Wait. Is our little sister finally in love?" Luke leaned over and clinked his glass against my almost empty one.

"Luke, stop teasing your sister." My father finally spoke up. I wanted more from him, but he remained quiet.

"That's it? Nobody has anything else to say?" I asked.

"What about harvest?" Ethan asked.

"We can hire somebody in Camila's place," Bisnonna said.

Nobody fought her. We ate in silence for about a minute until Mateo said something.

"I love this family very much, but I think Camila following her dreams is the best thing. Staying here will only keep her in the same cycle of working during the week and partying on the weekends. This way she gets to leave the villa for a bit, get an education, and see the woman she loves. She won't be gone forever. This place is in her blood."

Mateo's words must have hit home for my family because everyone got quiet. I was a nervous wreck waiting for somebody, anyone else to say something. My mom held her glass up. "Congratulations to my daughter. May all of her dreams come true."

The entire family raised their glasses to me. I got choked up but held my glass high. "Thank you so much for your support."

"When do you leave?"

"In two weeks. I want to get a feel for the campus and the town and figure out where I'm going to live."

"If you need anything from us, let us know. We're proud of you, Camila. Not everybody takes that sort of leap." My father looked sad, but he put on a smile for my benefit. I was going to miss my family, especially Bisnonna, but I was excited for the big change and doing exactly what I wanted to do.

Bisnonna tapped me on the arm. I leaned closer so I could hear her better.

"You know what to do first."

"What?"

"Find her."

I pushed through the door with two suitcases, my messenger bag, and a small tote. I couldn't have felt or looked more lost. The woman at the front desk gaped at me.

"Can I help you?" she asked.

"Yes. I have an appointment at two."

The woman looked me up and down, glanced at the stack of luggage, and shrugged. She pulled up the calendar on her computer, clicked the mouse too many times, and tried not to look alarmed. I could tell her computer was frozen. It was like trying to teach Nonna how to work a computer but watching her fail every time. "Well, if you say so. Please take a seat. What is this in regard to?"

"I was promised a tour."

"Are you sure you're in the right place?"

"Definitely." I sat because my legs were weak. I was too excited to be exhausted, but once the adrenaline left my body, I would crash hard.

The receptionist picked up the intra-office phone. "Yes, your two o'clock appointment is here. I locked up the computer again so I can't tell you for sure."

After a pause the woman smiled at me and softly hung up the phone. "It'll just be a moment."

I checked my phone for messages. When I'd landed, I texted my mom, Mateo, and Bisnonna that I made it safely. It was dinner time, so none of them had responded. I heard a door open and saw Peri walk out of her office while straightening the collar of her shirt. She looked up and stopped. Her mouth opened and closed.

"Hi."

Tears immediately gathered in her eyes, causing me to tear up, too. She walked straight into my arms and started sobbing.

"What's going on?" The receptionist stood and clutched her eclectic costume jewelry. She stared at us with alarm. "Do I need to call anyone, Peri? Like your mom or the police?"

"No, Ginger. Thanks though." Peri turned back to me. "What are you doing here?" She wiped her tears on her cuff. I handed her Isabel's handkerchief. "Don't ruin your shirt."

She cried even harder and gently took the handkerchief but refused to use it. "Why do you have Isabel's handkerchief? Please tell me she's okay."

I cupped her face and kissed her softly. "She's fine. She just wanted me to give this to you as a gift."

"What are you doing here?" She brushed away her tears and clutched me as though she couldn't believe I was here.

"Maybe we should go to your office?"

"Yes. Good idea." She pulled me toward the office door.

I stopped and pointed to my luggage. "Is it okay for me to leave my things here?"

The receptionist nodded very seriously. "I'll make sure nobody takes anything. And I'll lock the door if you're still in there when I leave."

Peri took my hand and pulled me into her office. She touched my face, my hair, and my arms as though not believing I was standing in front of her.

"I'm here. I'm really here."

"But why? Why didn't you tell me you were coming? I could have picked you up. I could have taken the day off."

"A lot of things are going on that I need to explain. Can we sit down?" I pulled her over to a small couch she had tucked into the corner. "This is a nice office."

"I don't want to talk about me. I want to talk about you."

I held her hands and took a deep breath. "Peri, I realized, even before you left, that I was in love with you, but I didn't know how to say it without throwing a wrench into both of our lives."

"You love me?"

"With all of my heart, but let me finish." She playfully zipped her lips but kissed me before she allowed me to continue. "I needed to make sure it wasn't just Bisnonna and Hilde's story that made me emotional and question everything. It was all you. I can't let you go."

"I have to stop you, or else I'll burst. I love you, too, Camila, and I knew it when I was there. It hit me the night we read the last letter, but I didn't want to mess up your perfect life by complicating it with a long-distance relationship or promises we couldn't keep," Peri said. She reached for a tissue from a box on the small end table. "I want only the best for you."

"I felt it in my heart. I knew you did, but I didn't know what to do about it. Now I do."

"You're here."

I'd missed those blue eyes and those full lips. I kissed her hard. "I'm here, and I'm going to have to take you up on your offer."

"What offer? I mean, you can have anything you want."

"I'm here to attend WFAA."

"You're staying?" Peri jumped up. "You're here to stay?" Fresh tears formed in her eyes.

I stood and pulled her close. "I'm here to stay. I start school in a month, but I thought we could spend some time together before school kicks in. I believe you told me you would give me a tour? Kind of like how I gave you a tour of my town, only you're nicer and will definitely do a better job?"

Her delightful laughter was amazing to hear in person. "We'll get to know the campus, find the bus schedule from my house, or I can drop you off every day. I'm my own boss, so I make my own hours."

"You want me to stay with you?"

"Of course I do. I love you, and I want to go to sleep every night and wake up with you every single day."

"I want the same, too."

"And we'll visit your family as often as we need to so you don't miss them so much."

The receptionist knocked on the door, cleared her throat, and spoke loudly enough for us to hear. "I'm leaving now but I'll lock up. I moved the luggage to behind my desk so nobody would be tempted to take it if they see it through the front window."

Peri giggled. "Thank you, Ginger. I'll see you tomorrow."

"But she might be late," I quickly added.

"Have a good night," Ginger said.

We waited until we heard the lock click into place on the main door. Peri straddled me and kissed me with a hunger that I knew all too well. I wanted to undress her and make love to her here, but this wasn't the place.

"Can you shut down early? Can we go back to your place?" I asked between deep kisses and heavy caresses.

"Our place? Yes, yes. Let me flip it over to the answering service, and we can be home in fifteen minutes. Are you hungry? Do you want to stop for food anywhere?" she asked.

"I'm hungry for you." I was eager to show her all the ways I missed her.

"Let's get out of here."

We pulled into the driveway of a cute bungalow cottage with flowerbeds and rosebushes trimmed to just below the line of the windows. "This is adorable." It was completely different from anything I'd seen or expected.

"It's not much, but I love it."

She helped bring my luggage in and gave me a quick tour.

"I have two bedrooms, but nobody ever visits, so we can make one your studio. Unless you want your own room? I don't want to be presumptuous."

I pulled her to me and slipped off her suit jacket, placing it gently on the bed. "I don't want my own room. Ask me what I want?" I unbuttoned her starched shirt, frowning at how impossible the buttons were to loosen. She pretended to think hard about my question while she unbuttoned my jeans.

"What do you want, Camila?"

"Mmm. I love it when you say my name. I want you naked and in the shower with me in thirty seconds."

She pulled me into the small bathroom and adjusted the water temperature until she thought it was acceptable. "Why are you still dressed?" She slipped out of her bra and panties and disappeared behind the shower curtain.

I wasted no time shedding the rest of my clothes and taking off my jewelry.

"What's taking you so long?"

"Ack. Stupid bracelet. I wanted to look beautiful for you, but now I can't get anything off."

She peeked around the curtain. "When you get frustrated, your accent comes out, and it's super sexy."

I forgot about the bracelet and joined her. "Hi."

"Hi. I've missed you," she said. She moved so that I was under the stream. This was perfect. In between kisses I managed to clean up, turn the water off, and wrap us both in towels. I followed her onto the bed and relaxed for the first time in almost a full day.

"I'm apologizing now if I fall asleep on you." I moaned as she massaged my tense back and legs. When I felt her tongue on the back of my thighs, I woke up. The closer she got to my core, the more my energy level ramped up. She used her knees to spread my legs apart and slid her fingers up and down my wet, swollen slit. I was ready for her. She slipped two fingers inside and stretched out so she was on top of me. Her teeth grazed my shoulder, and I gasped at the pleasure that rolled over me.

"I love you," she whispered.

I knew this wasn't a dream, even though it happened in a flash. One minute I was in Italy sitting in the shop, thinking my life had only one direction, and the next I was in Connecticut with my girlfriend on a completely different path. "I love you, too." I was overcome.

"You feel so good."

She nibbled my earlobe as she moved her fingers in and out. Everything about this felt right. I moved my hips against her hand. She kissed her way down my body and flipped me. I pulled the towel away and opened my legs. Her warm mouth on my thighs undid me. The moment her lips touched my clit I knew I was exactly where I was meant to be. She held my hips down while she brought me to the edge with her tongue several times. When I came, I grabbed the slats in the headboard and moaned out my orgasm. I was too tired to yell but strong enough to pull her into my arms. "You're the best decision of my life."

She kissed me softly and ran her fingertips lightly over my breasts. "I can't tell you how happy I am that you're here."

"I wasn't going to let true love slip away. I know how important it is. We both do."

She curled up next to me and pulled a light cover over us. "It's amazing how all of this happened. It makes for such a wonderful love story."

"It really does. I promise to never take us or our love for granted." I was serious.

"I promise the same." She leaned up. "Always?"

The love I felt for her roared and throbbed in my heart. That one word meant everything to both of us. It was our history, our beginning, and our forever. I kissed her hard enough to let her know I was serious, yet soft enough so she could feel it in her heart. "Always."

Epilogue One

One year later—Peri

"Ouch. What's in your pocket that's so sharp?" I asked. Camila smacked my hand away, but I kept feeling it. She pulled over and got off the bike and walked a few feet away. "Hey, wait. What're you doing?" I had to yell as traffic buzzed by.

Living and working at a winery had its benefits. Going home for lunch was a five-minute walk, and I was learning Italian at a fast pace. I wasn't an aggressive driver yet, but Camila always kissed my temple when I showed rage of any kind behind the wheel. She said it was cute. She tried to convince me to get matching motorcycles, but once I saw the Ducati she wanted, I balked. I was fine being a passenger, which was how we ended up on the side of the road in rush-hour traffic. I got off the bike and followed her.

"Nothing's the matter. It just hurt when you pressed into me."

"Well, whatever's in your pocket was hurting me, too. What is it?" I was completely oblivious. I just knew it was small and sharp. She took off her helmet, straddled the bike backward, and crooked her finger. I happily walked over, took off my helmet, and straddled the bike facing her. "Oh, I like this. And I'm sure all the people driving by do, too." When she kissed me, I forgot how close we were to the road and ignored the sound of the traffic speeding by. I could only hear my heart pumping faster and faster and feel her hands on my thighs.

"Can we talk about it in a few miles when we reach the beach?" Camila loved her beach. Even without the draw of her family and the villa, it was worth moving back here to see her lounging on the beach. I would never tire of seeing her in a bikini or how she tried to tame her wild hair when it was breezy by the water. She was completely oblivious to how other people stared at her. It sounded clichéd, but she only had eyes for me.

When Nerissa called me one night and offered me a job at the winery because her chemist was moving back to the United States, I told her I'd have to think about it. Italy had plenty of enologists with tons of experience that Rossini Winery could easily hire, but Camila was homesick, and Nerissa had offered me the job to get Camila home rather than because of my excellence at chemistry. As much as she was learning at the academy, she struggled with being distanced from her family.

At first Camila was angry at her family's meddling, but we'd learned about real sacrifice from Isabel and Amma. My business was okay. It had been my dream job years ago, but I didn't have the same professional drive I had from day one. My life had changed so much that nothing was more important than making Camila happy and being with her.

The rest was history. Now I was using my degree and learning about stabilizers and acid control and how to make wine without the chemicals. People were demanding organic wine, and I convinced the family to get a jump on it. Nerissa said I was a natural.

Camila spent most of her time at Isabel's Oils. What a beautiful transformation. Once she came back, she threw herself into the business, and on the nights I worked late, she painted. We set up the extra bedroom in the apartment we were building at the villa as a studio for her. Even though we were busy, we always made time for each other. Knowing Amma and Isabel's story and the pain and heartache they experienced over the course of their lives, we vowed to check in and have date nights every week. This week's date night was apparently happening with half the population of Sequina speeding by us.

Still oblivious, I shrugged. "I don't understand why you can't just show me here. I mean, we're pulled over already."

"Why are you so stubborn all of the sudden? I thought that was my strength?"

"You're rubbing off on me." I smirked.

"I noticed a lot of that this morning, for sure."

I grabbed the lapels of her jacket and reached into the pocket to find whatever was poking me. She stopped me.

"At least let me do this right."

"What do you mean?"

She pulled out the ring. "Okay, Peri Logan. Since you can't wait the five minutes it will take to get to the beach, this will have to do."

Her hand was slightly trembling as I sat in complete shock.

"We can wait," I said once I realized what was happening.

"Nope. It's going to happen right here."

I swallowed hard and looked at her instead of the ring.

"I love you, and I love our history. You were given a job and because you were so good at it, we're together now. I did everything I could to keep you from finding out the truth, but we both know I'm an idiot. You came into our lives and gave us all hope and happiness and, most importantly, love. I learned what true love is because of our great-grandmothers, but I feel it with you. You are everything to me and I want to marry you and have a beautiful life and have beautiful children with you. Will you marry me?"

I took a deep breath. "I love you and everything about us. Of course, I will marry you." I kissed her so hard, I almost knocked us off the bike.

She slipped the ring on my finger. "Do you still want to go to the beach?" she asked.

"Not now. I want to go home and celebrate properly," I said. I got off the bike so she could turn around, slipped my arms around her waist and smiled as she tapped the ring with her finger.

"*Ti amo.* I love you," she said.

"I love you, too. Let's go home and tell everyone the news," I said. I was thinking about Isabel and how excited she was going to be.

"Bisnonna is waiting," Camila said.

"She knows?"

"I had to ask her for the ring."

Tears sprang to my eyes. Nothing could ever match the cycle of love between our families. We were able to live our lives the way we wanted, unlike our great-grandmothers who had to sacrifice their hearts and true love because the world wasn't open to them. Seventy-five years later, we had the right to love each other, and I intended to live every day with my heart wide open and by Camila's side.

Epilogue Two

Two years Later—Camila

Bisnonna passed away three days after Isabel Hilde Rossini Logan was born. She died peacefully after spending the afternoon holding her great-great granddaughter. She was surrounded by every single person she loved. The pain of losing her was more than I anticipated. If it weren't for my wife, who loved her just as much as I did, the loss would have been unbearable. But baby Izzy and Peri needed me. I collapsed only at night, when just Peri and I were alone in our bed, with Izzy in the bassinet nearby. Bisnonna was my rock, the reason I believed in true love and chased Peri halfway around the globe. Had I never heard her story, I would probably still be partying at the beach with Mateo and running from relationships.

Hundreds of people attended Bisnonna's funeral. I didn't realize so many people in town knew her, but the crowd inside the enormous church and the people outside paying their respects gave me something else to think about other than extreme loss. People I had never met before came up to hug me and tell me things Bisnonna did for them. She donated a lot of the profit from Isabel's Oils to help local families who suffered in the war get back on their feet. She also donated to churches, helped build the town library, and gave periodically to The Florence Academy of Art.

When Isabel's Oils transferred to me upon her death, I was determined to make it even more successful so that Peri, Izzy, and I could have a comfortable life, and Izzy would have a college fund. I would always have the winery and the income from it, but Isabel's Oils was special. It was the one thing Bisnonna had control over, and she gave it to me.

"You're doing the far-away-stare thing. How are you doing?"

Peri's hands circled my waist, and her lips pressed into my shoulder. "I'm as well as can be expected." She squeezed me tighter. "Don't let me go."

"I'm never letting you go. I promise you."

She knew I was strong, but sometimes I needed to hear it. Our love was everything to me. The moment I opened up to her, I never looked back. My heart grew every time I looked at Peri, and I thought for sure it would burst with all the love it held. When she gave birth to our daughter, my heart couldn't take the kaleidoscope of emotions twirling inside. I cried at the beauty of our love. I wept at the perfection nestled in Peri's arms. An eight-pound two-ounce blond-haired baby with eyes bluer than her mother's stared at me with awe and pure love. I never expected this life and wouldn't trade it for anything.

"Will you love me forever?"

She brushed her lips across mine. "Not only forever but always."

Hilde,

It's been a long time, my love. So much has happened in my life since your last letter. I met your wonderful great-granddaughter Peri, and she's every bit as perfect as you. She's smart, funny, beautiful, and when she introduced herself, I thought she was you. I thought time had transported me back and we were together again. She gave me the locket, Hilde. You kept it all these years. She showed me photos of your family, and it filled my heart that you lived your life fully.

I need to tell you about my great-granddaughter, Camila. She's almost Peri's opposite, but they are beautiful to watch together. Very loving. They remind me so much of us. Who would have thought our great-granddaughters would meet and fall in love just like we did so many years ago?

I shared our letters with Peri, Camila, and our sweet friend Mateo, who wrote an historical romance novel based upon our love. He used the letters as inspiration, and now people are reading our story worldwide.

My world has changed so much in the last few years, all because you sent Peri to me. Camila and Peri are married. Today Peri is at the hospital giving birth to our great-great granddaughter. How wonderful is it that they are living the lives we wanted but could never have? They live at the villa, and I see them every day and watch their love grow. My time is limited, and I'm going to see you soon, but I want to meet the baby first so I can tell you about her. I hope she has thick, dark hair like Camila's, but blue eyes like you and Peri. Or maybe blond hair and brown eyes. I don't really care. I just want her to be healthy and happy.

We both did great things with our lives. When Peri first got here, we spent weeks talking about your life since the war. I'm so proud of you, Hilde. Your family is wonderful, kind, and successful. She told me about how you became a nurse and all the lives you saved and how your child and hers were all nurses, too. Peri was the one to break the chain, but she's found a good home at the winery. Even my granddaughter, Nerissa, thinks she's wonderful.

I'm tired, Hilde, and I'm ready to see you again. We've been apart too long. I know you told me to move on, and I did, but you always had my heart. I'm ready to share it with you again.

Always,
Isabel

About the Author

Kris Bryant grew up a military brat living in several different countries before her family settled down in the Midwest when she was twelve. Books were her only form of entertainment overseas, and she read anything and everything within her reach. Reading eventually turned into writing when she decided she didn't like the way some of the novels ended and wanted to give the characters she fell in love with the endings she thought they so deserved.

Earning a BA in English from the University of Missouri, Kris focused on poetry, and eventually decided to write her own happily ever after books.

Her debut novel, *Jolt*, was short-listed for a Lambda Literary Award. Her second novel, *Whirlwind Romance*, was a Rainbow Award finalist.

Kris can be reached at krisbryantbooks@gmail.com, @KrisBryant2014, and krisbryant.net.

Books Available from Bold Strokes Books

#shedeservedit by Greg Herren. When his gay best friend, and high school football star, is murdered, Alex Wheeler is a suspect and must find the truth to clear himself. (978-1-63555-996-5)

Always by Kris Bryant. When a pushy American private investigator shows up demanding to meet the woman in Camila's artwork, instead of introducing her to her great-grandmother, Camila decides to lead her on a wild goose chase all over Italy. (978-1-63679-027-5)

Exes and O's by Joy Argento. Ali and Madison really only have one thing in common. The girl who broke their heart may be the only one who can put it back together. (978-1-63679-017-6)

One Verse Multi by Sander Santiago. Life was good: promotion, friends, falling in love, discovering that the multi-verse is on a fast track to collision—wait, what? Good thing Martin King works for a company that can fix the problem, right…um…right? (978-1-63679-069-5)

Paris Rules by Jaime Maddox. Carly Becker has been searching for the perfect woman all her life, but no one ever seems to be just right until Paige Waterford checks all her boxes, except the most important one—she's married. (978-1-63679-077-0)

Shadow Dancers by Suzie Clarke. In this third and final book in the Moon Shadow series, Rachel must find a way to become the hunter and not the hunted, and this time she will meet Ehsee Yumiko head-on. (978-1-63555-829-6)

The Kiss by C.A. Popovich. When her wife refuses their divorce and begins to stalk her, threatening her life, Kate realizes to protect her new love, Leslie, she has to let her go, even if it breaks her heart. (978-1-63679-079-4)

The Wedding Setup by Charlotte Greene. When Ryann, a big-time New York executive, goes to Colorado to help out with her best friend's wedding, she never expects to fall for the maid of honor. (978-1-63679-033-6)

Velocity by Gun Brooke. Holly and Claire work toward an uncertain future preparing for an alien space mission, and only one thing is for certain, they will have to risk their lives, and their hearts, to discover the truth. (978-1-63555-983-5)

Wildflower Words by Sam Ledel. Lida Jones treks West with her father in search of a better life on the rapidly developing American frontier, but finds home when she meets Hazel Thompson. (978-1-63679-055-8)

A Fairer Tomorrow by Kathleen Knowles. For Maddie Weeks and Gerry Stern, the Second World War brought them together, but the end of the war might rip them apart. (978-1-63555-874-6)

Holiday Hearts by Diana Day-Admire and Lyn Cole. Opposites attract during Christmastime chaos in Kansas City. (978-1-63679-128-9)

Changing Majors by Ana Hartnett Reichardt. Beyond a love, beyond a coming-out, Bailey Sullivan discovers what lies beyond the shame and self-doubt imposed on her by traditional Southern ideals. (978-1-63679-081-7)

Fresh Grave in Grand Canyon by Lee Patton. The age-old Grand Canyon becomes more and more ominous as a group of volunteers fight to survive alone in nature and uncover a murderer among them. (978-1-63679-047-3)

Highland Whirl by Anna Larner. Opposites attract in the Scottish Highlands, when feisty Alice Campbell falls for city-girl-about-town Roxanne Barns. (978-1-63555-892-0)

Humbug by Amanda Radley. With the corporate Christmas party in jeopardy, CEO Rosalind Caldwell hires Christmas Girl Ellie Pearce as her personal assistant. The only problem is, Ellie isn't a PA, has never planned a party, and develops a ridiculous crush on her totally intimidating new boss. (978-1-63555-965-1)

On the Rocks by Georgia Beers. Schoolteacher Vanessa Martini makes no apologies for her dating checklist, and newly single mom Grace Chapman ticks all Vanessa's Do Not Date boxes. Of course, they're never going to fall in love. (978-1-63555-989-7)

Song of Serenity by Brey Willows. Arguing with the Muse of music and justice is complicated, falling in love with her even more so. (978-1-63679-015-2)

The Christmas Proposal by Lisa Moreau. Stranded together in a Christmas village on a snowy mountain, Grace and Bridget face their past and question their dreams for the future. (978-1-63555-648-3)

The Infinite Summer by Morgan Lee Miller. While spending the summer with her dad in a small beach town, Remi Brenner falls for Harper Hebert and accidentally finds herself tangled up in an intense restaurant rivalry between her famous stepmom and her first love. (978-1-63555-969-9)

Wisdom by Jesse J. Thoma. When Sophia and Reggie are chosen for the governor's new community design team and tasked with tackling substance abuse and mental health issues, battle lines are drawn even as sparks fly. (978-1-63555-886-9)

A Convenient Arrangement by Aurora Rey and Jaime Clevenger. Cuffing season has come for lesbians, and for Jess Archer and Cody Dawson, their convenient arrangement becomes anything but. (978-1-63555-818-0)

An Alaskan Wedding by Nance Sparks. The last thing either Andrea or Riley expects is to bump into the one who broke her heart fifteen years ago, but when they meet at the welcome party, their feelings come rushing back. (978-1-63679-053-4)

Beulah Lodge by Cathy Dunnell. It's 1874, and newly engaged Ruth Mallowes is set on marriage and life as a missionary...until she falls in love with the housemaid at Beulah Lodge. (978-1-63679-007-7)

Gia's Gems by Toni Logan. When Lindsey Speyer discovers that popular travel columnist Gia Williams is a complete fake and threatens to expose her, blackmail has never been so sexy. (978-1-63555-917-0)

Holiday Wishes & Mistletoe Kisses by M. Ullrich. Four holidays, four couples, four chances to make their wishes come true. (978-1-63555-760-2)

Love By Proxy by Dena Blake. Tess has a secret crush on her best friend, Sophie, so the last thing she wants is to help Sophie fall in love with someone else, but how can she stand in the way of her happiness? (978-1-63555-973-6)

Loyalty, Love, & Vermouth by Eric Peterson. A comic valentine to a gay man's family of choice, including the ones with cold noses and four paws. (978-1-63555-997-2)

Marry Me by Melissa Brayden. Allison Hale attempts to plan the wedding of the century to a man who could save her family's business, if only she wasn't falling for her wedding planner, Megan Kinkaid. (978-1-63555-932-3)

Pathway to Love by Radclyffe. Courtney Valentine is looking for a woman exactly like Ben—smart, sexy, and not in the market for anything serious. All she has to do is convince Ben that sex-without-strings is the perfect pathway to pleasure. (978-1-63679-110-4)

Sweet Surprise by Jenny Frame. Flora and Mac never thought they'd ever see each other again, but when Mac opens up her barber shop right next to Flora's sweet shop, their connection comes roaring back. (978-1-63679-001-5)

The Edge of Yesterday by CJ Birch. Easton Gray is sent from the future to save humanity from technological disaster. When she's forced to target the woman she's falling in love with, can Easton do what's needed to save humanity? (978-1-63679-025-1)

The Scout and the Scoundrel by Barbara Ann Wright. With unexpected danger surrounding them, Zara and Roni are stuck between duty and survival, with little room for exploring their feelings, especially love. (978-1-63555-978-1)

Bury Me in Shadows by Greg Herren. College student Jake Chapman is forced to spend the summer at his dying grandmother's home and soon finds danger from long-buried family secrets. (978-1-63555-993-4)

Can't Leave Love by Kimberly Cooper Griffin. Sophia and Pru have no intention of falling in love, but sometimes love happens when and where you least expect it. (978-1-636790041-1)

Free Fall at Angel Creek by Julie Tizard. Detective Dee Rawlings and aircraft accident investigator Dr. River Dawson use conflicting methods to find answers when a plane goes missing, while overcoming surprising threats, and discovering an unlikely chance at love. (978-1-63555-884-5)

Love's Compromise by Cass Sellars. For Piper Holthaus and Brook Myers, will professional dreams and past baggage stop two hearts from realizing they are meant for each other? (978-1-63555-942-2)

Not All a Dream by Sophia Kell Hagin. Hester has lost the woman she loved and the world has descended into relentless dark and cold. But giving up will have to wait when she stumbles upon people who help her survive. (978-1-63679-067-1)

Protecting the Lady by Amanda Radley. If Eve Webb had known she'd be protecting royalty, she'd never have taken the job as bodyguard, but as the threat to Lady Katherine's life draws closer, she'll do whatever it takes to save her, and may just lose her heart in the process. (978-1-63679-003-9)

The Secrets of Willowra by Kadyan. A family saga of three women, their homestead called Willowra in the Australian outback, and the secrets that link them all. (978-1-63679-064-0)

Trial by Fire by Carsen Taite. When prosecutor Lennox Roy and public defender Wren Bishop become fierce adversaries in a headline-grabbing arson case, their attraction ignites a passion that leads them both to question their assumptions about the law, the truth, and each other. (978-1-63555-860-9)

Turbulent Waves by Ali Vali. Kai Merlin and Vivien Palmer plan their future together as hostile forces make their own plans to destroy what they have, as well as all those they love. (978-1-63679-011-4)

Unbreakable by Cari Hunter. When Dr. Grace Kendal is forced at gunpoint to help an injured woman, she is dragged into a nightmare where nothing is quite as it seems, and their lives aren't the only ones on the line. (978-1-63555-961-3)

Veterinary Surgeon by Nancy Wheelton. When dangerous drugs are stolen from the veterinary clinic, Mitch investigates and Kay becomes a suspect. As pride and professions clash, love seems impossible. (978-1-63679-043-5)

A Different Man by Andrew L. Huerta. This diverse collection of stories chronicling the challenges of gay life at various ages shines a light on the progress made and the progress still to come. (978-1-63555-977-4)

All That Remains by Sheri Lewis Wohl. Johnnie and Shantel might have to risk their lives—and their love—to stop a werewolf intent on killing. (978-1-63555-949-1)

Beginner's Bet by Fiona Riley. Phenom luxury Realtor Ellison Gamble has everything, except a family to share it with, so when a mix-up brings youthful Katie Crawford into her life, she bets the house on love. (978-1-63555-733-6)

Dangerous Without You by Lexus Grey. Throughout their senior year in high school, Aspen, Remington, Denna, and Raleigh face challenges in life and romance that they never expect. (978-1-63555-947-7)

Desiring More by Raven Sky. In this collection of steamy stories, a rich variety of lovers find themselves desiring more, more from a lover, more from themselves, and more from life. (978-1-63679-037-4)

Jordan's Kiss by Nanisi Barrett D'Arnuck. After losing everything in a fire, Jordan Phelps joins a small lounge band and meets pianist Morgan Sparks, who lights another blaze, this time in Jordan's heart. (978-1-63555-980-4)

Late City Summer by Jeanette Bears. Forced together for her wedding, Emily Stanton and Kate Alessi navigate their lingering passion for one another against the backdrop of New York City and World War II, and a summer romance they left behind. (978-1-63555-968-2)

Love and Lotus Blossoms by Anne Shade. On her path to self-acceptance and true passion, Janesse will risk everything—and possibly everyone—she loves. (978-1-63555-985-9)

Love in the Limelight by Ashley Moore. Marion Hargreaves, the finest actress of her generation, and Jessica Carmichael, the world's biggest pop star, rediscover each other twenty years after an ill-fated affair. (978-1-63679-051-0)

Suspecting Her by Mary P. Burns. Complications ensue when Erin O'Connor falls for top real estate saleswoman Catherine Williams while investigating racism in the real estate industry; the fallout could end their chance at happiness. (978-1-63555-960-6)

Two Winters by Lauren Emily Whalen. A modern YA retelling of Shakespeare's *The Winter's Tale* about birth, death, Catholic school, improv comedy, and the healing nature of time. (978-1-63679-019-0)